DARK KILL

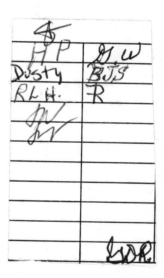

8-12

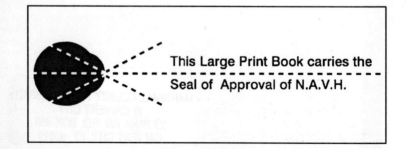

This Large Print Book carries the
Seal of Approval of N.A.V.H.

DARK KILL

A WESTERN DUO

TODHUNTER BALLARD

WHEELER PUBLISHING
A part of Gale, Cengage Learning

GALE
CENGAGE Learning·

Detroit • New York • San Francisco • New Haven, Conn • Waterville, Maine • London

GALE
CENGAGE Learning

LIBRARY OF CONGRESS CATALOGING-IN-PUBLICATION DATA

Ballard, Todhunter, 1903-1980.
    Dark kill : a western duo / by Todhunter Ballard. — Large print ed.
        p. cm. — (Wheeler Publishing large print Western)
    ISBN 978-1-4104-4986-3 (softcover) — ISBN 1-4104-4986-6 (softcover) 1. Large type books. I. Ballard, Todhunter, 1903-1980. Railroad doctor. II. Title.
PS3503.A5575D37 2012
813'.52—dc23   2012018155

Published in 2012 by arrangement with Golden West Literary Agency.

Printed in the United States of America
    1 2 3 4 5   16 15 14 13 12
FD202

ACKNOWLEDGMENTS

"Dark Kill" first appeared in *Western Magazine* (10/56). Copyright © 1956 by Bard Publishing Corp. Copyright © renewed 1984 by Phoebe Dwiggins Ballard. Copyright © 2008 by Sue Dwiggins Worsley for restored material.

"Railroad Doctor" first appeared as a four-part serial in *Ranch Romances* (2nd August Number=8/14/53)-(3rd September Number=9/25/53). Copyright © 1953 by Warner Publications, Inc. Copyright © renewed 1981 Phoebe Dwiggins Ballard. Copyright © 2008 by Sue Dwiggins Worsley for restored material.

TABLE OF CONTENTS

DARK KILL

I

When Lew Lander first came into Colorado he had a horse, a gun, and a rope. He also had five hundred head of the hungriest, trail-weary cattle that this world has ever seen. There wasn't anyone in the valley at the time. People said Lander was crazy to try and settle there. The Indians weren't yet on their reservations; there wasn't a railroad within five hundred miles. If a man managed to raise his cattle, and keep his hair, he had the problem of marketing his beef.

Lander solved this in his own way. He sold beef to the Indian agents and by the time the rail line came through he was one of the biggest cattlemen in the territory. He had a crew of thirty riders, and 3 million acres of graze, and so many cattle that he made no real effort to count them. And then, he died.

The boys weren't very old when their father passed on. Jerry was twenty. Wolf was two years younger, but they had been raised in the saddle, and they knew as much about beef as men twice their age, and the chances are that, if they had done as the old man planned and hung together, they would not have had any trouble.

Jerry was tall, and dark-haired, and he had a way of smiling quietly that made people like him. Wolf was different. Wolf took after his mother's people. Wolf had red hair, and blue eyes, and he was always getting into fights. Not that he wasn't agreeable. It was, as Jerry once said, that Wolf just seemed to like to fight.

They fought as kids, and it was in the cards that they would fight as men, but they still might have held the ranch together if it had not been for Judy Parker. Judy came out from Denver that summer to teach school. The winters were rough in that country, and school ran through the summer months.

Jerry it was who saw her first, and Jerry took her to the Clogtown dance. He was twenty-three then, and his father had been buried for three years. He took her to the dance, but Wolf stole her and took her home. It was as simple as that, and people in the valley who liked to gossip shook their heads and said that you could not really blame the girl because Wolf had always had a way with people, especially women.

The dance was on Saturday night. Sunday noon Wolf came riding into town with Hy Burner and two other friends. Jerry was sitting on the hotel porch.

Jerry saw his brother coming, and he got up from his chair and moved down the steps to the sidewalk and stood there, waiting until they came abreast of him.

Wolf was laughing at something Hy had said, and his head was turned and he had not seen his brother. Jerry's voice hit him like the slap of an open hand.

"Kid," he said, "climb down off that horse. I'm going to lick you until you can't crawl."

Wolf swung around. He looked at his brother and his wide mouth got its derisive grin and his blue eyes turned a little wicked and he said to Hy: "Look, here's Romeo, but I heard tell somewhere that he lost his Juliet." Wolf had been down to Denver and he had seen two Shakespearean plays and he was always talking about them.

The three riders with Wolf laughed. There was always someone with Wolf, even when he was small. He was the kind of man who attracts friends, who is always surrounded by people ready to laugh at his jokes.

Jerry wasn't that type. Older people usually respected Jerry while they frowned a little on Wolf. Jerry was steady, hardworking, dependable, and slow to anger, but he was angry now. He reached out suddenly and grabbed his brother's leg. The horse, startled by the sudden movement bolted, and Jerry, setting his heels in the deep dust, dragged Wolf out of the saddle.

Wolf lit flat, his arms wide, with a jar that might have knocked out an ordinary man. But Wolf rebounded off the ground as if he had been made of rubber. He was grinning when he came to his feet, and grinning as he charged, both arms swinging. They still talk about the fight in the valley. It was a fight the like of which is seldom seen. Both men weighed over one hundred eighty, both stood nearly six feet tall, both were hard-muscled and flat-stomached from much riding, and neither knew what the word fear meant. They stood and slugged each other until their arms were so weary that they could hardly lift them, and then they grappled, falling together into the dust, rolling over and over as they tried for advantage. No one knows how long the fight might have continued. A big crowd had gathered, making a kind of ring about the fighters, but suddenly this ring parted and Judy Parker forced her way through.

She was a small girl, with dark hair and an intent face that looked very serious until she smiled, then her eyes lighted and her face warmed, and she was suddenly beautiful. But she was not smiling now. She was very serious and extremely angry. She ran in, grabbing Wolf's shoulder. Wolf happened to be on top at the moment. The next instant Jerry heaved and they rolled over, reversing the position, nearly knocking the girl from her feet.

"Stop it!" She now had hold of Jerry's hair and was trying to pull him off his younger brother. Neither of the men paid the least attention to her. Their sole interest at the moment was to inflict as much damage on the other as they possibly could.

Judy seemed to realize this. She stood for an instant, her small hands on her hips, glaring at them, then she looked around. Hurl Poke, the town's marshal, was standing behind her, enjoying the fight as much as the rest of the spectators. It never occurred to Hurl Poke that his duty was to stop them. In his eyes, this was strictly a family affair. If the two Lander boys wanted to pummel each other in the middle of the town street that was their business.

"Stop it!" Judy had his arm and was shaking him. "What's the matter with you?

15

Don't you see they are killing each other?"

Poke looked at her, slightly annoyed. He had seen them fight this way before and they had never seriously injured one another yet. "Let them alone." He turned to glance again at the fight.

Judy stared at him a little helplessly. Then she saw the gun in its holster on his belt. Before he realized what she was about, she had reached out, pulled the gun free, and using both hands fired it twice into the air.

The heavy sound of the .45 cut the afternoon like an explosion of dynamite. It caught the crowd unprepared. It even reached through the battered senses of the fighters. For an instant they forgot each other and turned to see what had happened. Neither of them was prepared to face the angry girl. She stood before them, the gun looking very large in her small hands, its heavy barrel pointing directly at them.

"Get up."

Slowly they dragged themselves to their feet. Their clothes were layered with dust; Jerry had a cut over one eye, and Wolf's nose was bleeding. They glared at each other, and then at the girl. Had they been allowed to finish the fight, to continue until both were exhausted, the trouble might have been over, as it had been over after previous fights. Or if they had been halted by a man, they might have turned on him, but to be stopped by a girl. . . .

Neither of them blamed her, but both knew that the fact that a woman had halted them would be told and retold all over the valley. They did not blame her, but they blamed each other and there was only one answer they could think of. They split the ranch.

II

Old Judge Pinkley had been Lew Lander's lawyer ever since the town had been founded with the coming of the railroad. He had watched both boys grow up, and he had helped handle the ranch business affairs since their father's death. But he knew better than to try to act as peacemaker when they showed up in his office.

They weren't speaking to each other, not any more than was necessary. Both of them had puffed faces, and the cut above Jerry's eye sported a piece of plaster.

"It's this way," said Jerry. "Me and Wolf never did get along." He really believed it at the moment. "So, we've decided to split the ranch."

The judge who was a small man with a

goatee merely looked from one to the other. "That what you want?"

Wolf was staring at the floor between his feet, probably so he would not have to look at his brother. "That's it," he said. "We figured to divide the place at the river. The one who gets the north half can use the north line camp for headquarters, the one south gets the ranch buildings."

The judge nodded. The Mesquel River divided the range nearly in half. "That seems fair enough. Which takes the north, which the south?"

They looked at each other.

"Suppose," said the judge, who did not want the quarrel to flare into new violence, "you flip a coin."

They flipped a coin, and Wolf won, and Wolf chose the south with the ranch buildings. "We'll count the cattle," he said, "and split them even down the middle. Who keeps the brand?"

"You got the buildings," Jerry said. "I should keep the brand."

It was so decided, and they hired every spare rider in the country to help with the roundup. The final tally showed that there were nearly twenty thousand animals wearing the Box L brand. Half of these were vented with a Wolf Head that was the brand

Wolf Lander chose.

The older, steadier hands stayed with Jerry. The younger, wilder fringe of the Box L crew went to the Wolf Head, and a friction developed almost at once between the two outfits as if the riders were taking on the hate with which their bosses regarded each other. Even the other inhabitants of the valley lined up, some for Wolf, some for Jerry, and it seemed that there was a war building.

Judge Pinkley tried to stop it. The judge sent for Judy Parker, and, when the young teacher came to his office, he put it to her bluntly. "I suppose you know this is all your fault."

She glared back at him. Her mother was Irish and Judy had a temper of her own, and she showed it now. "My fault, because two grown men are acting like a couple of children?"

He said: "I've watched those boys grow up." There was a note of sadness in his old voice. "There isn't a mean bone in either of their bodies."

She didn't answer him.

"It was a mistake," he told her, "to go to that dance with Jerry and leave it with Wolf. Maybe where you come from small things like that aren't important, but out here one man doesn't take another man's girl without causing trouble."

She smiled, thinking he was joking, and, when she smiled, the small dimple showed in her left cheek and her eyes seemed to dance. Then she realized that he was deadly serious, and the smile went away. "I didn't mean anything. Wolf said he'd show me the twin peaks by moonlight. He said we'd be back in plenty of time. I didn't realize it would take almost until daylight."

"Did you tell Jerry that?"

"I tried. He wouldn't even talk to me."

The judge should have realized when he was licked, but he was a stubborn man. He went down to talk to Martin Heller at the bank.

Martin was small, and dark, and sharp. A cowboy once, he owed his position in the bank to old Lew Lander who had started it. He heard what the judge had to say, but shook his head.

"There's nothing I can do," he said. "Neither of those boys will ever listen to me. They are as headstrong as two unbroken colts and they hate each other thoroughly."

This last the judge did not believe. He knew that the boys had always quarreled, but he had always believed there was more high spirits than malice in their arguments.

20

The judge got into his buckboard and drove out to the old northern line camp that Jerry was busy converting into a ranch headquarters. He pulled into the yard, tied his horses to the pole fence of the corral, and walked across the hard-baked surface of the yard to where Jerry was supervising the building of a blacksmith's shed.

"Jerry," he said, "come over here a ways. I want to talk to you."

Jerry hesitated for a moment as if he knew what the judge had in mind and did not want to talk about it. Then he slowly followed Pinkley back across the yard.

"What is it?"

The judge said: "Your father was the best friend I ever had. He took me in when I came out here to die. He fed me, and clothed me while I read for the law."

Jerry knew all this.

"And the last thing your father told me before he died was to look after you boys."

Jerry stared down at the little judge. It did not strike him as funny that two men, nearly six feet tall, should be looked after by one who was hardly more than five. He said: "It's no use, Judge. Wolf's gone bad. He always had a wild streak in him and it's coming out."

The judge was suddenly angry. "I never

thought I'd hear you talk about anyone like that, Jerry . . . anyone. Just because you're sore at Wolf."

Jerry's voice hardened suddenly and his dark eyes looked like chips of black flint. "Come over here."

He led the way to a corner of the yard behind a row of buildings. There, spread out on the ground, was a hide. The judge saw that it was from a freshly cut animal. Jerry turned it over. It showed a Box L that had been vented to a Wolf Head. The judge looked at it for a long minute, then raised his eyes questioningly.

Jerry said: "One of the boys ran across this yearling yesterday. It's nearly eight weeks now since we split the ranch and rounded up and re-branded the stock Wolf kept. That yearling was branded not later than day before yesterday."

The old judge studied the hide and the brand, showing raw, a fresh burn. Even to his inexperienced eyes the evidence was plain. He lifted his head and looked searchingly at Jerry. "I can't believe it. There must be some explanation. Wolf, no matter what his faults, is not a thief."

Jerry's face had a wicked cast. "Not a thief in the ordinary sense of the word, Judge, but maybe he doesn't consider it stealing when he takes my cows. He bragged last week in the Roundtop Saloon that I'd be broke within three years. He said I didn't have the guts to run a big outfit without his help."

The judge said bitterly: "It's the girl."

Jerry's face tightened again. "Let's forget about her."

"You can't," said the judge. "I've watched you. You can't, and neither can Wolf. I've watched him, too. It would be easier if she were no good, but she is. There's nothing wrong with her except that both you and Wolf fell in love with the same woman."

Jerry shook his head. "She won't have anything to do with me. I've tried to talk to her and she simply won't talk."

"She won't talk to Wolf, either. I think she figures that this is all her fault. I think she would have thrown up the school and gone back to Denver, if Martin Heller hadn't talked her out of it. Martin is now president of the school board."

Jerry had no interest in Martin Heller. He had never had a great deal of respect for the small banker. It was his brother he was thinking about.

"Wolf's hired Pete Clouse as foreman," Jerry said. "That should show us all the way the wind is blowing."

The judge sighed. "I don't like Pete Clouse," he admitted. "The man is a natural-born killer with the instincts of a horned toad and the dependability of a rattlesnake. But you have to remember that most of your father's old crew elected to stay with you when the ranch was split, and Wolf had to take what he could get in the way of riders."

"That's no reason to hire Clouse. My old man ran him out of this valley and he didn't dare come back until after Dad was dead. Clouse brought six toughs with him and from what I'm told they are all riding for the Wolf Head."

The judge made one last effort. "If I can get Wolf over here and show him this hide, will you talk to him?"

Jerry shrugged. "If he wants to talk. But I'll tell you right now . . . you're wasting your time."

He was right, as Judge Pinkley found out two hours later when he drove his buckboard into the headquarters of the Wolf Head Ranch. Even before he climbed from the sagging seat, he noted the difference that only a few short weeks had made. There was an unkempt look about the place that Lew Lander would not have tolerated during his lifetime, and that Jerry had not allowed to happen, a careless look as if the crew did not take the trouble to fix anything or put anything away.

Wolf was talking to Pete Clouse when the judge pulled in. Clouse gave Pinkley a sly look, and then turned and moved off.

Clouse was a big man, dark as an Indian, with straight hair and a sallow, ugly face. He walked with an insolent swagger as if he dared the world to interfere with him. He was known to be ugly and unmanageable when drinking. Before Lew Lander had driven him from the valley, Clouse had been arrested three times and brought before Pinkley. Once he was accused of stealing a horse, once for shooting up Blackwell's store, and once for killing a man. But each time he had gone free because no witnesses would testify against him. He had walked out of the courtroom, sneering at both the judge and jury.

Judge Pinkley followed the solid figure with his eyes until Clouse disappeared around the corner of the bunkhouse, then he turned to find that Wolf Lander was watching him, and that the blue-green eyes that were usually smiling had a hard, remote look.

"Well, Judge. This isn't a social visit, I guess?"

Pinkley reflected that in all the years he had visited this ranch he had never had as cold a greeting. But he held his temper, although it was difficult.

"Look, Wolf. I remember you when you weren't big enough to top a horse. Don't put on airs with me."

The red-headed man looked at him, and then looked away. "Things have changed, Judge."

"I see they have." Pinkley's eyes went around the littered yard. "And not for the better, either. Your father would rise straight up out of his grave if he knew that Pete Clouse was sleeping in the bunkhouse and eating his grub in the cook shack. Have you lost your mind, Wolf? There's an old saying, lie down with dogs and you get fleas. Lie down with thieves and you get your throat cut."

Wolf laughed, but the rollicking sound that had been so good to hear was missing. "It takes certain tools to do certain things, Judge. Don't worry about Pete. I can handle him."

In a fair fight the judge had no doubt that Wolf could handle Pete Clouse. The trouble was that, when Clouse fought, he did not fight fair. He said: "Wolf, I was over to see Jerry."

He saw Wolf's green eyes go bleak and cold. "I don't want to hear about him."

"You want to hear this," the judge said. "Jerry found a yearling wearing the Box L brand changed to a Wolf Head, and the change was made no earlier than the day before yesterday."

Wolf stared at him. "Are you accusing me of rustling my brother's cattle?"

"I'm not," the old man said. "But someone did. I think I'd keep a sharper watch on my men."

Wolf laughed shortly. "Don't worry. They're too lazy to do anything unless I order them to, and I haven't started rustling just yet."

"I said that someone did."

Wolf was suddenly very angry. "Look, Judge. I've heard talk, too. Someone did, and I'll make you a small bet that it was done by Jerry's orders. All he wants to do is put me in the wrong. Well, it isn't going to work. This valley isn't big enough for both of us, and I'm the one who is going to stay. Just mark that down in your little black book."

III

Martin Heller sat at his desk in the front part of the bank office and stared out at the town's main street with thoughtful eyes. He was thirty-two years old, and he had achieved success far above anything that anyone who knew him had expected. But Martin was not surprised. Long ago he had made up his mind that he was going to be one of the most powerful men in the territory. At that time it had seemed a foolish dream.

He had been riding for old man Lander for $30 a month and found; he had been eighteen years old and did not weigh ninety pounds dripping wet. The crew had used him as a butt for their jokes and he had hated them, but more than he hated the rest of the riders he hated Jerry and Wolf Lander, for they had by birth everything that he wanted, everything that he hoped to get.

His time had come at an odd moment. It had happened fourteen long years ago. Lew Lander had just shipped a train load of cattle to Chicago and was cursing because he had to ride the hundred miles to Cheyenne to draw a slight draft on a distant Chicago bank. It was then Martin had made his suggestion, standing in the dust of the shipping pens, watching the freight pull away. He'd said: "If there was a bank in the valley, you wouldn't have to ride all the way to Cheyenne."

Wolf Lander had been a bare-legged kid then. He'd heard the remark and snickered, but old Lew had turned his head and he wasn't laughing. "The valley needs a bank," Lew had said. "Only trouble is . . . to find a man to run it."

Martin Heller had gulped. He'd thought: *If the old fool laughs at me, I'll kill him.* But aloud he'd managed to say: "What's the matter with me?"

Wolf had really howled then. That was where Wolf had gotten the nickname, because he could actually howl like a wolf. "What do you know about running a bank?" Lew had asked.

Martin Heller had looked at the boy, wanting to murder him, but he'd kept his voice level. "I can figure," he had said, "and I can write, and I'm honest."

This last had decided Lew Lander, this and the nerve of the scrawny kid standing up for himself. Lander had gotten the other ranchers in the district together, and they had put up $50,000 and started their bank.

That had been fourteen years ago, and in those fourteen years Martin Heller had transformed himself from an undersized cowhand into one of the most important men in the state. He had pinched and saved, and he had gradually bought up the bank stock — from the ranchers who knew little about banking operations and cared less — until he controlled the institution. He granted mortgages and acquired some cattle of his own. He was the third most important man in the valley, but he had sense enough to realize that he would remain the third man as long as the Lander brothers held their ranch.

The feud, utterly unexpected, came at a proper moment in Heller's plans, and the news that Wolf Lander had hired Pete Clouse as foreman was almost too good for Heller to believe. Heller had used Clouse for small errands in the past.

Now, Heller was waiting for Pete Clouse. Heller had managed to get word to the new Wolf Head foreman that he wanted to see him at once.

"It's this way," Heller said, when he and Clouse were seated together in the rear room of the bank. "I'm going to break both of the Lander brothers."

Clouse was not a man who wasted words. "How?"

Heller told him: "They have all the cattle

30

in the world but not much money. No one in the valley ever has any ready cash. That's what the bank is for, to make loans against their cattle."

Clouse nodded.

"So you steal their cattle. No one is going to bother you. Wolf trusts you completely. You steal from both of them and drive the cattle up into the mountains, and, if you can manage to stir up trouble between them, by making each one think that his brother is behind the thefts, so much the better."

Clouse helped himself to a drink and squinted at Heller. "And then what happens?"

Heller smiled. "Don't worry about that. Both of them look on me as a friend, both come to me for advice on financial affairs. Before they know it, they will have borrowed so much money from the bank that they'll never be able to pay off."

Clouse considered this. "And if they find out, they'll kill you."

Heller's face was suddenly drawn and ugly. "Maybe it would be a good thing if an accident happened to Jerry. He's the smarter of the two. Maybe we could make it look as if he were murdered by his brother. In that case, the valley might just hang Wolf. And the bank then would have to foreclose . . . to protect its loans, of course."

A week later, Heller sat at his desk, his eyes on the street where Jerry and his foreman Ed Irish had just ridden up to the bank's hitching rail. Irish had been on the Box L when Jerry was born, and he would probably die on the ranch. A good cattleman, loyal to the ranch, the split between the brothers had been hard on him. He was arguing when they came into the bank. "I don't believe it," he was saying. "I don't believe Wolf is a thief. He may hate you, but he wouldn't sneak behind your back to steal a steer. He'd brace you with a gun."

Heller rose and came forward to the wooden fence that separated his office from the main part of the bank. His small, dark eyes turned questioningly from one man to the other. "What's this all about?" He spoke with the easy assurance of an old friend.

Jerry turned toward him. "We found a yearling," he said. He went on to tell how they had run across the animal with the fresh brand. "Someone stole it from us and ran the Wolf Head on it. Why should anyone do that unless Wolf ordered him to?"

Ed Irish said: "I don't trust Pete Clouse."

"I don't, either." Jerry's eyes were hard.

"But what good would it do Clouse to rustle my stock? The only one it would benefit is Wolf."

"And Clouse is working for him."

Heller said: "Let's don't do anything hasty, Jerry. This could be some kind of an accident. You and Wolf are having enough trouble now without stirring up more."

"You haven't seen any trouble yet," said Jerry. "I haven't told you the rest. You know how our range lies. The mountains make a kind of natural fence. Some of the stock drifts up into the timber, but they don't go far and they come back down with the first snow."

The banker was watching him intently. "Yes?"

"So, we don't pay too much attention to the stock during the summer. The crew is busy with haying, and fixing the buildings, and breaking out horses. I haven't really looked at the stock for a couple of months until yesterday."

Heller said slowly: "So?"

Jerry's tone tightened. "A good third of them are gone. I can't tell how many until the roundup. And we found the trail up through the hills over which they had been driven. They are probably scattered across Wyoming by now."

Heller wet his lips. He had not expected that Jerry would miss the cattle so soon. "What are you going to do?"

Jerry said grimly: "I sent a message for Wolf to meet me here in town. If he doesn't come, I'll take the crew and ride out to the ranch and settle it once and for all."

Heller was thinking rapidly. He did not want Wolf and Jerry Lander to get together. If they did, if they started to compare notes, they might realize that there was a third force in the valley, stealing from both of them, for as many cattle had been taken from Wolf's range as from that of his older brother. Heller said: "If you and Wolf meet, only one thing will happen, and a fight never solves anything. The best thing for you to do is to ride back to the ranch and cool off. I'll talk to Wolf. I'll try and bring him to his senses."

Jerry started to shake his head, but Ed Irish cut in: "Heller's right. You and Wolf would rather argue with each other than try to get along. Let Heller talk to him. You don't want a shooting war blowing up this valley, do you?"

Jerry stared from one to the other, feeling slightly trapped. It was not that he was afraid of a shooting war. But he was thinking of his crew. They were loyal to a man, but they were mostly middle age, and they were cowhands, not gunfighters. They were certainly not qualified to go up against the toughs and brush jumpers that Pete Clouse had brought with him when he took over as foreman of the Wolf Head. Jerry said slowly: "I guess you're right. But listen, Heller. You tell Wolf that this has got to stop, that I've ordered every man to carry a rifle, and the first member of his crew that we catch on our side of the river gets shot."

He turned then, and walked out. He fully expected to climb on his horse and get out of town as soon as he could, but, just as he was moving down toward his horse, he saw Judy Parker come out of Blackwell's store. The girl turned the other way, apparently not seeing him, and walked slowly up the street. With a muttered word to Ed Irish to go on and he'd catch up, Jerry started after the girl. He knew that half a dozen people watched him from the store windows he passed.

"Judy!"

The girl glanced across her shoulder, but she gave no sign of recognition, and she did not stop. If anything she walked faster.

Jerry went after her. He was nearly running when he came up to her, saying: "You'd better stop or I'll put a rope on you."

She stopped, turning, looking up with eyes bright with anger. "I suppose it makes you happy to get me talked about?"

He said: "Now, look, I haven't done anything."

"Haven't you? Everyone on Main Street is watching us at this moment. It wasn't enough that you pulled your brother off his horse and fought in the dust like a couple of animals. It isn't enough that you've carried on your silly feud until everyone in the valley thinks there will be a war, and everyone says that I'm responsible."

"Well, we. . . ."

"And now you have to chase me on the street."

He said: "For a nickel I'd turn you over my knee and spank you, right here."

"You wouldn't dare." The small hands at her sides were doubled into fists, and Jerry had the sudden idea that she both would and knew how to use them. He grinned a little, and said: "All I wanted to do was to ask you if you'd go with me to the dance Saturday night."

"You know I won't."

He tried to be reasonable. "Now, listen. All I did was to fall in love with you."

"I'm sorry. I'm not interested." She was still angry. "I want nothing to do with you or with that crazy brother of yours, either, and you can tell him for me that I don't want him riding out to the schoolhouse again."

Jerry hadn't known that Wolf had been riding over to the schoolhouse, but at least his brother did not seem to be making any better time with her than he was. The fact made him feel a little better toward Wolf.

"So you're not going with Wolf Saturday night?"

"I most certainly am not."

"But you are going to the dance?"

She hesitated for just a moment, then she nodded. "I'm going with Martin Heller."

For an instant Jerry stared at her, then he started to laugh.

She asked waspishly: "What's the matter with that?"

"Why," he said, "nothing at all. It's kind of tough to have to compete with a man like Wolf, but no trouble to handle a runt like Heller. I'll be at the dance Saturday night. Save me most of your dances."

She said angrily: "I wouldn't dance with you if you were the last man in the valley."

He just grinned, watching her move away. The idea that Heller would take a girl to a dance amused him. "The little runt," he muttered. "He's getting big for his britches."

He was still chuckling. He wished Wolf was here to share the joke with him. Wolf in the old days would have thought up some trick to play on Heller.

Jerry felt real good for the first time since the fight with his brother. He hesitated for a moment, then moved across toward the Cattleman's Saloon. He was not usually a drinking man, but for some reason at the moment he felt the need to celebrate.

The long, semidark room, with its many odors coloring the stale air was deserted save for Tonopah Joe, the bartender. Jerry did not know where the man had gotten the name. Tonopah had been the bartender at the Cattleman's ever since Jerry could remember. A short man, nearly as wide as he was tall, his head was entirely bare of hair save for the bushy eyebrows that jutted out over his small eyes. Jerry did not like him very well, but he wanted to talk to someone.

He ordered whiskey, and told Tonopah to pour one for himself.

The bartender, a little surprised, complied, staring at his sole customer thoughtfully. "What's got you busting all your buttons, Jerry?"

Jerry downed his drink. He grinned, wiping his mouth with the back of his hand.

"It's a nice day, Tonopah, and I just naturally feel good."

Tonopah shrugged. Tending bar for nearly forty years had soured most of the human kindness out of him. He was a morose man who had no true friend in the whole valley. "You're crazy, Jerry."

Jerry didn't take offense.

Tonopah added: "If I were in your trouble, I wouldn't smile."

Jerry helped himself to another drink. The batwing doors behind him swung open. He glanced up at the mirror on the back bar, and then he froze. Pete Clouse had come into the room, Pete Clouse followed by four other Wolf Head riders.

IV

Slowly Jerry set the glass on the bar. He did not know that Martin Heller had sent Clouse to the bar to start trouble. But Jerry did not need to know this to realize that he was in a spot. He and Clouse had never gotten along, and the man's eyes, as they swept around the room, held an expression that should have been warning enough.

Jerry stood there, his back to the door, not moving, yet very ready, his hand not far from the butt of the heavy gun that swung at his hip. Clouse had paused for just a minute, and then came forward slowly, the four men fanning out behind him until they made a semicircle. Tonopah had glanced up. Tonopah was too old a hand not to recognize the signs of trouble. He said in his tight, old voice: "Take your fight outside, Pete. I don't want this bar wrecked."

Clouse looked at him, his eyes cold and deadly, and Tonopah was suddenly silent. Clouse came forward five steps and stopped. "Turn around, Lander, I want to talk to you."

Jerry turned slowly, keeping his hand well away from his gun. He knew that any move on his part would turn the barroom into a crashing inferno.

He looked at Clouse, and then at the fanned-out men. He was caught, and he knew it, and his mouth had a sudden dry metallic taste. But his voice was level and unhurried as he said: "What do you want?"

Clouse grinned. He was thoroughly enjoying himself. He was at heart a bully, and he liked nothing better than to toy with a victim, trying to make him crawl. He said: "I understand you've been talking about me."

Jerry looked blank. "You must be mistaken, Pete. I only talk about people I think are important." He was trying to goad Clouse into anger, trying to make the Wolf Head foreman lose his head, for he recognized now that this was a perfectly planned attack, and that they would never have braced him if they expected him to walk out of here alive. He had the bitter thought that Wolf must have ordered his murder. It was hard to believe, but if Wolf would stoop to stealing, he might not be above murder.

Pete Clouse's heavy face darkened, but he managed to hold his temper. "You're a liar." He said this clearly, distinctly. "You've been going around saying that we have been stealing your stock."

Jerry tried to recall who he had talked to. As far as he could remember, he had mentioned it only to the judge and to Martin Heller. But he knew that this meant nothing since any member of his crew might have told of the discovery that stock had been stolen. Jerry didn't answer. He watched the man in front of him. He knew that with five guns against him he had little or no chance of surviving. But if he had to die, he certainly meant to take Pete Clouse with him.

Clouse was saying wickedly: "No one calls me a thief and gets away with it. You're going to apologize, Jerry. You're going to get down on your knees and crawl over here and say that you are a liar."

A quiet voice behind Clouse said: "You're having pipe dreams, Pete!" The men behind Clouse turned their heads. Ed Irish was standing in the saloon doorway, a shotgun in his old hands. He smiled a little at them, his gray eyes hard and mocking. "Go ahead, tough men, open the ball. Let's see which of you wants to die first."

It was evident that none of them wanted to die. They had been very brave, very fierce when they had five guns to Jerry's one. But now, under the frowning barrels of Ed Irish's weapon, they slowly raised their hands to show peaceful intent. Only Clouse kept his hands at his side, standing half turned toward the door, motionless.

Ed Irish said: "You've got exactly ten seconds to get them up, Pete. I've always promised myself that someday I'd have the pleasure of blowing a hole in your belly, and it might as well be now."

Clouse said through tight teeth: "Old man, I won't forget this soon."

"I hope you don't," said Irish. "I hope you never forget it. Get your hands up."

Clouse read the determination in the old eyes and slowly raised his hands. Jerry Lander stepped away from the bar and lifted the gun out of Clouse's holster. He tossed it over the counter to fall with a *clatter* on the worn boards at Tonopah's feet. Then he moved around the half circle, lifting one gun and then another, tossing them into a pile in the far corner.

"OK, boys, get over against the wall."

They stared at him uncertainly, not at all sure what he meant to do.

"Get over there."

They obeyed slowly, sullenly.

"Watch them, Ed."

Ed Irish's eyes had a dancing quality as if he were thoroughly enjoying himself. "I'll watch them."

Jerry pulled his own gun. He walked to the bar and laid it on the scarred counter, then he faced around. "All right, Pete. I'm going to whip you until you can't crawl."

Clouse glared back at him, hardly believing his ears. He was twenty pounds heavier than Jerry, the veteran of a hundred barroom fights. Then a pleased, hungry look came into his face, his lips pulling back into a smile. He charged, his big arms flailing, his reddened fists looking like two blocks of knotted wood.

Jerry ducked the first swing and drove his right fist into Clouse's belly. The force of the blow halted the big man for an instant and air *whooshed* out of his open mouth. But he shook his head like a wounded bull and charged again. This time one of his lumbering blows caught Jerry on the ear and sent him spinning back against the bar.

Clouse followed, lowering his head and diving in an effort to trap Jerry between the bar and the pile-driving thrust of the big, shaggy head. At the last instant Jerry stepped to one side and Clouse butted the bar edge so hard that it knocked the whole counter a good half foot out of line. He dropped to his knees, but he was not out. He stayed there for a full minute as if trying to clear his addled senses, then he dragged himself up and turned, just as Jerry came in, both fists working.

There was no mercy in Jerry. He beat the big man as few men have been beaten. But he did not escape punishment himself. One eye was swollen, there was a cut above the other where Clouse had succeeded in butting him, and he was painfully bruised around the body. The blow that put Clouse down was one under the heart. It was a blow of desperation, for Jerry's arms were so tired that his hands seemed to be made of lead. It was all he could do to raise them high enough to strike. He sank the fist into Clouse's side and watched him go over onto his face and lie, quiet and unmoving, on the dirty floor.

Jerry stood there, wiping the blood away from his eye and staring down at the fallen man. Clouse had gotten up many times, and, if he rose this time, Jerry doubted that he had enough left to put him down again. But Clouse did not rise. In fact, he did not stir. He lay as if he were dead and there were those among his men against the wall who thought he was.

Jerry turned slowly then. He picked up his gun from the bar top and shoved it into his holster, and came around and looked at the men along the wall with his good eye, as if he were engraving their faces in his memory.

"You're through in this valley," he said, and his voice was little more than an exhausted croak. "I mean that. If I catch any of you again, I'll shoot first and ask questions later. Pick up their guns, Ed."

Irish moved over to the corner and scooped up the captured weapons.

"Come on." Jerry did not glance again at the men along the wall. He led the way out into the street. The glare of the sunlight hurt his eyes, and he squinted against it, trying to remember where he had left his horse.

"Over there." Ed Irish pointed toward the

rack in front of the bank.

Jerry walked down the middle of the dusty street. He did not see Heller watching him from the window of the bank. He did not see anyone. Somehow he reached his horse and lifted himself painfully into the saddle and rode out of town, Ed Irish following. Ed was still carrying the captured guns.

At the first creek Jerry pulled off the road and dismounted. He used his neckerchief, dipping it in the cool water and bathing the blood from his face. The water stung the cuts but it revived him, clearing his head, making it easier for him to think.

Ed Irish had stepped out of the saddle. With a stick he dug a small hole beside the creek and dumped the captured guns into it. Then he kicked dirt over them and stomped the sod in place.

Jerry had turned to watch him. "Looks like we pulled part of their teeth."

Ed Irish answered without looking up. "They can buy more guns."

"You think Pete Clouse will stay in the valley after the beating I gave him?"

The older man nodded soberly. "He's got to. The only thing in the world a man like Clouse has is his pride. He can't take a beating and lie down. Nothing will satisfy him but killing you."

Jerry again dipped the neckerchief in the water and held it over his bruised face. When he took it away, he said, "I'll have to be ready for him."

The old man frowned. "I've watched you use your gun. You're fast, but you never pulled it on a man, Jerry. There's a lot of difference, and Pete Clouse has had a lot of practice." Jerry did not answer and the old man went on: "Maybe I should ride over to the county seat and have a talk with the sheriff."

At once Jerry was affronted. "We never have needed any outside law in this valley."

"Things are different now." Ed Irish sounded stubborn.

"Not that different. I'll take care of Pete Clouse when I have to. How'd you happen to show up in that saloon just at the right time?"

"I didn't happen to," Irish said. "I was riding for home and I passed those jaspers. They didn't bother me, but I got to thinking of you alone in town, so I rode back and borrowed the shotgun from Bechwell."

"Lucky for me you did."

"There's something else. Pete Clouse stopped for a minute at the bank and spoke to Heller."

Jerry looked at him. "What are you trying to say?"

The old man shrugged. "I don't rightly know. Maybe nothing, but from the bank they went directly to that saloon, as if they knew where you were, as if they were hunting you."

Jerry shook his head. "Are you trying to say that Martin Heller is mixed up with Pete Clouse? You know that isn't true. Martin may be a runt, but he's one of the most respectable citizens of the valley. Why, he's done everything in his power to bring Wolf and me back together."

Ed Irish did not argue, but he looked thoughtful.

V

The version that Wolf Lander got was very different from what had actually happened in the saloon. The crew came home, having mounted the battered Clouse on his horse and half holding him in the saddle during the long ride. They came into the yard to see Wolf standing on the porch. George Neff elected to tell the ranch owner what had happened:

"Your brother was in the saloon, talking to Tonopah, calling you a rustler and saying

48

that anyone who rode for the Wolf Head was nothing but an outlaw."

Wolf came down off the porch, his face setting in hard lines. "What happened?"

Neff took a long breath. He was a practiced liar and he knew that he was getting his story across. "We were at a back table, just having a quiet drink. Pete stood it as long as he could, then he got up and walked over and told Jerry he was a liar. Jerry swung around quick as a wink and hit him with a bottle. That knocked Pete down. He was only about half conscious but he struggled up and Jerry beat him."

Wolf's eyes glinted. "And what were you doing all this time?"

Neff said: "Nothing. We started to, but that damn' Ed Irish came in with a shotgun and backed us over against the wall. Jerry beat Pete until he dropped unconscious, then he turned around and ordered us all out of the country. Said that he'd kill any of us on sight."

Wolf's face was grim.

Neff went on: "And he said he was going to brand you as a rustler and run you out of the valley before the fall roundup."

Wolf stood for a long moment, thoughtful. Then he said slowly: "You pulling out?"

Neff stared at him. "You want us to?"

49

Wolf shook his head. "But I don't want any shooting trouble, either. It's one thing for us to split the ranch, but it's something else to start a shooting war. You stay on the place and keep the rest of the crew in. I'm going to town to see Heller. This thing is getting out of hand."

He said as much to Martin Heller when he walked into the bank just before closing that afternoon. "I suppose you heard about the fight?"

Heller nodded, measuring Wolf with his shrewd eyes. "They aren't talking about much else in town."

"What's the matter? Has Jerry gone crazy?"

Heller took a long time to answer. Finally he said: "I'm afraid it's the girl. I should have let her go back to Denver when she wanted to, instead of insisting that she finish out the school term."

The words caught Wolf off guard. "What's she got to do with this latest fight? Did Pete Clouse insult her or something?"

Heller shook his head. "No, Clouse wasn't in town when it happened. Jerry chased her down the street. I couldn't hear what was said, but I could see that they were arguing, and then, when she went on, Jerry turned into the saloon. I could see by the way he walked that he was very angry."

"So he took it out on Clouse?"

Heller nodded. "That's about the way I figure it."

"I've got to be sure." Wolf was talking, half to himself. "I'll go down and ask Tonopah exactly what happened."

"Do that." Heller had already talked to Tonopah. Heller had paid the bartender $100 to swear that Jerry started the fight. He watched Wolf leave the bank and move up the street. He did not rub his hands together in pleasure, but his face told plainly that he was very satisfied with the way things were going.

But even as he watched Wolf, someone was watching him. Fred Bates was a man old before his time. He had come West, a bookkeeper who could no longer take the Eastern dampness. He had gotten a job with the newly opened bank and had been there ever since, a combination teller, bookkeeper, and general handyman. He had no friends, and he seldom spoke to anyone save the customers who came to his window. Martin Heller treated him with contempt, working him long hours, and showing him no more courtesy than if he had been a piece of furniture. If Heller had been asked, he would have laughed and said that Fred

51

Bates was a spineless fool who hardly had sense enough to feed himself. But he underestimated Fred Bates.

Fred knew exactly what was going on. He had watched silently as Heller strengthened his grip on the bank, and he guessed that Heller was purposely pushing the fight between the Lander brothers with the idea of eventually grabbing both sections of the big ranch. Bates had not spoken of this to anyone. He had little love for the people in the valley, especially the Lander boys, who in their younger days had not hesitated to play their practical jokes on him, but he watched with a growing bitterness, engendered by his dislike of Heller. He thought now: *If I just told them what he is doing they'd fix him, they'd kill him.* And he reasoned with himself: *But what if they wouldn't believe me? What if they told Heller, and he sent Pete Clouse and his boys after me?* He shivered. He was not a brave man.

Wolf Lander knew nothing of this. He crossed the street and walked into the Cattleman's Saloon and nodded to Tonopah, looking around the room. There were five men playing poker at a rear table. Aside from them and the bartender the place was empty.

He walked over to the bar and ordered

whiskey, and watched in silence as the bartender set out the small glass and bottle. There was something in Tonopah's manner that bothered him, a nervousness that was not normal with the man. "What's the matter, Tonopah?"

The bartender lifted unwilling eyes to meet his. "It wasn't my fault."

"What wasn't?"

Tonopah licked his dry lips. "I couldn't stop him. He was like a crazy man."

"You mean Jerry?"

Tonopah nodded. He seemed eager to talk, almost too eager. "I don't want you to think I helped against your crew. I don't take no sides in the fight, Wolf. I serve anyone who comes in with the money."

"That's all right."

"Never thought I'd live to see the day Pete Clouse would get licked," said Tonopah.

"Getting hit with the bottle didn't help him."

Tonopah had not heard that version of the story but he agreed readily, meanwhile cursing Heller under his breath for not warning him. "Jerry did a real thorough job," he added. "Is Pete going to pull out?"

Wolf's face darkened. "He is not. What gave you that idea?"

Tonopah said: "From the way Jerry talked

I kind of got the idea that he meant it. He said that he'd shoot the first one of the crew he met on sight."

Wolf said tightly: "Jerry isn't running this valley. He may think he is, but he's got another think coming." He downed the whiskey at a single gulp, tossed a silver dollar on the bar, and turned out of the saloon. Tonopah stared after him thoughtfully. *I wonder,* he mused, *just what Martin Heller thinks he's up to. Now why should a banker want me to lie to Wolf about who started that fight?* He was silent, considering, wondering how best to turn his small knowledge to his advantage.

Wolf went back to the bank and got his horse. He rode it down to the edge of town where the small schoolhouse squatted in its fenced yard. He had to talk to Judy Parker and he was not at all sure of his reception.

He saw as he came in sight of the small building that school was already dismissed, the children stringing across the yard. He idled until the last one had gone, then rode through the gate and up to the doorway, stepping down.

Judy Parker had heard him. She was at the high desk at the front of the room, correcting papers. She looked up, and, when she realized who it was, her eyes darkened and her face flushed. "I told you that I never wanted to see you again."

Wolf had paused in the doorway. He came on now, down the center aisle between the rows of desks, not stopping until he was directly before her. "I understand you talked to my brother this morning."

She said levelly: "He talked to me. I walked down to the store during recess and he followed me."

"Is that why he went on into the saloon and whipped my crew?"

She had not heard of the fight. "I know nothing about it. He asked me to go to the dance Saturday night and I refused. Then he said I'd better save most of the dances for him. That was all he said."

Wolf had forgotten the Saturday night dance, but he pretended not to have. "I'm glad you refused because you are going with me."

"I'm going with Martin Heller."

"Heller?" Wolf ran a hand through his red hair. "Well that ties it."

She said angrily: "And what is the matter with Martin Heller? I understand he's a friend of yours."

Wolf grinned. "Oh, Martin's all right, I guess, but not to take my girl dancing."

"I'm not your girl."

"You're going to be," said Wolf. "Remember, I expect at least half the dances on Saturday, and maybe you and I will ride out and see another sunrise."

Judy controlled her temper, saying in a strained voice: "Listen, Wolf, this whole thing has gone far enough. Why don't you and Jerry get together? If it's because of me . . . forget it. I wouldn't marry either of you for all the cattle in the valley."

"Sure you will, if I have to kidnap you." He was grinning at her "You're right pretty when you're angry."

She picked up a ruler and threw it at him. He caught it expertly, then leaned across the desk and, grasping her shoulders, kissed her hard. Her lips under his kiss were cool and unresponsive, but she did not struggle to get away and after a moment he released her. "Remember, I get half your dances on Saturday night."

He was gone then, and the girl sat where she was, unmoving until she heard the *thud* of hoofs as he turned his horse out of the sun-baked yard.

VI

Pete Clouse was up and around the next morning despite his aching muscles. The vitality of the man was enormous, and he seemed to have absorbed the beating without any real physical damage. But the damage to his pride was a burning thing that ate at him and turned his whole insides to hate. He snarled at every member of the crew who dared speak to him, and ignored Wolf when the young rancher gave him orders about the day's work. Only to the four men he had brought to the ranch with him and who had been at the saloon during the fight, was he even half civil.

They rode out to repair a stretch of fence, and once away from the house Clouse turned to Neff. "We're going over across the river tonight," he said. "We're going to burn Jerry out. We're going to shoot him and that foreman of his."

Neff had no softness in him. He had ridden shady trails ever since he was a boy and he was well over forty, but he protested now. "Heller won't like it," he said. "Heller don't mind if you kill Jerry. In fact, I think he wants you to, but he doesn't want anything which might stir up the country, and a fight like that would."

"Hell with Heller."

Neff knew Pete Clouse well enough not to push the argument too far, but he tried once more. "Better wait for a couple of days until you're feeling better."

"I'm feeling well enough for this job." He glared at the other men. "Tonight, when you ride in, don't put your horses in the corral, tie them in the brush down by the creek so we can slip away without Wolf knowing."

"Some of the rest of the crowd in the bunkhouse will tell him."

Pete Clouse stared at Neff. "Not if I tell them not to. There isn't one who wants trouble with me." He said this last, not as a boast, but as a simple fact, and Neff knew that he was speaking the truth. There was no more argument.

At midnight, when Clouse crawled out of his bunk, the four men were awake and ready. Clouse lighted a lamp and stared around as the other sleeping men stirred. He called to them: "You all wake up!"

They came grumblingly awake.

He looked big and bulky and formidable in his bunchy coat. "We're taking a little ride," he told them. "I don't want it mentioned to anyone, not even Wolf. Do you understand?"

They understood.

He blew out the lamp and led his four men through the door and across the dark yard. There was no moon, and the stars were far away and gave but little light. They reached their horses without incident and turned toward the river, Neff and Clouse riding ahead, the other three following.

The river was not large, some forty feet across and shallow enough in most places so that the swiftly running water did not come much above the horses' knees. It was a cold, clear stream, fed by the mountain snows that clung to the higher peaks until well into August each season and afforded plenty of water for that whole section of the valley. They splashed across and, keeping their horses at a steady jog, mounted the rising swell of the rolling range, heading toward the mountains that made a dark smudge in the north.

The line camp Jerry was transforming into his home ranch stood in the wide mouth of a side valley. It was not in timber, but the trees grew down the slope to within five hundred feet of the yard on three sides. Pete Clouse swung his men up into the timber, climbing one of the side ridges and circling to come down at the rear of the log buildings.

There were three big stacks of hay in the yard, freshly cut, stored against the deep snow of the coming winter, and at sight of them Clouse's eyes glistened. He posted Neff above the house on the ridge so that he could cover the front yard and led the rest around to fire the stacks.

They were burning brightly before their light disturbed one of Jerry's sleeping crew, and he woke the bunkhouse with his rising shout. Men, half dressed and still drugged by sleep, tumbled out into the yard that was now nearly as light as day from the leaping flames of the haystacks. The first to appear drew a rifle shot from Neff, and fell backwards against the man who had been following him through the door. The others, inside, not understanding what was happening, tried to push their way out.

Jerry Landers had not been sleeping in the bunkhouse. His bed was in a small shack, far to the right that he had set up as an office and had been using until the main house could be finished. The light of the flames had not awakened him, since the shack's window was on the far side. But the first shot did. He rolled out, unconsciously feeling for his boots, pulled them on, and then moved to the door, picking up his rifle as he passed its resting place.

He stopped in the doorway, surveying the yard and the bunkhouse and the timber beyond. He saw Neff then, for the man, feeling secure from below, had stepped out of his hiding place to get a clearer shot at the bunkhouse door.

Jerry raised his rifle, letting it come up until he caught the dark shadow of Neff's bulk in his sights. Then he squeezed away his shot. He heard the mushy *thud* as his bullet struck even before he caught the man's wild, high yell of surprise. But he did not wait for either. As soon as he fired, he was running forward, headed for the shelter of the timber, knowing that he had to make it or they all were dead. With the Box L trapped in the buildings, the fire lighting the yard, the attackers could take their time, sniping at anyone who showed his face. But with Jerry loose in the trees it would be another story.

He had traveled more than half the distance before Pete Clouse and the men with him in the growth above the bunkhouse realized what was happening and turned their attentions to him. A bullet *thudded* into the turf on his right, another struck ahead of him, a third tore through the loose fabric of his shirt just as he reached the shelter of the first trunks and threw himself into their shadow.

He stayed there, flat on his belly for a full three minutes, recovering his shortened breath. Then he rose cautiously and worked around through the timber to where Neff had been. The man was gone, but blood on the ground, and a dropped rifle showed where he had been. Jerry paused, listening, and heard the *crash* of a horse ahead of him and guessed that the wounded man had managed to drag himself to his mount and was pulling out.

He forgot him at once. No more bullets came searching him from the raiders. They seemed to have turned their attention to the Box L men still penned in the bunkhouse below. Jerry saw the flash of their guns as they fired at spaced intervals in an effort to keep his crew from breaking out.

Grimly he started to circle through the trees. In him was a deep burning anger that grew as he moved ahead. He had no way of knowing who had ordered this attack, whether it was Pete Clouse's idea or whether his brother had been in on it. As he moved forward, he remembered the times he and Wolf had played in these same hills, riding their horses up and down the shallow draws, shooting and howling out the high spirits of their youth. He knew every inch of the terrain, knew it as he knew the lines in the back of his own hand, and he took advantage of it to find himself a high rock face from which he could command the position of the men below him.

He waited then, coldly, deliberately. He had no fear of them although he judged that there must be four or five in the raiding party. He waited until someone below fired at the bunkhouse, and then sent his own bullet searching downward toward the point from which the shot had come. There was a sharp, startled yell, and then a curse, and then a man's deep belligerent voice that he had no difficulty in identifying as belonging to Pete Clouse.

"He's on the ridge above us!"

At once they turned their guns upward, sending their fire splattering among the trees to rebound from the rocks about him. He grinned, levered another shell into the chamber, and fired at one of the gun flashes. Then quickly he shifted along the ridge to pause with a tree for shelter and send another shot.

There was the high, neighing cry of a hit horse, and cursing and thrashing in the brush, and then Pete Clouse's order, plain to hear: "Let's get out of this!"

They went, making no attempt to conceal their passage, and Jerry sped them on their way with a few well-placed shots. Then, when he was certain they were entirely gone, he climbed back down into the yard, calling to his crew as he came. They boiled out around him. These were peaceful men, all of them with the fire of youth burned out of them, replaced by solidness and responsibility. But they were angry now. They tried to save the haystacks, but it was too late. Already the fire had eaten so deeply into the dried grass that it would smolder for days.

It was Ed Irish who made the suggestion, just as light was breaking in the eastern sky: "Are we going to take this lying down, or are we going after them?"

Jerry stared at him bleakly. "Ed," he said, "you boys were hired to work on the ranch, not to fight, not to go up against gunmen like Pete Clouse's crowd."

The older man sighed. "You don't seem to understand, Jerry. This is personal with us now. We were the ones in that bunkhouse, being shot at. If you hadn't managed to sneak out and get up onto that ridge, some of us would probably be dead."

Jerry looked at them, at their grave, set faces. These were men he had known all his life, men who had ridden for his father. He said slowly: "I won't order you to ride after them, but I will ride with you."

VII

Wolf Lander came out of the ranch house just in time to see the ten horsemen top the crest of the small rise. He stopped, blinking as they rode forward into the yard. He recognized all of them, his brother in the lead, Ed Irish at Jerry's side, and the rest of the crew grim-faced and silent. He walked down the porch steps and across to where Jerry had halted his horse and now sat, staring down at him. "What do you want?" He had already noted the guns across the saddles, the alertness of the men.

Jerry said: "Check the bunkhouse."

At once his men circled away, leaving Irish and Jerry to face Wolf.

Wolf's anger was rising. "I ask again, what do you want?"

Ed Irish answered for Jerry: "Clouse."

Wolf said tightly: "Listen, Jerry, no matter what is between us, no man rides on my land and takes my crew without me trying to stop him. Didn't you do enough to Clouse yesterday?"

"To give him the excuse to burn my stacks and try and shoot up my crew?"

Wolf's mouth opened. "What are you talking about?"

It dawned on Jerry that Wolf knew nothing of the night raid. Whatever other faults Wolf had, he was not a liar, and, if he had planned the raid, he would have said so and damned them to do anything about it. Jerry said: "Clouse and four or five men swooped down on us last night. They fired the haystacks and shot up the bunkhouse. Ace Dorn got a bullet in his shoulder."

Wolf was gaping up at his brother. "You're certain it was Pete?"

"I heard his voice. I wasn't sleeping in the bunkhouse but in the old wood shack I've made into an office. I got out and winged Neff."

Wolf swore under his breath. "This is none of my doing. It's because of that fight you had with Clouse in the saloon yesterday. Come on, I'm going to find out about this." He turned without waiting for an answer and stalked toward the bunkhouse, but he learned very little, for Clouse and the men who had followed him were not there. Some of his crew were just getting up; others were already in the cook shack. They could tell him nothing except that shortly after midnight Clouse and four men had walked out of the bunkhouse warning them to tell no one, not even Wolf.

Wolf Lander walked back across the yard with his brother, his face more serious than

Jerry had ever seen it. Wolf said slowly: "They've probably made for the hills. They probably knew that I wouldn't stand for anything like this."

Jerry said suddenly: "Look, Wolf, we've been making fools of ourselves. You haven't been branding any of my stock, have you?"

The redhead shook his head.

"Someone has," said Jerry. "About a third of my steers are gone. We found a plain trail leading up into the hills."

Wolf hunched his shoulders. "Let's have a look, but first, have your men eaten?"

Jerry shook his head and Wolf called to his cook, giving his orders.

Afterward, they rode, Jerry's men and those of Wolf's who had not been with Clouse. They had no difficulty in following the trail. It led up the cañon where the river came out of the hills, well marked by the hundreds of hoofs that had passed over it, but they did not find the cattle. Instead, high in a mountain meadow they came upon a cabin and a newly built corral, and the marks of a branding fire. Studying the tracks, Ed Irish said: "I guess about four or five men brought the critters this far, then they re-branded them, and another crew, maybe a dozen men, picked them up and drove them north. The others turned back."

The two brothers looked at each other, and Wolf's tone was bitter. "Seems like Pete Clouse made a sucker out of me."

"Or me," Jerry said. "They were mostly my cows he took."

Wolf said tightly: "He was riding for me, and I feel responsible for all his acts. You take a tally and let me know how many head you think are missing. I'll make them good."

Jerry hesitated for a moment. "Wolf, this whole thing is a little silly. Just because you tried to steal my girl."

"Your girl? Now wait a minute."

Ed Irish said angrily: "You two pups shut up, will you? Supposing you let the girl decide. It isn't going to help her make up her mind you two giving each other black eyes."

They turned to glare at him.

"Meanwhile them jaspers, whoever they are, are making off with the cattle they stole."

Wolf and Jerry were both listening to him now.

"If they were mine" — the old man was speaking with studied carelessness — "I'd ride out after them and find who took them and where they went."

Jerry said: "You think Pete Clouse is with them?"

The old man shook his head. "Not unless he caught up with them. Those tracks are a good week old, maybe more. If you ask me, Clouse has holed up somewhere in the hills."

"Then I'm not leaving the valley until I find him. I tell you, Wolf, you go with the boys."

Wolf shook his head. "Clouse is mine. He belongs to me. You go."

Ed Irish said in disgust: "Both of you stay. I'll find those damn' cows." He turned, his eyes ranging over the crew, picking out the men he wanted. He chose six. "That's enough," he said. "I'm not leading an army out to take them back single-handed. I just want to find where they went and who got them. You'll hear from me when I know anything."

He rode away then, leaving the brothers with the remaining members of their crews. Wolf said: "What do we do now?"

Jerry shrugged. "We scout the country I guess. Pete and his boys haven't gone too far. They have at least one wounded man with them and I think I hit one of the horses. We should pick up their trail without too much trouble."

But in this Jerry was wrong, for although they broke into small groups and searched the timber all along the north and west rim of the valley, they found no trace of Pete Clouse or his men.

There was a very good reason for this. Clouse, as soon as he rode away from the Box L, knew instinctively that he dared not go back to the Wolf Head. He guessed that as soon as Jerry could collect his crew from the bunkhouse they would do exactly as they did. And he was faced with the need for a quick decision. He could ride up into the hills and follow the trail that had been made when the cattle were driven away. But Neff had been shot through the body, and one of the horses had a bullet in its flank. He chose, instead, to ride to Heller's place, knowing that the banker would not dare refuse him shelter.

The Heller place was small, only a couple of thousand acres, sitting on a small creek two miles to the north of town. But there were a number of buildings, and their horses would pass unnoticed in Heller's corral. They reached it an hour after daylight, having cut across country and avoided the town, and Clouse was reasonably certain that they had not been seen.

The sound of their arrival woke the small banker and he stormed out onto the porch furious at the invasion. Clouse had dismounted and was helping the wounded Neff out of the saddle.

Heller came down off the steps, glaring at him. "What do you think you're doing here?"

Clouse turned on him. He had no real liking for this small man whom he found it profitable to do business with. "We ran into trouble at the Box L," he said mildly. "We had to have some place to hole up until it quiets down a little."

"You'll not stay here."

"We've got to. If I'm any judge, the first thing Jerry will do is to ride over to the Wolf Head. And if I guess right, Wolf will join him in jumping us."

"But what if they find you here?" Heller was pale now, his mouth drawn.

"They won't," said Clouse. "No one ever comes out here to see you. You aren't that well liked."

A spot of angry color appeared in each of the banker's sallow cheeks, but he controlled himself with an effort. "What about him?" He jerked his thumb toward Neff who had been helped to the edge of the porch.

"I'm a pretty good doctor," Clouse said. "I'll dig the bullet out of him. That's about all we can do."

For one sick moment Martin Heller

71

wished that he had never seen any of these men. He was not a coward, and he had handled a gun in his time, but he had thought that he had grown past any personal involvement in this. Actually what Pete Clouse said was true. Almost no one ever came out to the ranch, and the two hands he hired were old, sour men who seldom went to town. The chance that Clouse and his followers would be discovered was very small.

He said: "All right. All right, get him inside, and keep out of sight yourselves. Clouse, I want to talk to you." He led Pete away from the house, out of hearing of the rest. He was furious, but he had learned to conceal his temper.

When they were alone, he said: "That was a stupid thing to do."

Pete Clouse stirred. In ordinary circumstances he would not have taken that kind of talk from anyone. But this was not an ordinary thing. He said sullenly: "I thought you wanted to get rid of Jerry?"

"I do, but I want to get rid of him, not mess up the job. Now we'll have to get rid of him and Wolf, too."

"I mean to." Clouse was grim. "Give me a couple of days and I'll try again."

"Supposing you let me do the planning."

Martin Heller's words were chill. "Things seem to work a little better when I make the decisions."

Pete Clouse glared at him, but he held his words. There was too much at stake for him to break with Heller now. But he stored up the thought in the rat nest of his mind. Someday, sometime he would settle with this small banker. Someday he would break Heller in two with his hands.

"All right," he said, "but don't wait too long."

VIII

Coming out of the hills with two men at his back, Jerry Lander rode into the Wolf Head yard late on Saturday afternoon. He was tired and hot and angry, for all their riding had drawn nothing but a blank.

Wolf had been beside the corral and he walked forward to meet his brother, his head showing red and fiery in the afternoon sun. "No luck?"

Jerry shook his head. He made no move to dismount, but eased himself in the saddle, hooking one leg over the horn. "Not a sign."

Wolf was morose. "No luck here, either. I've ridden three horses into the ground.

No sign of them. They must have pulled out of the country."

Jerry was thoughtful. "That isn't like Pete. He's too bullheaded to quit."

"Maybe one of your shots hit him." Wolf sounded hopeful.

Jerry shook his head. "I don't think so. His voice was real healthy. I guess you're right. They probably pulled out."

"Any word from Ed Irish?"

Jerry shook his head again. "I suppose he's trailing those cows. They must have driven them clear to Canada. Well, I've got to be moving along."

Wolf was instantly alert. "Going to town?"

Jerry pretended surprise. "Why would I be going to town?"

"The dance."

"Oh, I forgot about it." He yawned. "Guess I've had too much riding these last few days to be interested in any dance. I'll head home and hit the blankets."

He turned away and motioned to his two men, and they rode over the rise.

Wolf watched him go, a half smile on his freckled face. He thought: *Jerry likes to pretend. Jerry thinks he's fooled me into believing he isn't going to that dance.* He whistled softly to himself and, turning into the corral, saddled a horse. He meant to be at the dance when Jerry arrived. . . .

Martin Heller saw Wolf ride into town just before dark, and watched as Wolf progressed up the street to leave his horse at the livery. He watched him intently as he came back down the street, wondering if Wolf would seek him out at the bank, but instead the red-headed man turned into the saloon. Heller hesitated. He seldom invaded the saloon, but he felt that he had to talk to Wolf. He had not talked to him since the attack on Jerry's ranch.

He rose and put on his hat and turned and found Fred Bates watching him from the teller's window. "You can close up," he told Bates. "Be sure and lock the safe." He went out then into the late afternoon, too wrapped in his own thoughts to be conscious that Bates had come around the counter and stood at the front window, watching him as he crossed to the saloon.

Tonopah was behind the bar. Two card games were going at the rear of the room, and Joey Dirkson, the blacksmith, was having a drink with Wolf. Heller moved over to them, nodding to Dirkson. "A small one, Tonopah."

Tonopah served the banker with no change of expression. Heller downed it neat.

75

There was something dainty about the way he took the liquor, no drop spilling from the small glass as if he deplored waste to the extent that he could not stand to spill anything.

Dirkson finished his drink and wiped his mouth with the back of a none-too-clean hand. He said: "The old lady will skin me if I don't get home." He left the saloon. Heller watched in the mirror until the batwing doors flapped shut behind him, then said idly to Wolf: "In for the dance?"

Wolf had been thinking something else. His mind came back to the present with a start, and he grinned. "I understand you're taking my girl."

Heller considered him, saying carefully: "Someone had to take her. It's hard enough to keep schoolteachers in this part of the country, and I am head of the school board."

Wolf laughed. "Martin," he said, "you're the first man I ever knew who had to find an excuse for wanting to take a pretty girl to a dance. You have to show more steam than that if you expect to hold her."

Martin Heller flushed slightly. Not even to himself had he admitted a real interest in Judy Parker, and it came as a kind of shock, brought on by Wolf's careless words, that he was actually interested in the girl. But he could not let Wolf know. "Someone had to take her, and certainly she wouldn't go with either you or your brother."

Wolf grinned. "All right, Martin." He winked at Tonopah. "You take her, but you don't have to dance with her. You never were a very good dancer, anyhow."

Heller knew what he meant. He had a vision of the girl, floating around the hall in Wolf's arms while he stood on the sidelines and a little of his dislike of the idea showed in his voice. "Don't worry, I'll dance with her."

"Want to bet on it?" Wolf's grin was mocking. "Jerry will be there, and I'll be there, and she'll have trouble enough with us without having to worry about you."

Heller motioned Tonopah to fill their glasses. "I'll bet," he said. He downed his drink and with a muttered excuse he left the saloon.

Wolf grinned after him, and then wandered over to watch the card game.

Outside, Heller walked to the stable and got his horse. He rode slowly, thinking as he rode. When he turned into his own yard, he saw Pete Clouse come to the door and his resolve hardened into purpose.

"They'll be at the dance," he said to

Clouse when they were standing in the cluttered living room of his house. Neff lay on a pile of blankets in the far corner, his eyes still bright with fever.

Pete Clouse looked a little like a hungry cat as he listened.

"It's the girl," Heller went on. "They can't stay away from her. If we could get them into another fight. . . ."

Clouse said: "Get them out on the street. I'll take care of the rest of it. I want them both." He turned to his three men who were still on their feet. "We'll ride in after the dance starts."

IX

Jerry Lander rode into town at 8:00 p.m. He came alone, leaving his horse at the stable and asking the hostler: "My brother come in yet?"

The man nodded. "He came in early."

Jerry grinned, and moved out along the darkened street, lighted only by the lamps in the store windows. The dance hall stood at the south end of town, a square, frame building some forty feet in length. Outside its door a group of riders was gossiping with friends they had not seen in weeks. They parted as Jerry came up, several of them

78

speaking to him.

He grinned, pushed his way through, and stopped just inside the doorway to look at the long room. Four swinging lamps gave it radiance, and on the small stand the two fiddlers and the man with the guitar worked industriously while the caller mopped his red face and chanted his rhythmic words. Jerry saw his brother's red head, and then Judy Parker's dark one, and his questing eyes found Martin Heller against the far wall, talking to Hurl Poke, the marshal.

Jerry moved over, and, as he came up, the marshal went away, striding across the room with a purposeful air. Jerry looked after him.

"What's the matter with Hurl?"

Heller said: "Trouble at one of the Indian shacks below town." He sounded as if he had little interest. The music ended; the couples thronged off the floor. Judy Parker, looking flushed and excited, came up with Wolf and for an instant the two brothers faced each other.

The music started, and Jerry took hold of the girl's arm, saying: "My dance."

Martin Heller objected. "This one is mine."

Jerry winked at him. "You brought her, Martin, that's enough of a break for one

79

man." He swung her away before she could protest.

She said, half angrily: "That wasn't very nice."

He grinned. "Why wasn't it? You ran out on me once. Remember? I'm taking you home tonight."

"No."

He had steered her toward the door without her being aware of his intention, and suddenly his voice was deadly serious. "Yes, Judy. We're leaving, now."

She said: "No, wait. I haven't got my shawl. I haven't. . . ." But he was already easing her through the crowd around the door and she did not know how to object further without creating a scene that would make more talk.

They came out through the crowd and a boy appeared suddenly at Jerry's elbow, saying urgently: "Hey, a man just sent me to find you, Jerry. Hurl Poke needs your help, down by the Indian shacks."

Jerry stared at him. "What's the trouble?"

The boy shook his head. "I don't know. He just said to get you. He needs help bad."

Jerry turned to the girl. "OK, go on back inside and wait for me." He did not pause for her answer but started quickly along the dark street. Judy Parker took one step after him. She did not know why but suddenly she was seized with a feeling of premonition, a feeling of approaching disaster. She started to call his name, then she turned and pushed back through the crowd into the hall. She saw Wolf over beside the bandstand, still talking to Heller, and hurried toward them, grabbing Wolf's arm.

They both turned and Wolf saw her white face. "Why, Judy, what's happened? Where's Jerry?"

She told them quickly, and Heller laughed, a dry, rustling sound. "Hurl's getting old." He said this a little loudly. "When he can't handle one Indian without help, he'd better turn in that badge."

Wolf laughed, also. "Come on and dance." He had the girl's arm and was leading her toward the floor.

"Wolf. Hadn't you better go help your brother?"

He grinned. "Heller and I sent that boy. We called to him out of the window and had him circle the building and catch you outside. We saw you sneaking out with Jerry."

She stared. "You mean there isn't any trouble?"

He shrugged. "Oh, I guess there's some trouble down in shack town. Hurl went down there a while back, but he didn't send for help."

She said suddenly: "I think I hate you. That's twice you've pulled me away from Jerry . . . twice." She started to turn away and suddenly the sound of a shot hammered in from the dark street, sounding loud and explosive above the din of the music.

"It's Jerry!" The girl gave a little cry and was running toward the door. Wolf shoved her out of the way. He charged at the crowd that was gathered around the entrance and forced his way through the scrambling men by main force, bursting out into the dark street, shouting Jerry's name as he ran.

Jerry, from a block down the street, saw him come, straightened from where he had ducked behind the corner of Bechwell's store and yelled his warning. But the warning came too late, for one of Pete Clouse's men, crouching on the roof of the black-smith shop, caught Wolf in his rifle sights as the red-haired man ran through a patch of light thrown from the saloon door, and squeezed off his shot.

Wolf Lander died in the middle of the street, falling face forward into the deep cushion of the dust. Jerry saw him fall. Jerry also saw the dark shape against the lighter sky as the rifleman straightened for a better look at his victim. Jerry steadied his short gun, taking his time, standing to get a clearer shot, heedless of the men concealed somewhere across the street who had already taken a shot at him, and fired. He saw the figure on the blacksmith's shop throw up his arms, and heard his cry, and the *clatter* as the rifle fell, and saw him pitch forward into the street.

And then all sound was lost in the yammer of guns that broke loose from the shadows on the far side of the street. Jerry dropped, the movement entirely instinctive. When the first shot had come, as he hurried down the street in an effort to help the marshal, he had assumed that it had been fired by one of the Indians who inhabited the section known as shack town. But now he realized that this must be a trap, set for his brother and himself, and that the men who were firing at him from the shadows on the far side of the dark street must be Pete Clouse's men.

This all sped through his mind in the seconds that burned away as the guns flashed at him. A slug broke the glass window of the store before which he had been standing, another *plunked* into the wooden side of the watering trough at the edge of the board sidewalk. A third, lower than the rest, burned a shallow trough across his back, tearing the shirt but doing little more than breaking the skin. And then, as suddenly as the sound had crashed out, it ceased, and the street was plunged in silence. The crowd before the dance hall had ducked back out of sight as the firing started, and no one moved.

Jerry knew that the men across the street were waiting. They did not know whether they had hit him or not. They were waiting for some motion on his part that would give them a clue. He knew that he could not stay where he was. Sooner or later they would come after him. They might be circling back through the darkness now, ready to slip across the street farther down and come up behind his position. He had to move.

He wiggled backward across the board-walk, an inch at a time. The planks were covered with glass shattered from the broken window. It gave him an idea. Cautiously he came up to his knees, and then rose. His back was beginning to burn where the bullet had seared its course. It was very dark where he stood with the unlighted store behind him. He felt carefully along the window, trying to learn how much of a hole had been broken in the store glass. Apparently most of the big pane was gone, leaving only jagged edges along the frame. He stepped through. The smell of rope and ground coffee and dry-goods mingled to fill the air. He knocked against something in the darkness that *clattered* to the board floor and at once a gun hammered from the far side of the street; the slug passed him to pound a tinny *gonging* noise from a stack of pails in the far corner. A voice which he thought was Pete Clouse's shouted through the night: "He's in the store. Head him off!"

Jerry was running now toward the rear. He found the door locked with a padlock and smashed at it with his gun barrel and, failing to break it, smashed the window above, crawling through, cutting his hand in the process, and dropping on one shoulder to the dirt of the alley. He was up, almost at once, sprinting down the alley. Fortunately he knew every foot of the straggling town. As a boy he had raced up and down these self-same alleys, playing during the long Saturday afternoons when the whole countryside had come in to visit and gossip with their friends.

The bar of light, cast from the saloon's rear doorway, was ahead of him, and he halted, not wanting to cross it, and stood listening, his ears sharpened by his urgency, but at the moment he could hear nothing except the thumping of his own heart. He was not worried for his own safety. He wanted to catch Pete Clouse and his men, one at a time, and make them pay for Wolf's death, for he never doubted that his brother was dead.

He circled backward away from the line of stores, through a littered vacant lot, coming between two shoddy cabins and making a wide sweep that brought him to the street two blocks above where Wolf had fallen in the dust. Here he crossed and came back down the alley on the far side until he saw the two-story structure of the livery barn loom out of the night. There was a corral beyond the alley and he had almost reached the corner of this when a dark figure, suddenly rising out of the gloom, called Clouse's name.

Jerry fired almost as soon as the man spoke. He heard his bullet strike and a shrill scream. Then, someone beyond him, at the far corner of the corral, was driving shots at him through the darkness, bullets that clipped away at the posts beside him. Suddenly, from the barn at his back, a gun opened up and he knew he was caught in a crossfire. He dropped again, feeling the soft cushion of the dust, and crept around so that he could crawl under the bars of the pole fence. There were a dozen horses in the enclosure, spooked by the hammer of the gunfire, shifting uneasily away from him in the shadows, the sound of their movements covering any noise that he might make.

A voice called from beyond the corral: "He's in with the horses, Pete, watch it!"

He knew then where Pete Clouse was, and he turned back to face the open rear doors of the barn across the alley. Someone had extinguished the lantern that usually burned in the runway and the whole place was in full darkness. Jerry watched the building with narrow attention, and then turned again and moved carefully across the rutted ground of the corral, his gun ready, his eyes searching for the man who was somewhere beyond the rear fence.

X

The minutes dragged. He did not know how many men were with Clouse, but Wolf had told him there had been four when they rode away from the Wolf Head. One he had shot off the blacksmith's roof, the one who had killed Wolf; one here at the corner of the corral, who had screamed into the darkness; and one he was certain he had hit at his own ranch during the raid. That could mean that there was only Clouse and the man behind the corral left, two against one. He could not be certain of course, but he thought he was probably right. The tension was building up within him, but it was also building up within the other two. The man behind the corral was safe, for Jerry had not been able to see him in the gloom, but this man could not stand the pressure of being alone, of not knowing what crept against him in the quiet night.

"Do you see him, Pete?" The man's voice was high with nervousness, sounding almost like that of a woman.

Clouse did not answer. But Jerry spotted the other man. He stood at the corner of a small shed some fifty feet away from the corral's near fence. He stood in the deep shadow that the shed gave, but he had stepped forward to see better and a gleam of light from the distant dance hall windows struck the lightness of his face. Jerry shot beneath that face, aiming at where he judged the unseen chest would be, and he heard the man's high, despairing yell.

Clouse, who had been waiting at the corner of the barn's open door, fired at the flash of Jerry's gun. He missed by inches and the bullet struck one of the nervous, shifting horses. The horse reared and the other animals broke into a circling run that carried them around the square of the fence as if it had been a racecourse. Their movement confused Clouse and probably saved Jerry's life. Jerry ducked under the rear fence and ran around it, traveling along the length of the barn until he reached the street end, and along the sidewalk until he came to the open double doors of the runway. Here he stopped, and breathed deeply three times in an effort to steady his pulsing heart. Then he peered around the door frame.

The runway was dark, and the doorway at the alley end showed a rectangle of faintness, a glimpse of the lighter sky. Against this lightness at the left side was a vague shape, hardly noticeable in the gloom. For a moment Jerry could not be certain that this was Pete Clouse, standing partly sheltered by the door frame, peering outward in an effort to locate his intended victim. Then the shape shifted a little and Jerry said in a low voice: "Behind you, Pete." He stepped into the center of the doorway.

Clouse spun, firing as he turned, the squeezing of the trigger an entirely instinctive act. He fired without aiming, without truly seeing the man he shot at. The bullet, by some lucky chance, struck Jerry in the right shoulder. The force of the heavy slug spun him half around, and his gun slipped from his nerveless fingers, and he went down, not so much from the shock of the wound but in an effort to find the gun he had dropped.

Clouse sensed that he was down. Clouse ran forward with a cry of triumph, firing twice as he came. He missed both times, shooting too high, as the fumbling fingers of Jerry's left hand found the gun in the litter of the runway floor. Jerry came up to his knees as Clouse's gun blasted almost in his face, the bullet *humming* past his ear. Jerry did not hurry. Grimly he took his time. He had the feeling that he would die, but in dying he meant to take Clouse with him.

He fired, and pulled the trigger back and fired again, and yet again. Clouse was falling, so close to him that one outstretched hand brushed Jerry's shoulder as the big man went down. And then everything was quiet in the runway, quiet with the stillness that suggests death.

Slowly Jerry rose. Never afterward could he recall exactly how long it took him to come to his feet. He rose, and thrust the gun into the front of his belt. His right arm hung, limp and useless, and the shoulder was beginning to burn. He saw that Clouse was dead.

Somewhere out in the street he heard a rising tide of excited voices and, turning, moved slowly toward the door through which he had entered. Lanterns bobbed in the street outside, and a knot of people had formed around Wolf's motionless body. Jerry moved toward them, and heard someone suddenly calling his name.

Judy came out of the darkness into the lantern light. "Jerry!" She was against him, crying softly, yet deeply as if she could not stop. "Jerry, you're all right. . . ."

His good arm was around her, holding her close. She did not realize for the moment that he was wounded. "Wolf," he said, and, turning, led her toward where his brother lay.

Hurl Poke, the marshal, was bending above Wolf's body. The crowd separated to let Jerry pass. Poke rose and, seeing him, shook his head.

The girl at Jerry's side said: "It's my fault. I told him you were on the street. I was worried."

Jerry turned to look down at her. "It isn't your fault. It isn't anyone's fault. You couldn't know that Clouse and his men were out here waiting for us." He looked

91

again at Poke. "Did you send a kid asking me to come and help?"

The marshal's face was blank.

Judy said: "He didn't send the boy. Wolf and Martin Heller did."

Jerry turned to glance down at her again.

"It was their idea of a joke." Her voice caught. "Wolf told me. It was a way to get you out of the hall so he could dance with me. They called to the boy through the dance hall window." She broke off then, for there was the *drum* of hoofs at the end of the street and Ed Irish rode into the glow cast by the circle of lanterns. His horse was sweat-stained and his old face showed lines of fatigue as if he had been in the saddle too long. He stared at the grouped men, and then at Jerry and his voice was harsh: "What's going on?"

They told him then, a dozen men, all trying to talk at once. He listened, his eyes still on Jerry's face. Afterward, he dismounted slowly, saying as he did so: "We found the cattle."

Jerry had released his arm from around the girl. He took a step to face the old foreman. "Where?"

"Clear on the other side of the Medicine Bows."

They stared at each other.

Ed Irish said: "I got some help and we rounded up the crew, and I found out who they were working for."

"Clouse?"

"Martin Heller."

It took a full minute for the name to sink through Jerry's consciousness. "Heller." He repeated the name as if he did not quite believe it. Both he and Wolf had always looked upon the banker as a rather helpless figure, a man who needed to be taken care of. "Heller?"

The old foreman nodded. "I talked to the riding boss. He was kind of scared. The local sheriff was all for hanging him, and he told the whole thing. He said that Heller has been rustling a few head every year for over six years. Seems he bought this ranch beyond the divide and was stocking it gradually, but when you and Wolf split this year, he saw his chance to fill his own herd and ruin you both at the same time. He even hired Pete Clouse to go to work for Wolf, just to stir up trouble."

"Heller." Jerry was looking around the crowd, searching for the small banker. "Have any of you seen Heller?"

"He's over at the bank, cleaning out the safe." It was Fred Bates.

They turned to stare at the bank's teller.

"I've been watching him." There was a vengeful gleam in Bates's eyes. "I knew that it would catch up with him sometime."

No one said anything. They were too stunned. There was not a man in the whole crowd who did not have money in that bank, who did not believe. Hurl Poke turned and started for the bank, but Jerry caught his arm.

"No you don't. He's mine."

Poke stared at him hard, started to object, then his eyes fell on Wolf's huddled body. Someone had thrown a blanket over it, but it was still there, a silent witness. Poke nodded. "Your business," he said, then his eyes went to Jerry's shattered shoulder. "Sure you don't want help?"

Jerry did not answer. He turned and started down the street toward the bank. His shoulder was paining severely now, feeling as if someone were probing the wound with a red-hot iron. His mind was a sea of bitterness as he thought of the things his father had done for the man in the bank. But mostly the bitterness was directed against himself. He realized that he had been careless, that both he and Wolf had been careless. They had not had to work for what they had. Old Lew Lander had left them the ranch and they had both been too

94

young to accept the responsibilities that were justly theirs. The fight with Wolf, he felt, was his fault. Wolf had run off with his girl, but to Wolf life had always been a kind of game, a huge joke. Even tonight Wolf had helped Martin Heller send him out onto the dark street by relaying the false message from the boy. Wolf had thought it only a joke, to separate him from Judy. But Heller. Heller, he realized now, had known that Clouse and his men were waiting out there in the darkness to kill him. Heller had sent him to his death. But they had missed him. And Wolf, hearing the shot, had raced out to die in his place.

He reached the front of the bank and peered through the window. The safe was in the rear corner, behind the teller's counter. There was light coming from that corner as if someone had placed a lamp on the floor beside the safe, but the high counter blocked his vision, hiding not only the lamp and the safe but the man who must be kneeling before it. He tried the bank door, turning the latch gingerly so as not to alert the man at the safe, if there was a man. Perhaps Heller had come and had already gone. Perhaps Heller was even now creeping along the dark alley toward the livery and a horse that might carry him to safety.

The door swung open, and with it came a little gust of air from the dark street that was more warning than any clicking of the latch. The man behind the counter shifted. The scrape of his boot was very plain in the quiet room, and then the lamp went out as he leaned over and blew down the hot chimney. Then there was silence for a full moment before the gun roared from behind the counter, the bullet striking the half open door, shattering the glass. But Jerry wasn't there. He had shifted quickly to the right, so that he was now crouched behind Heller's own desk, his gun in his left hand, ready.

"Martin. . . ." He tried to pitch his voice so that it would be difficult for the man beside the safe to know from what exact spot it came. "You're finished, Martin. Light that lamp and walk out with your hands up."

He had no hope that Heller would obey. He actually hoped that he would not, for the prospect of dragging out a murder trial, of trying to convict the banker of Wolf's death was a dreary thing. But he had to give the man a chance. It was not in him to do otherwise. He got a shot for answer, a shot still directed toward the building's door. Apparently Heller did not realize that Jerry had moved. The flash of his gun was very plain in the dark room. A low counter separated the space occupied by Heller's desk from the teller's corner and Jerry fired over this, resting his left arm against the corner of the desk to steady it.

He heard a shout and then a cry, and then the *pound* of feet as Heller raced across the room, vaulted the counter, and dived past him for the door. He fired as Heller was framed for a moment in the entrance against the light that came in from the lanterns farther down the street. He saw the banker stagger, and then go on, and heard a gun roar outside. Then he saw Ed Irish move into view and stare down at the dead banker.

Jerry pulled himself upright with his good arm, and stood, leaning shakily against the desk. Now that it was all over he knew suddenly that he was very weak. He steadied himself for a moment, and then walked slowly to the door. Judy was there to meet him. Judy had her arm around him, leading him back into the room, calling sharply for a doctor. Judy, white-faced, scared as the doctor stripped away the shirt to look at the shattered shoulder.

When it was finished, when they would have taken him down to the hotel and to bed, the girl started to turn away. He caught her arm with his good hand, saying carefully to control his weakness: "Where are you going?"

She turned back then. She said in a low voice that even the doctor could not hear: "This was all my fault. If it hadn't been for me, none of it would have happened."

He thought of Wolf's grin, of the way his brother's eyes had crinkled at the corners when he laughed, of the way the sun had shone on his red hair. He shook his head slowly. "It wasn't your fault. Wolf wouldn't want you to think it was. There were only a few things in this life that Wolf ever really cared for. You, the ranch, and me."

She didn't answer.

He said: "You can't leave now. Without Wolf I'll have a lot to do, a lot to take care of. You'll have to stay and help." She looked at him then and he flushed uncomfortably. "That is of course if you want to stay."

Her eyes told him that she did. She did not argue further; she bent and kissed him gently.

■ ■ ■ ■

Railroad Doctor

■ ■ ■ ■

I

Andy Lawrence perched himself comfortably on the top of the empty baggage truck to watch the arrival of the through sleeper from the East. It was a daily ritual for him, since like most of the boys in Soda Springs he fully intended to become a railroad man. Originally he had planned to be an engineer. The men who ran the locomotive equipment were considered the princes of the road, but Andy had already figured out that, while the engine man might be the more colorful, the dispatcher exercised the real power, and with this in mind he had gone out of his way to make friends with Boone Grantline.

The dispatcher lived at the hotel that was run by Andy's mother, and he had readily agreed to teach Andy the code and how to use the key. The offer had come only that morning, and Andy was thinking about it as the heavy train rolled in and the passengers hurried down the steps and dashed toward the lunchroom. Andy had a true desert boy's contempt for these Eastern travelers with their white, unburned skins and their odd uncomfortable clothes, and he paid little attention until the tall man came up to him.

"Hi, son." The voice was friendly. "Don't they run the hack any more?"

Andy came out of his daydream, in which he had pictured himself as running the whole division, and looked at the newcomer. He decided the man was a drummer. "You looking for a hotel?" The man nodded, and the boy's interest came to life. "You've got three choices," he said. "The Railroad Hotel is noisy. The Palmer House is quieter, but they rob you. Now, if you want a quiet place with good food and clean beds, why, my mother runs the Apache."

The man grinned. "I guess the Apache sounds about right."

Andy slid from his perch. "You won't be sorry. I'm Andy Lawrence."

The man showed surprise. "You Dave Lawrence's boy? How is Dave?"

"He's dead," Andy said, and the warmth had gone from his voice.

"Dead?" All expression faded from the man's face, leaving it cold, a little bleak.

"Dead. But he wasn't old. . . ."

"He was murdered, a year ago Christmas morning."

The man stared down at the small face, as taut and resolute as his own. "Dave murdered. But who . . . ?"

"If I knew, I'd shoot them." Andy was trying to mask his grief by sullenness as he stooped to pick up the man's bags. "And when we get to the hotel, don't tell Ma I said anything. I'm not supposed to talk about it."

The man took the heavy bags from the boy's hands. "Why not, Andy?"

Andy shrugged. "Ma says that it won't bring Pa back, and they never found out who shot him, and they never will, and she just doesn't want it to make me bitter."

The man's voice was soft. "I knew your father very well, Andy. In fact, I came back here, partly to prove that he hadn't made a mistake in giving me his help. I'm Hippocrates West."

Andy, who had been leading the way across the station yard, turned to stare at him. He had heard the name all his life. The town still gossiped about West, about the nameless boy who had been raised by the Bentons in the northern breaks, who had helped the older Benton boys hold up a train and been knocked from his saddle by a posse bullet. Yes, Andy knew the full story: how the boy had been brought to town more dead than alive and how he had nearly been sent to the Territorial Prison, along with Prince and Duke Benton. He would have gone to prison if it had not been for Andy's father and for Doc Condon, who had taken the youthful outlaw into his own home. Condon had taken him in and given him a name. He had called him Hippocrates West, and the name had amused the town. But it had not amused Andy's father, who had snorted: "Hippocrates West! Hippocrates, my foot. I don't care if this Hippocrates did start the medical business. It's a hell of a name to mark a kid with. Why couldn't Condon have called him Bill, or Pete, or Frank? It will mark him, and no one will ever forget who he was or that he helped hold up that train."

Andy hadn't forgotten, although it was more than six years since West had run away. There had been some loose talk about trailing him then, about bringing him back and sending him to the prison, but nothing had ever come of it. And now West was back, and Andy was as excited at meeting him as if he had seen Billy the Kid or one of the Earps. He stuttered as he said: "Doc

Condon will sure be surprised to see you."

West looked down at him. "How is Doc?"

"Mean as ever. Ma says he'll never change, and he'll never die. He keeps himself pickled all the time." They crossed the broad street and came into the narrow lobby of the Apache Hotel, Andy racing ahead to shout: "Ma! Hey, Ma! Guess who's here!"

Mary Lawrence was small and quick and bird-like, and her face in spite of its crown of white hair was still young-looking. She came from the dining room, wiping her hands on her apron, saying in a reproving voice: "Don't shout. What will the gentleman think?"

"He's not a gentleman," Andy said. "He's Hippocrates West."

Mary Lawrence stopped. Then her face warmed and she came forward to stand on tiptoe and peck a kiss against West's cheek. For an instant the action startled him. Then he dropped his bags, picked her up in his powerful arms, and swung her around, her feet well clear of the floor. "That's the finest homecoming a man ever had." He kissed her then, fully on the lips.

Mary Lawrence was flustered. "Hy West, you put me down. I'm old enough to be your mother."

"But too pretty," he said. The laughter

died from his eyes. He set her gently on her feet and said softly: "I wish you were, ma'am. I do for a fact. Andy doesn't know how lucky he is."

II

Andy Lawrence retreated to the kitchen as his mother showed West up to his room. Andy was anxious to spread the news of West's sudden return, but his eagerness was tempered by his appetite and he was helping himself to a slice of bread and jam when Belle Callahan came from the laundry and caught him.

She was a large girl and her face was slightly broad and her features had the irregularity that so often marks the Irish, but her mouth was wide and generous, her gray-blue eyes kind and friendly and understanding.

"Andy!" She caught him by the back of his jacket. "You know you aren't allowed to eat between meals."

He struggled to keep the bread out of her reach. "I know something you don't know. Hy West just came back, and old Doc Condon don't even know he's home."

She let go her grip in surprise. "Hy West?"

"That's right."

She said in a strange voice: "What did the fool come back here for?"

Andy retreated to a corner, but he was puzzled. To him, Soda Springs was the greatest town on earth. "Why shouldn't he come back?"

"Why should he? They treated him like a dog, and the kids at school made fun of him until he wore his guns one day. They stopped mighty quick, believe me."

Andy was staring at her. "You knew him? You knew the Orphan Kid?"

"I went to school with him."

"Gee, you're old."

She laughed at him then. She had to. She was twenty-two. Then she turned and the laughter died, for West was standing in the dining room doorway.

He came forward, and neither spoke for a moment. Then he said softly: "Hi, Belle."

"Hello," she said, her eyes studying him, noting the changes that six years had wrought. "I never expected to see you here again."

"Why not?" he said. "I told you I was going away and get to be a doctor, and then come back and show them all."

She walked over to lean one hand against the table. "And are you a doctor, Hy?"

He nodded, his tight lips smiling a little.

"Even have a paper to prove it."

"But why did you come back?"

"Why not? I said I would."

This stopped her for a moment. There was a hard core in this man that had always frightened her a little, a hard purpose that carried him forward against all and any odds. She said, slowly: "You'll get no practice here. It surely would have been easier to stay in the East."

He considered in silence. She had been his only friend in school, the only one of sixty children who had not looked on him as a kind of freak, and he had been bitter and lonely, not allowed to return to the Benton ranch by the court that had paroled him in Dr. Condon's care. Belle had been something of an outcast herself. Her father had been a sergeant in the cavalry, stationed at the nearby fort, her mother a laundress for the officers, and the town children had considered that she was not one of them. On this their friendship had been based, and it was to her that he had bragged that he would run away and become a doctor. She had not believed him. She had jeered at him until he struck her. Then they had fought, for in the hard world in which Belle had been raised you asked no quarter simply because you happened to be a girl.

The town marshal had pulled them apart. The town marshal had locked him up, claiming that he was a danger to everyone in Soda Springs. And Callahan had come down and made the marshal turn the boy loose. Callahan was no longer in the Army. He had bought himself out and started a saloon, and was already becoming something of a power in the politics of the town. Callahan had gotten the boy free and walked down the street with him.

"It was my girl made me come," Callahan said. "She claims the fight was her fault. She says you're planning to run away."

West's cheek was puffed where Belle's hard little fist had caught him squarely. He did not answer. He did not trust Callahan. He did not trust anyone. He was bitter, and hurt, and savage as a cornered bear.

Callahan looked at him shrewdly. "I ran away," he said. "Nearly forty years ago. I met the squire as I was leaving, and somehow he guessed and he gave me a shilling. A man should not be without money. I'm doing the same thing for you." He reached out and put a $20 gold piece into West's palm. The boy's first impulse was to run after the Irishman and throw the money in his face, but he did not. He left Soda Springs that night and now he was back.

He told her this, and said: "The first thing I want to do is to give your father back his money, to prove to him that it was not wasted."

"So that's what brought you back?"

His jaw set. "Look, Belle, you know what I took from this town, better than anyone else. It would have been simple to stay in the East, but all my life I'd have been haunted by the knowledge that I'd run away, that I was afraid to come back."

"But you'll starve," she said. "You can't expect the people here to accept an outlaw kid as a doctor."

He grinned then. "If that is all that worries you, forget it. I knew what the town's reaction would be. I have no plans to go into general practice. I'm the new assistant at the Railroad Hospital."

She was startled. "Gruber's assistant?"

"I guess that's his name."

"Oh." She could think of nothing more to say.

It was his turn to ask a question. "What are you doing here?"

She told him levelly: "I'm the hired girl."

He was surprised. Even before he had left Soda Springs, Callahan's saloon was prospering and he said in some embarrassment: "Your father . . . I thought. . . ."

"That I would not have to work?" She did not pretend to misunderstand. "I don't . . . not if I were willing to live on what the saloon makes . . . but I don't like that kind of money. I don't hold with liquor any more than my mother did. She left Callahan when he started the place, and I'd be a hypocrite if I were willing to live on money that was made in a way I don't approve of." He stared at her, and she smiled. "Don't worry about me. Mary Lawrence, bless her, is wonderful to work for." She glanced at the watch pinned to the front of her shirtwaist. "Which reminds me. It's time to start supper. We can talk later."

West turned away slowly, knowing he had been dismissed. For six years he had pictured his return, and for some reason that he did not clearly understand he felt let down. He left the kitchen, crossed the lobby, and stepped out into the street. As soon as he left the shelter of the wooden gallery, the afternoon sun beat down upon him with fierce intensity. Under the whitish glare the town still dozed in its late *siesta*. Even the shrill whistles of the slowly moving switch engines in the big yards had taken on a sleepy note.

Soda Springs was a railroad town, a division point, with all the faults and vices and dirtiness that went with such a place. It was not different from a hundred other such towns, but its setting was different in that it perched uneasily on the desert that stretched out to the south and east like the irregular folds of a carelessly spread blanket. Only to the north and west was there a hint of beauty, for here in the near distance rose the timbered peaks of the higher watered country, dark mountains edging a broken land which was so rough that men seldom rode through it. Along the edges of this plateau-like formation were the tumbled cañons that corkscrewed their watercourses into the flat lands below. Small ranchers had built their homesteads in these cañons, battling the thin feed, the rocky soil, and the howling winters. Above them were a few mines, their starving owners following the faulted veins that laced their circuitous way through the volcanic torture of the rock. It was a poor country, a troubled country, a place that had known violence and strife long before the railroad punched through its right of way, and built the town by establishing its shops, its division point, and its hotel.

But the coming of the railroad had not changed the basic pattern of local life. The railroad workers battled the ranchers and the miners. The outlaws lurking in the rough country swept down occasionally, raiding the more prosperous ranches and the railroad alike, ignoring the fact that the Territorial Prison reared its grim walls less than thirty miles to the west. And to highlight the uncertainty the Indians were continually restless on their unproductive reservations, kept in check by a nervous and understaffed Army. This was the land in which West had been raised, and this was the land to which he had returned, feeling as much a stranger as if he had never lived here. It was difficult for him to associate himself with the reckless boy who had ridden with the Bentons, who had sneered at the court after the train robbery, and who had run away.

He glanced along the street, seeing no activity in the grip of the afternoon heat. A dozen horses, apparently forgotten by their owners, stood hip-shot at the rails, their heads bowed, the only sign of life the constant switching of their tails to drive away the persistently *buzzing* flies. West's movements were unhurried and he breathed the dusty air sparingly, already feeling the parched dryness that seemed to sear his lungs. He was glad to turn out of the glare into the comparative coolness of Callahan's saloon.

The room into which he came was semi-dark and he paused an instant to allow his contracted pupils to accustom themselves to the gloom. It was an old trick, born of those early years when each room he entered might hold an enemy and where sun blindness might bring a quick, sharp, jarring death. He no longer felt that he was hunted, or that every man's hand was against him, but his pause was an instinct of those other days when he had ridden the outlaw trail. As soon as his vision sharpened, he saw that the big room was hardly changed. It seemed a little dirtier, its bar a little more scuffed, its swinging lamps a little more dented. But the same smell still lingered, a mingling of old dust and tobacco smoke, and spilled beer and human sweat.

Callahan was behind the bar, his bulging middle under its dirty apron giving the lie to the fact that only ten years before he had been the hardest riding sergeant in the old 3rd Cavalry. He was a moose of a man, his dark hair cut so short that the scars that marred his round skull showed plainly in remembrance of a thousand fights. An explosive man, handsome in his own way, his features reminding West of Belle Callahan. Callahan had been watching the game at one of the rear poker tables when West entered. Standing behind the bar, his big hands resting on the dark surface, he was tall enough to see over the heads of the small crowd.

He turned his head and, failing to recognize the newcomer, turned back to watch the play of the cards. West walked back along the bar toward him, drew a gold $20 piece from his pocket, and laid it before the saloon man.

"I'm returning the loan with thanks."

Callahan looked at the gold piece, then lifted his eyes to the younger man's face. "Well, I'll be damned." His voice had an explosive quality that filled the big room and turned every head at the card table toward them. "You're the kid that ran away to be a doctor." He extended a thick palm. "When did you get back?"

West shook hands. "At noon."

"How'd you make out, getting to be a doctor?"

"I made out. I am one."

"The saints preserve us. Belle said you would, but I didn't believe it." He stared at the gold piece, frowning. "That wasn't a loan. A man gave me a shilling once. I passed it on to you. You pass it to someone else for luck."

West hesitated for the barest instant, then picked up the coin with a nod, and dropped it into his vest pocket. In place of the gold he drew out a handful of change. "I'll buy a drink for the house."

He turned to glance at the men around the poker table. None of them nodded in greeting. None of them seemed to know who he was, none but an untidy man who sat at an otherwise empty table to the left of the card game. He had been taking no part in the play, but he had watched the fall of each card with the same concentrated attention that he might have used if the chips in the center of the table had all been his. He was Dr. Condon, and West looked at him with real attention. The old doctor had saved his life by digging a bullet out of him, and then taken him into his home rather than let the court send a boy to prison. But in some ways living with Condon had been worse than prison. He had never understood the man. Sometimes, when deep in drink, Condon would discuss medicine. He had a real love for his profession, although he would scoff at it when he was sober. At other times he would rail at West, calling him ignorant and stupid and dumb, a brush jumper without education. It was these attacks that had decided West that at all costs he would become a doctor. He had never told Condon of his ambition. He had told no one but Belle, and she had jeered, and they had fought, and he had run away.

Beside Condon lay a dirty, white dog with a long-nosed head and yellow coyote eyes. West did not need to be told that it was a mean dog, a vicious dog. He knew the strain, guessing that it was a grandson or great-grandson of the bitch that had nipped at his legs when he lived with Condon. The dog was ugly, but no uglier than its master. Condon's head was bald, save for a fringe of mouse-colored hair around the edge. His eyes were bloodshot and he was untidy. He looked older than he was because of personal sloppiness. He sat at the table, not moving beyond a fluttery gesture of his fingers on the dog's neck, showing no expression as he stared at West.

But West knew Condon was surprised. It was very evident that the news of his return had not yet reached this saloon. Then Condon said: "So you're a doctor?" Apparently he had heard what West had said to Callahan. "I never expected to live to drink to your being a doctor." He watched as Callahan set the filled glass at his elbow, then lifted it slowly. "It's a strange world, full of strange turnings." He downed the drink at a gulp, set the glass on the table, and added in his rumbling voice: "So you've come back. You're going to repay my care by taking my practice away from me?"

West shook his head. He had expected no greeting from Condon save sarcasm and jeers; that was the way the older doctor greeted the whole world. But it had not occurred to him that Condon would think that he had returned to rob the older man of his practice. "I'm not going into private practice," he said. "I'm here to work at the Railroad Hospital."

For the first time a gleam of real interest showed in Condon's yellowish eyes. "Don't tell me the railroad finally got some sense and fired Gruber?"

"I'm to be his assistant."

Condon started to laugh then, the sound appearing to originate far down in his big belly. The laughter rose in a cascade of noise that seemed to fill the long, smoky room. "Well, I'll be damned," he said when he had recovered enough breath to speak. "This is the end. That snot-nosed bastard hasn't enough to do to keep one man busy so they send him an assistant. No wonder they say the whole road is going broke. It's a good thing they don't have a hospital in every town. There wouldn't be enough doctors in the world to keep them going."

The men at the near table laughed. Callahan didn't. West sensed that Callahan was watching him, and he knew that in the saloon man's eyes he was undergoing his first test. If he allowed Condon to make a fool of him, the story would be told all over town by evening. Each action he took would be watched, for he was marked. He had known this before he returned and he knew that in this country a man was judged by his ability to handle himself in any situation. Inside he felt grim, but he managed a laugh, knowing that it was not too good an effort, knowing that it had a forced sound. But when he spoke, his tone was easy. "Sounds like I won't be overworked," he said. "Sounds like I'll have plenty of time to take care of the mistakes you've been making around here for years, Doc."

The laughter in the room grew, and for the moment he had turned it against Condon. He had no intention of losing his advantage. He nodded to Callahan, said to Condon — "See you later." — and moved easily down the room toward the door. Behind him the laughter had died. Behind him was no sound but the growling of the white dog.

On the street Hy West felt better. Condon was known as the sharpest wit in town. To turn the laugh on him was an achievement. He crossed to the hotel, entered it, and crossed the lobby. He had reached the bottom of the stairs and was just starting upward toward the room when he heard the noise from the kitchen: a man swearing sharply, and Belle Callahan's muffled answer.

He moved quickly through the dining room to the kitchen door. He pushed it open and found Belle struggling in a man's arms. The man's back was toward West, and he did not know that the doctor was in the room until West seized his shoulders, jerking him free of the girl.

West held him for an instant, then spun him across the room. He stumbled over the ironing board that had been standing beside the table and went crashing into the big range, his hands outstretched in an effort to break his fall. They came down flat on the smoking top. He jerked erect with a high shout of pain, and pivoted to meet the newcomer. As he turned, West realized that it was Bo Benton, the youngest of the family.

For an instant Benton was motionless, surprised at seeing West. Then he swore hoarsely. "The Kid!"

West waited, his powerful body a little crouched. Of all the Bentons he had liked Bo the least. Bo was a braggart; Bo had picked on him when he was a child because West had been smaller. Bo had stolen his things, and made him do work that was rightfully Bo's. He felt a surge of anger rise through him, but he curbed it, saying in a flat voice: "Get out of here, Bo."

The youngest Benton showed his teeth in a wicked smile. Like all of his breed he would fight at any time, merely for the love of fighting, and he had always disliked the younger man. He had not understood this dislike himself, nor realized that it stemmed from his inner knowledge that West was smarter than he, and that he was actually jealous of the orphan. He had had several drinks, priming himself to enter the hotel kitchen, and the drinks inflamed him now. Without answering he charged, throwing a wicked left into West's stomach that doubled the doctor over. As West bent forward, Bo grabbed his shoulders, holding him thus for an instant as he brought up his knee sharply for West's jaw. But he missed, for although his first blow had driven most of the air from the doctor's body, West still had enough sense left to catch the lifting leg and throw himself backward, heaving upward as he did so, thus dumping Bo onto his back on the scrubbed floor.

He knew from long experience that no Benton would ever stop a fight as long as he could move. He dived onto the fallen man, using his weight and the strength of his arms in an effort to smother him. There was no science. They fought as they had fought always, like two young animals. But they were both much bigger now, much heavier, and their fists did far more damage. The advantage lay with Benton. He was heavier, the veteran of a hundred barroom fights, and his muscles were the harder since West had done little physical work during the last six years. But a determination rode West. There was something in him that drove him forward, even when it seemed that he was beaten. They broke finally, rolling clear and struggling to their feet to stand toe to toe, slugging until Benton was forced to clinch. Then they went down again, locked in each other's arms. This time Benton landed on top.

West lay for an instant, gasping for breath. Then he twisted, arched, and managed to throw Benton from him. Benton rolled over and over until he was near the stove. He came to his knees, and made no effort to rise farther. Instead, his hand dropped to the heavy gun in his belt and dragged it clear of the holster. He raised it, using the last of his faltering strength, and centered the heavy barrel on West's chest, saying in a ragged voice: "I'm going to kill you, Kid."

West stood beside the center table. He had used it to drag himself to his feet. He swayed, his eyes bloodshot. He was not in much better shape than Benton, but in his own heart he knew that he had won. The very fact that Bo Benton had been forced to pull his gun proved he admitted West was the better man. Still, the knowledge would be of little good to one who was dead, and he never thought for an instant that Bo would hesitate to shoot. He was too far away to dive for the gun. There was no possible weapon on the table, not even a bread knife.

He stood staring at Benton, watching for the man's finger to tighten on the trigger. Belle Callahan was watching, also. Belle had been raised in a hard school, and she looked around quickly for a weapon. The first thing she saw was a flatiron, smoking on the heated stove. Without hesitation she seized a pot-holder and then snatched up the iron. Leaning across one corner of the stove, she pressed the iron squarely between Bo Benton's shoulder blades.

The gun in Bo's hand exploded as he jumped straight into the air, the bullet digging into the floor at West's feet. Then Bo fell, squirming onto his back as if by so doing he could stop the burning sensation between his shoulders. West jumped, even as the girl swung up the iron, and grabbed the gun that had dropped from Bo's hand. He watched Bo Benton try to dance upon his back, and for the life of him he could not help laughing.

Bo gave up trying to rub out the burn against the floorboards. He struggled to his knees, glaring upward at the man who now held his gun. "I'll kill you for this, Kid."

"Get out."

Benton rose slowly. "I'll kill you."

West didn't bother to answer. He squeezed the heavy gun's trigger. The noise of the explosion filled the kitchen, and a neat hole appeared in the scrubbed boards between Benton's booted feet. Bo stared at the hole as if he did not believe his eyes. West fired again. This time the bullet knocked the heel off of Bo's right boot. Benton had had enough. He turned and leaped out through the kitchen door to the alley beyond. He had never before run from any man, but he ran now.

West made no move to follow. Belle Callahan was suddenly laughing as if she could not stop. Andy came racing in from the main room, attracted by the shots, just as Hy West thrust the big gun into the waistband of his trousers.

"What happened? Who'd you kill?"

Belle Callahan told him. The story was too good to keep. She picked up the iron she had dropped and returned it to the stove. Andy was gazing at West with big eyes. He said slowly: "I wouldn't want the Bentons after me. I sure wouldn't. That Bo is bad."

West didn't answer. He knew that Andy spoke the truth.

III

Andy Lawrence was having a wonderful time. He had traveled from one end of Railroad Avenue to the other, telling the story of Hy West's homecoming and of Bo Benton's fight and branding. It was not often that the town heard such a funny story, especially about the Bentons, and it spread like wildfire. Andy loved to talk, and he loved to be the center of attention, but suddenly he lost interest in furthering the spreading of news. His quick eye had seen two riders turn in to the foot of the street, and he identified them almost at once as Bentons. He stopped before a grocery store, and, standing under the shelter of its gallery, partly hidden by a barrel of potatoes, he watched them come toward him.

The Bentons usually left the town pretty much alone, but once or twice each month they rode in, generally quarrelsome, especially after they had had a few drinks, and they seldom left without trouble of some kind. Andy watched them, then turned to see Bruce Gimble coming toward him from the opposite direction. Gimble habitually rode the streets at this hour of the evening, looking big and important behind the glitter of his marshal's star.

Andy did not like Gimble. With the ability of the adolescent to ferret out the weakness of adults he had long ago decided that Bruce Gimble, behind all his bluster, was a coward. He and his friend, Sam Dillon, had waited for months, hoping that Gimble and the Bentons would meet head-on sometime when the outlaws were feeling mean. Like most of the boys in Soda Springs, Andy was both a little afraid and also a little proud of the Bentons. He marveled at the way they came and went, careless of the fact that half the people in the territory hated them for their arrogance, their bullying ways, and the occasions when they shot up the town for pure meanness.

He looked again at them, and then back at Gimble. A sneer grew on his young lips, for the marshal had sighted the oncoming riders and swung south onto Fremont, obviously to avoid meeting them. It was not a new thing for Gimble to remain practically invisible when the outlaws were in town. He was only following his cautious custom, so that he would not be called upon to enforce the local ordinance that forbade the wearing of guns within the town limits.

Andy watched the Bentons pass. There were only two of them and they seemed very peaceful, so Andy decided that there would be no excitement from them, at least until later. Disappointed, he moved on up Wichita Avenue to the Dillon house, but Sam was not at home. Andy turned back aimlessly, feeling lonely. He drifted across Railroad Avenue to the station platform just as the night limited rolled in from the east.

He noticed the girl first because she was pretty, small, and blonde, and very striking in her city clothes. The rest of the passengers did not bring luggage as they stepped down and headed for the lunchroom, but a trainman followed her down the steps carrying her bags. He set them on the platform, and she looked around as if for help.

Andy was at her side in a moment, sensing a chance for profit. "Help you, ma'am?"

She turned to smile at him. "Why, perhaps you can. I'm looking for a Doctor West. He used to live here and he just came home recently."

Andy's interest jumped. "Of course I know him. He's staying at our hotel." He stooped and picked up her bag, finding it surprisingly light. "Is he a friend of yours?"

He was already piloting her through the crowd, and her laugh made him turn. "I guess you'd call him a friend," she said. "At least I came out here to marry him."

Andy had absorbed more surprises that day than he usually did in a month. He recovered enough to ask: "What's your name?"

"Laura Hall."

"You knew Hy at Chicago?"

"I was a nurse there. Do you think Hy will be at the hotel now?"

The boy nodded. "He's lying down in his room."

Laura Hall was surprised. West was not the kind to go to bed early. "Is he sick?"

This was the opening Andy had been playing for. "Well, I wouldn't say that he was exactly sick. He had a fight with Bo Benton, and he's a mite battered up."

"Fight?" Laura Hall stopped. In the years she had known West he had never fought anyone. "What in the world was he fighting about?"

"Well, Bo tried to kiss our hired girl, and Doc stopped him, and they fought, and then Bo pulled his gun, and Belle . . . that's the hired girl . . . she branded Bo with a hot iron, and Doc grabbed Bo's gun and shot his heel off."

Laura was staring at him. "You aren't making this up?"

Andy was indignant. "You can ask Hy. That's just the way it happened, so help me."

Laura Hall bit her lip. The boy's words, more than the people they passed as they moved up Railroad Avenue, made her realize what a different world this was from the one she knew. The sun had dropped behind the western mountains, but there was still enough light for her to see the people on the street: shirt-sleeved men, their wide-brimmed hats pushed back from sunburned faces, ten men for every woman. She wondered again if she had not made a mistake in coming here. In the lobby, facing Mary Lawrence as she wrote her name in the smudged register, her doubt grew. She must see West at once.

Mary Lawrence was having one of her spells, and Andy showed the new guest to her room, lit the lamp, and made certain the pitcher on the washstand contained water.

She opened her purse and put a silver dollar into his small hand. Andy stared at it as if he had never seen a dollar before. Certainly no one at the hotel had ever given him one. The usual reward for carrying their bags was a dime, or a quarter at most.

"That . . . that's too much."

She smiled. Laura Hall had used the same smile on older men with good results and it captivated Andy. "Which is Doctor West's room?"

Andy hesitated. He was old enough to know why his mother had such a strict rule about women in men's rooms, but with this girl he thought that it was different. Certainly she looked like a lady, not like Straight-Edge Ella's girls. Andy knew all about the big house on the side street. He had run errands for them more than once. There were few things about Soda Springs and its citizens that Andy and Sam Dillon did not know. He said slowly: "You're not supposed to go to a man's room unless you're married to him."

She smiled again. "But Hy and I are going to be married."

Andy was still a little dubious, but he felt that there was small chance that his mother would find out, and Laura had given him the dollar. In the end he led her along the hall toward West's room.

Hy West had been lying in the warm darkness. He was fully dressed and he had no intention of going to bed, but his face was marked by Bo Benton's fists. He knew the story was probably all over town, and he wondered if it would be wise for him to leave the hotel on this night. He heard their steps, and the knock on his door, and he said — "Come in." — automatically.

The door opened. He saw Laura Hall standing in the oblong of light. "Laura!" He came off the bed at once, fumbling for a friction match, lighting the lamp. "Laura, where did you come from?"

Andy was an interested spectator, standing in the doorway as the girl entered the lighted room. West saw him and said: "Thanks for bringing her up, Andy." He walked over and shut the door. He stood there for a moment, listening. There was no sound of footsteps from the hall. He reopened the door.

"That's all, Andy."

The boy turned reluctantly and moved toward the head of the stairs. West waited until he started down, then closed the door again and turned back to the girl. He looked at her for a long moment in silence. "I thought we said good bye."

Tears were close behind her eyes, and she came forward uncertainly. "You asked me to come out here with you. I said I wouldn't, and then, when I realized you were gone, I couldn't bear being alone. I got the next train."

Still he made no move to touch her. It was as if he had turned to stone. She hesitated for an instant, then stepped against him, her young body alive beneath the tightness of her dress, pressing against him, warming him, turning him alive. He crushed her to him.

She pushed him away, laughing up into his face. "You do still want me?"

He kissed her. All the loneliness that he had known through the years was welling up within him. That's what Laura had meant to him, a cure for loneliness. He really knew very little about her, for she talked only sketchily about herself. He knew that she was Polish with a name that was not Hall; that her father had been a stockyard worker with seven children; that she had run away from home at fourteen and managed to take nurses' training at a time when there were still few women in the profession. She had not told him why she left home, how one of her father's drunken friends had taken her to bed with him. These things she had kept to herself. Nor was she in love with West. She, too, had been lonely, and they had drifted together, two strangers in a large city. At least, she realized, he was honest, and he had ability. He would go far once he was out of school, and she had attached herself to him, planning to marry him, hunting the security of being a successful doctor's wife.

Their affair had run through his school years, and it had come as a distinct shock to her when, after his graduation, West turned down a resident's job to accept a position in a railroad hospital in a remote Western town. She had railed at him then. She had told him that he was crazy, that she did not mean to bury herself in any sagebrush village. But as soon as he was gone, she realized that without him she had no future. All the fine plans she had made collapsed, and never being one to hesitate when her comfort was involved, she had caught the next train for Soda Springs.

Now, standing in the bare hotel room, she was certain that she had again made a mistake. She said in a choked voice: "Why did you ever come back here?"

His voice was low, even. "I had to show them."

She pushed back so that she could see his face. "Had to show who? Had to show them what?"

He hesitated. "Look, Laura. I never talked much about myself at the hospital, about who I am or where I came from."

She realized that this was so, but she had never given it much thought. She had not talked much about her own early years, either. "What difference does it make?"

He shrugged. "It made a difference to me. I was raised by a family named Benton. I never had a name. Sometimes they called me the orphan, sometimes the Orphan Kid."

She was staring at him, feeling the bitterness in his level tone.

"They were outlaws. I don't mean they were in hiding all the time. A lot of the outlaws in this country have their own places, and, as long as they don't pull anything too raw, the authorities leave them alone."

She didn't understand. It showed in her face.

"That's because there isn't much law out here, and the country is big, and pretty empty. The Bentons stole a few cattle and held up a stage now and then. But no one could prove it, and all of them were dangerous. And then we held up a train."

She drew her breath sharply. "You held up a train?"

"Well, I stayed with the horses. I was only fourteen. Anyhow, we got away with the express box, and started for the hills. A posse trailed us and cornered us up in the peaks, and I got a bullet in the shoulder." He stripped off his coat, and then his shirt to show her the white, diamond-like scar. She had seen it before, but she had never questioned him. He went on, his voice still showing no emotion. "They caught us, Duke and Prince Benton and me. They had a trial and they sent Duke and Prince to prison for twenty years. But the sheriff told the judge I was too young, and a doctor named Condon offered to take me into his home and raise me. The court paroled me in his charge."

She said faintly: "That's where you got the idea of being a doctor?"

He nodded. "Condon was drunk half the

time, and he treated me the way he treated a couple of mean dogs he had. He used to tell me I was too stupid to be a doctor, too stupid to be anything. I had a bad time. The kids at school called me an outlaw. The town felt I should have gone to prison. There was only one person who was halfway decent to me, a girl, and I told her that I meant to be a doctor. Then she jeered at me. That was more than I could stand. We had a fight and the town marshal locked me up, and there was talk of them revoking my parole and sending me to prison. The girl's father came and got me out. He gave me twenty dollars and I ran away."

She was staring at him. "And after all that trouble you were fool enough to come back here?"

He said grimly: "I had to come back. I had to show this town and Condon that they were wrong about me, that I did have brains enough to become a doctor. I had to show the girl's father and the girl that I wasn't fooling, that I really meant to make something of myself."

Laura had a sudden thought. "That boy said you had a fight this afternoon, over some girl. Was that the same girl?"

He nodded.

She said: "Are you in love with her, Hy?"

He was startled. "In love with her? Of course not. I'm in love with you."

Laura had her own ideas about that. She had never been one to kid herself, and she was not kidding herself now. She knew that she had played upon West's loneliness, that she had purposely excited him and taken him to bed with her. She knew, or thought she knew, that she could still hold him, but she resolved to be careful. Either he was in love with this other girl and did not know it, or he really had hated the town so strongly that he needed to come back to get even. And Laura believed that love was a much stronger emotion than hate. Certainly it was emotion of some kind that had brought West back. Reason hadn't. Reason would have kept him in Chicago where his future was assured.

IV

Andy went unwillingly down the stairs. He was burning with curiosity and he resented the fact that West had sent him away. He turned through the dining room into the kitchen in search of his delayed supper, and Belle Callahan had to break off her ironing to feed him.

"One of these days, when you don't show

up at mealtime, you can go hungry."

The boy was not perturbed. He had heard the threat many times before. "How's Ma?"

"Not good. She's lying down in the back parlor. I don't like these spells. They seem to come oftener."

Andy's mind was on something else. "That's one swell girl who came out to marry Hy West. She gave me a dollar."

Belle made no attempt to hide her surprise. "Where is she now?"

Andy spoke without thinking. "Up in Hy's room."

Belle started to say something, then thought better of it. She gathered up the shirts she had ironed and moved toward the back parlor. She returned in less than a minute. "Andy" — there was nervousness in her voice — "your mother's worse. Get Doctor Condon right away."

"But. . . ."

"Hurry!"

The boy gulped the rest of his milk and started toward the door.

"Run!"

He ran then, suddenly frightened. He headed directly for Callahan's as the most likely place to find the doctor, but Condon was not there.

"You see him," he told the bartender, "tell

him Ma is took real bad." Then he ran on down the street toward the adobe house that served as Condon's combination office and living quarters. The sun-baked yard was surrounded by a high board fence to keep in the half dozen snarling dogs. Andy paused at the gate. He did not like the dogs. Although he had tried, it was impossible to make friends with them. But Condon must be home, for there was a light shining through the front window. He called, shouting Condon's name.

At the sound of his voice the dogs redoubled their clamor, rushing forward to leap against the gate in an effort to get out. The house door was pulled open and Condon roared at the dogs. They slunk back, their loud protest scaling downward to whines.

"What's wanted?" The doctor was an untidy, bulky figure in the yellow lamplight.

"It's Ma, she's took bad."

Condon answered him with a muffled curse. "Tell her to take a couple of her pills. I can't come now."

The boy was very frightened. "But you've gotta. Belle says she's real bad."

Condon was not impressed, but he thought of something and laughed suddenly. "Get Hy West. He's at your place.

139

Now's the time to find out what kind of a doctor he is." He slammed the door, thus cutting off the path of light that had lain across the yard. At once, the coyote dogs took up their brawling.

Andy hesitated, not knowing what to do. But it was plain that Condon was not coming, so he turned and ran back toward the Apache, muttering as he ran. He was very mad at Condon. He'd get even somehow, but he didn't quite know how.

He was crying as he burst into the lobby, tears that were a combination of his anger and his fear. He stopped when he saw Belle.

"Condon won't come."

Belle stared at him, not believing.

"He said to tell her to take her pills, and then he said to let Hy West doctor her."

It had not occurred to her to call West. The town was so used to depending on Condon. She ran up the stairs, knocked on West's door, then turned the knob and opened it quickly. She was startled to see West without his shirt, facing the strange girl. Belle had forgotten that Andy had said the girl was in West's room, and for a moment surprise and embarrassment held her silent. Then the urgency of her need made her say: "It's Mary. She's very sick and Condon won't come."

Of the three in the room West was the most at ease, the most business-like. Laura had guessed at once that this was the girl over whom West had fought. She eyed her possible rival with careful attention, but West wasted no time. He caught up his medicine bag without bothering to put on his shirt and came into the hall.

"Where is she?"

"Back parlor."

He went down the stairs two at a time, with Belle following more slowly. She turned once and looked back. Laura Hall was standing at the head of the stairs, her face expressionless. Then Belle forgot her as she followed West across the dining room and through the side door into the small parlor.

Mary Lawrence was past speech. The pain in her side was so acute that she could do nothing but moan. Belle gave West a careful but rapid description of the symptoms.

"This isn't her first spell. She gets dizzy, and then sick at her stomach, and the pain is in her right side, low down."

"What's Condon say?"

She shrugged. "Indigestion. He gives her pills."

West had stripped back the covers, bared the abdomen, and was prodding it gently as he watched the sick woman's face. He saw her wince, and turned toward the door where Andy stood nervously.

"Get Miss Hall." His voice was crisply professional. "Tell her I need her."

The boy ran toward the stairs. Belle said quickly: "What is it, Hy?"

West's words were shorter than he intended. "Heat some water, a lot of water. Clear off the kitchen table and get me all the light in there you can."

His manner frightened her. "You're . . . you're going to operate?"

He nodded.

"What's the matter with her?"

"Her vermiform appendix, I think. I'm afraid it's already ruptured." He broke off as Laura came in, trailed by Andy, and then gave her his orders.

Laura was not excited. She was a competent nurse. "Why not use the Railroad Hospital?"

He said: "I haven't been there yet. I don't know what facilities they have and I haven't met Doctor Gruber. We haven't time to waste. Show Belle what to do in the kitchen. The table will have to be scrubbed, my instruments boiled. You'll find a can of ether in my bag. It will have to do."

She nodded, turning toward the kitchen. West told Andy: "I need a couple of strong men, the first you can find on the street."

The boy was gone almost before the doctor finished speaking. He came back in a few minutes with two railroad brakemen. West had found a blanket. He showed them how to use it as a stretcher, and helped them move the sick woman to the kitchen table.

The men left reluctantly. They did not like the idea that West was going to operate. "Where's Condon?" asked the taller of the two. "Maybe we should stop him."

His partner shook his head. "You stop him. That's the Orphan Kid. I heard tonight that he'd come back, and I guess he's a doctor from what they were saying at Callahan's. Besides, I'll bet Condon's drunk right now."

His friend did not take the bet. They went out and up the street, telling the news. In five minutes a crowd began to gather before the hotel.

Inside, West had ordered Andy from the kitchen and closed the dining room door. Then he went to work, and, as he worked swiftly, he thanked Providence that Laura was there to help him. Had he had time he might have admired Belle's composure, but he had no time. This was the first operation the girl had ever witnessed, while he and

143

Laura had participated in many. But this was the first time he had acted entirely on his own without the hospital staff beside him. His actions were nearly automatic, deft and rapid. He heard Belle's sharply drawn breath as he made his first incision, and then it was very quiet in the big square room.

He sighed with relief when he found that the appendix had not yet ruptured. But it was extremely swollen and inflamed. He removed it, cleansed the cavity, and closed it neatly. But not until the sick woman had been swathed in rolled sheets and he had made a final check of her pulse did he look up.

Belle Callahan's face was dead white, and her even teeth had left sharp marks on the redness of her lower lip. Her eyes had darkened until they looked enormous and her voice was shaky. "Is . . . is she all right?"

It was Laura who answered, speaking not to the girl but to West. "A very creditable operation, Doctor. I don't think Doctor Forbes could have done better himself."

The words brought a quick pleasure to West. As he washed his hands, he felt that he had passed his first test. He thanked Laura by a quick kiss upon her cheek, then gathered up his instruments and packed them in his case.

Andy stood aside as they moved his mother through the wide doorway into the laundry where Belle had fixed a bed. The boy had recovered from his first fright, and his eyes showed the glint of hero worship.

"I was going to be a dispatcher, but I've changed my mind. Do you have to be very smart to be a doctor?"

West put a hand on his shoulder. "You're smart enough, Andy. Are you willing to work?"

"I'll work," Andy said. "I'll really, truly work. You just wait and see."

V

Condon shut the door after sending Andy away. He turned to face the three Benton boys. Outside, the yammering of the dogs was already dying to dispirited whines. He had become so used to the racket that he did not hear them.

Bo Benton stood, his shirt removed, his scorched hands showing red and blistery, his back marred by a red blotch where the hot iron had touched him. Vance and Fred were beyond the table, watching, and Condon looked at them in anger. "If that boy had found you hiding here, the story would

145

be all over town."

Vance grinned. Vance did not like Condon and took no trouble to hide his feelings. "I guess even the Bentons have a right to come to a doctor when they get burned." He grinned at Bo, who swore at him.

Condon glared, but did not answer as he started to examine Bo's back. The touch of his fingers was not gentle. Bo winced. "For God's sake, Doc, take it easy."

Condon grunted. "Now you know what a cow feels like when you sear her hide with your running iron. Fred, go into the kitchen, heat a pail of water, and dump in all the tea you can find. I want tea leaves, as many as there are, for a poultice."

Fred Benton disappeared into the kitchen. The doctor took a pair of scissors, punctured the blister, and started to trim away the wrinkled skin.

The pain made Bo curse. "So help me, I'll run a gun barrel down the Orphan Kid's throat."

Vance laughed. Vance was two years older than Bo, and of all the Bentons he had been friendliest with West. "Way I heard it," he said, "it wasn't the Kid who swung that hot iron. It was the Callahan girl. Seems like she don't appreciate your courting."

Bo turned so quickly that the point of

Condon's shears dug into his back. He yelped, then glowered at his grinning brother. "Keep your damn' mouth out of my business."

Vance shrugged and went on mocking him. "Getting kind of uppity, aren't you, boy? I hear her old man is coining money. What are you after, the girl or the saloon?"

Bo started for Vance, but his brother merely circled the table ahead of him. Condon laid down the shears deliberately. "To hell with you. I can't dress your back if you waltz around like a traveling bear. Come back here. And if you don't want me to be digging one of Callahan's bullets out of your no-good hide, you'll keep away from that girl."

Bo came back grudgingly. Fred appeared from the kitchen carrying the bucket of soaked tea leaves. Condon picked up his shears and removed the rest of the loose skin, saying as he worked: "None of you Bentons has a grain of sense. I curse the day I ever got mixed up with your family."

Fred's face darkened. He was the most quarrelsome of the Bentons and his face bore the scars of a dozen barroom fights. "You'd have starved to death without us, Doc."

Condon was fixing the tea leaf poultice on

Bo's back. He stopped, staring at Fred. "What's bothering you now?"

"Duke and Prince. They've been in prison nearly eight years. The Orphan Kid came back here today, free as air."

Condon said in a resigned tone: "I did all I could for them. I showed your mother the letter I got from the lawyer. We were hoping for a pardon by the new governor. No luck."

Fred said slowly: "You took your cut from every hold-up we ever pulled. You owe it to the boys to get them out."

Condon finished fastening the poultice in place. He did not answer until it was secure. Then he said in a tired voice: "If Duke and Prince had listened to me, they wouldn't have held up that train and they wouldn't have been caught. And after they were, I brought a lawyer clear from Fort Smith to defend them."

"You kept Hy West from going to prison."

"His age and Dave Lawrence saved him. All I did was to bring Hy here when the court decided he couldn't go back to your ranch. He never even knew I was mixed up with you. There was nothing any of us could do for Duke and Prince. They were lucky not to get life."

"What difference does it make . . . twenty

years . . . life? We're going to break them out."

Condon stared at him, realizing that this was not idle talk, that the Bentons actually planned to help their brothers escape. "How do you expect to do that?"

"You're going to figure that out," Fred told him. "Ma says you were all-fired smart, planning our hold-ups. It should be a cinch for you to figure out how to free the boys."

Condon's temper was seldom even and it flared now. He knew that the Bentons were not normal, that they were ignorant and bigoted and had never seen a town larger than Soda Springs. For years their very name had terrorized this part of the country until they had an exaggerated opinion of what they could accomplish. He glanced at Vance, knowing that he was the shrewdest member of the family. "Do you think this fool idea is possible, Vance?"

Vance shrugged. "When Ma gets an idea in her head, all the black powder in the world won't blow it out. You'd better start thinking, Doc, or you'll be in trouble."

Condon laughed suddenly. "Do you think I'm a fool? I've been damned careful that no one suspected I was connected with you, or with your hold-ups. Don't threaten me. Who do you think would take your word against mine? I never held up a stage or stole a cow in my life."

"You killed Dave Lawrence." Fred was leaning across the table now, his dark eyes glowing, his mouth an ugly line. "You thought no one saw you that Christmas morning. You thought there was no one else in town awake when you stepped out of the alley and shot him in the back."

Condon's mouth went dry. He tried to speak and found that his stiff lips would not form the words. Fred saw the shock on the doctor's face and grinned wolfishly.

"Bo and I were sleeping in your stable that night. It was too cold when we quit drinking to ride home. We heard the dogs when you left and came down to see what was going on. We trailed you up the alley and we weren't fifteen feet from you when you poked your gun into Dave Lawrence's back."

Under the lamplight Condon's face glistened with sweat. A lesser man might have crumpled at learning suddenly that a secret he had kept closely guarded was known. The Lawrence affair had been his one act of real violence, and he had cursed himself a thousand times for giving way to his fear. For Dave Lawrence's murder had grown out of Condon's fear that the sheriff had guessed his connection with the Bentons. He had never known what act of his had first aroused Lawrence's suspicion. But abruptly he became conscious that Lawrence was watching his every move, that each time he rode out of town, Lawrence trailed him. It was then that he had decided that the sheriff must die.

His plan had been simple, based on his knowledge of Lawrence's character. He had waited until a man wanted on a federal warrant was reported in the area, then he got word to Lawrence in the middle of the night that a stranger was hiding in the livery stable. Lawrence had reacted as Condon knew he would. He came alone to investigate, walking along the deserted Railroad Avenue. And as he passed the alley, Condon stepped from the shadows to poke a gun against his back, to shoot him before he could turn.

By the time they had come to tell the doctor of the murder and call him in his official capacity as coroner, he was safely home in bed, apparently drunk. Neither the new sheriff nor the town marshal had made any real effort to find the murderer, believing it to be some chance rider who had had trouble with Lawrence, and Condon had nearly forgotten the crime.

Now he studied Fred's face. The Bentons had remained silent for over a year, waiting until they needed something from him before they used their knowledge. He could deny it, of course. It would still be his word against theirs. But he could not afford to take the chance. It would be one thing to stand accused of planning a hold-up in which he had taken no active part, and quite another to be charged with the cold-blooded killing of as popular a man as Dave Lawrence had been. And other things would then come out. His long association with the Bentons. He said tonelessly: "What is it you expect me to do?"

"Work up some way to get Duke and Prince out of prison."

"That's impossible."

"You'd better try." It was Fred. "We aren't fooling, and you know Ma. When she gets an idea in her head, she's real impatient."

Condon wet his lips. He had to have time to think. He said: "You can't expect me to pull something out of my hat right now. Tell your ma I'll come out to the ranch and we'll talk it over."

He watched them go with real relief. He had no idea what he meant to do. His first impulse was to pack his things and get away from Soda Springs as fast as he could ride.

He could be a long way into the mountains before it dawned on the Bentons that he was gone.

He looked around the room. This was home, shabby as it was, and he was old. He did not want to change. Much as he mocked Soda Springs and its citizens, he had an acknowledged place here which he would never achieve anywhere else.

He sat down heavily before his desk and stared morosely at the tintype above the desk. It was the picture of a pretty, laughing woman, a pleasing picture. But it did not please Condon. "Laugh," he snarled, talking to it as he sometimes did. "Laugh your head off, but I'm not through yet. You thought I was through once, and you were wrong. You're wrong now because I'm not finished. You just wait and see."

VI

Bo was muttering to himself as they started down the dark street. Vance glanced at him curiously. "What's eating you?"

"The Kid's got my gun. Can't leave my gun in town. Whole darn' town will laugh."

Fred said: "Let's go get it."

Vance turned in the saddle. "You crazy fool. Haven't you had enough trouble for

153

one day?"

"I can take care of him," Bo promised. "If Belle hadn't burned me with that flatiron, I'd have blown his fool head off."

"And hung for it."

"Look," Bo said. "Are you with me or not? You ride up to the hotel and tell the Kid I'm waiting for him down by the livery. Lend me your gun."

Vance shook his head. "I don't want any part of it."

"I'll go," Fred said, and swung his horse toward the hotel.

Vance said: "To hell with it." He turned and rode away. Bo watched him go in sullen silence. Then he thought of something. He still had no gun.

He swung around, intending to go back to Condon's and borrow one, but as he turned, he saw his brother come down the hotel steps. He waited as Fred rode up.

Fred said: "He isn't there. He operated on the old lady. Then he went down to Callahan's for a drink."

Bo glanced up the street toward the saloon. "Let me have your gun."

Fred hesitated. "You aren't going in there by yourself?"

"Why not?"

"Callahan doesn't like trouble in there and

he keeps a shotgun under the bar."

Bo swore. "Are you going to give me that gun or am I going to take it away from you?"

Fred shrugged and silently passed the gun to his brother. Bo dropped it into his empty holster. They rode toward the saloon in silence.

Gimble watched them from the far corner of the livery. The town marshal had been looking for them most of the evening, wondering where they were. It wasn't that he wanted to see them. It was only that he would feel much safer once they were clear of town. He saw them dismount before Callahan's, saw Fred pull the rifle from the boot beneath the stirrup. He frowned. "What in the devil?" he muttered aloud. Surely even the Bentons weren't crazy enough to attempt to hold up Callahan.

He swore. He wished someone else was town marshal. He wished he was a good one hundred miles away. At least no one knew where he was, and he did not mean to be present when the trouble started. He pulled his horse back into the deeper shadows, rode down the alley behind the livery, and so toward the end of town.

Before the saloon door, Fred Benton halted and levered a shell into the rifle chamber. Then he nodded. Bo pushed the batwing doors wide with a sweeping gesture of both hands, like a swimmer using the breast stroke, and in the next second was in the long room, Fred close behind.

The room was poorly filled, for it was late. Two tables of poker still carried on at the back of the room, but the bar was deserted aside from West who stood near the center, talking to Callahan. He did not turn as Bo came in, but Callahan lifted his head and at once sensed danger. He was too old a hand not to recognize the signs and he said, hardly moving his lips, his voice little more than a whisper: "Watch it, Doc." As he spoke, his eyes dropped to West's belt. He noticed the absence of any weapon and he frowned.

West lifted his eyes to the mirror. He saw Bo standing inside the door. Fred was at his back, and he saw the rifle in Fred's hands. He knew at once that their arrival was no accident. Even the Bentons did not enter a saloon carrying a rifle unless they were after someone, and he guessed that someone was he. Under his breath he cursed himself for being so careless as to come out alone and unarmed. His years in the East had lulled him into a feeling of false security.

He stood there, not turning, waiting for what was going to happen, powerless to prevent it. He sensed that Callahan was reaching under the bar, and, when the big saloonkeeper straightened, he held a six-gun almost hidden in his big hand. This he slid across to West, keeping it screened from the view of the men behind West's body. Hy reached out and slipped it under his belt. As he did so, he glanced again in the mirror.

Fred had halted just inside the door. He stood with his rifle held down alongside his right leg as if he thought that by so standing no one in the saloon would notice it. Bo came on, moving carefully. His legs were stiff. He had pulled the wrappings from his burned hand and it hung, claw-like, at his side, below the butt of the holstered gun. He advanced until less than ten feet separated him from West. There he stopped, standing with his feet a little apart, his shoulders slightly hunched.

"Kid."

West said: "What is it?" He was conscious that the players at the card tables in the rear had ceased their games and were turning to watch.

"I've come for my gun."

"Oh, that." West sounded surprised. "Why, of course." He turned then, and to the men watching from the rear tables it seemed that

157

he whirled. As he came around, his long fingered right hand dropped to his belt. The gun seemed to grow into his hand. He jumped then, as Fred started to bring up his rifle. He jammed the gun hard into Bo's stomach, almost knocking the wind out of the youngest Benton.

Bo had started to draw as West turned, but the gun was hardly clear of the holster when the barrel of West's weapon jarred into his belt line. He stopped, frozen.

West said tonelessly: "Let it drop, Bo."

Benton stared into the doctor's eyes, finding them cold, a little mocking, but utterly unyielding. He knew West well enough to sense that, if he failed to obey, the gun against his stomach would explode. Suddenly he was scared. His burned fingers released their grip, and the gun slid from his grasp to *thud* onto the scarred floor at his feet.

Fred Benton had his rifle half raised, but Bo's body was between him and his target. For a minute he hesitated, and in that minute Callahan took a hand in the game, poking the twin barrels of his Greener across the bar top so that they covered Fred Benton. "Put it down, Fred."

Benton said savagely: "We won't forget this, Callahan."

"Remember it then." The big Irishman was unmoved. "Any time you think you or your brothers can walk into my place and shoot holes in my mirror you better think again. Lay the rifle on the floor and get out."

For an instant it seemed that Fred would refuse. Then with a muttered oath, he threw the rifle from him so that it *clattered* against the wall as it fell. Without even looking toward it, Fred Benton swung on his heel, knocked the doors aside, and plunged out into the night.

West used one hand to swing Bo around and push him after his retreating brother. He followed him clear to the door, and stood watching above the batwings as the Bentons mounted and spurred furiously out of town.

Not until he was certain that they were gone did he come back toward the bar, gathering the rifle and six-gun up from the floor as he passed. He dumped them on the bar and added the gun that Callahan had slid to him. "Thanks. Sorry you had to get in trouble with the Bentons because of me."

"Scum," Callahan said, depositing the firearms under the counter. "If the people in this town had the guts of rabbits, we'd have run the Bentons out of the country long ago. Drink?" He did not wait for an answer, but poured whiskey for two. "Why the devil did you come back to this mess anyhow?"

West didn't answer. He drank his whiskey, and then with a nod turned out into the night.

The following day the town's single paper asked the same question. Why had Dr. West come back to Soda Springs? It was seldom that Bert Borus, the editor, had much to write about, and he spread himself. He had pieced together most of the story, the fight West had had with Bo in the hotel kitchen, West's operation on Mary Lawrence, Laura's arrival to marry West, and the brush in Callahan's saloon. From there the editor went backward, reminding his readers that this was the boy who had once been called the Orphan Kid, who had only escaped going to prison with Duke and Prince Benton because of his youth; recalling how Dr. Condon had taken the boy, how the boy had run away East, and studied to be a doctor, and how he had now returned to serve as an assistant at the Railroad Hospital. On the whole the story pictured West in a favorable light, but it did point out that he had been raised by the Bentons, that as a boy he was sullen and quarrelsome, and that he had had two fights the very day he returned.

The town read and divided as most towns do. Some citizens were for leaving West alone. Others, including the minister of one church and the elder of another, met and decided that it was both illegal and an outrage that a man who should by rights be in prison was allowed to practice medicine in Soda Springs. These carried their complaint to the division superintendent.

Dr. Franz Gruber, head of the Railroad Hospital, read the paper as he stood at the bar in Callahan's having his morning drink. Gruber did not like Soda Springs, or the hospital, or the patients he was supposed to serve, and he would not have read the paper had not his eye caught the headline:

NEW DOCTOR FOR RAILROAD HOSPITAL

Gruber was a stuffy man, not quite middle-aged. He had graduated with honors in Vienna and had looked forward to a brilliant career. But drink and serious trouble with a woman forced him to flee the continent, and he might have starved had not a chance acquaintance in New York told him that the Pacific Railroad was building a chain of hospitals through the West and having difficulty finding enough doctors to staff them.

When he was sent to Soda Springs, the empty, barren country depressed him, the violence of the people frightened him, and only fear that he would not find another job made him stay. His hands trembled as he read the headline, for he thought at first that he was being removed. Then, after he had read the whole article, he was horrified. His new assistant was a former outlaw, a train robber. He laid the paper on the bar and hurriedly left the saloon.

And the first glimpse Gruber had of his new assistant was not reassuring. West was big. He weighed a good thirty pounds more than Gruber, and none of it was fat. His eyes were level and direct and unyielding, and Gruber had to steel himself to speak.

"You're new," he said, "so you may not know the strict company rule. None of us is allowed any private practice. The railroad doesn't want to antagonize the doctors in the towns along the right of way."

West said shortly: "Condon was called and refused to come. The operation could not be postponed."

Gruber flushed at his tone, but managed to say in a level voice: "It's nice to have you here. We will now keep the hospital open through the night. We will alternate. Every other week you will take the night shift, and it will also be part of your work to ride the wrecking train in case of accident. Now, I'll show you around."

He led West first into the second office, then through the ward. The hospital was nearly empty, the only bed patients being a brakeman whose crushed leg had been removed, and two section hands who had gotten into a fight on a work train and fallen to the ballast, lacerating themselves but breaking no bones.

West was seized by a feeling of depression. He had come here to work, to learn. A new doctor learned only by experience. And there did not seem to be enough here to keep one man occupied. He watched while Gruber examined the brakeman's stump. He could find no fault with Gruber's surgery, but it was evident that the administration at the hospital was very lax and he smelled the heavy odor of whiskey upon Gruber's breath. The floors were dirty and the kitchen worse. It was with a feeling of relief that he left, promising to report at 6:00 that evening.

Outside he found Andy and a small, sandy-haired boy waiting for him. Andy introduced his companion as Sam Dillon.

"He's going to be a doctor, too," Andy explained. "Sandy does everything I do."

West nodded, his mind busy on other things. "The world's a big place. It can use a lot of doctors."

Sam's voice had a piping quality. "We were going to be dispatchers yesterday," he explained, "but Andy says being a doctor is much more important. Does a doctor make more than a dispatcher?"

"Some do."

Sam considered, then brightened. "Say, have you still got your guns? My pa says that when you were a boy you were real fast with them."

West shook his head, and disappointment registered on the faces of both his companions.

"I've got my father's," Andy said. "Ma don't know it, but I've got them in my bureau. I practice with them real often."

West didn't answer. He could think of nothing appropriate to say.

"Would you show me how to use them some time?"

He stopped then, looking down into Andy's face. "I don't think I'd better," he said slowly. "I wore my guns to school once when I wasn't too much older than you are, and I almost got into bad trouble. Your father took them away from me, and he made me promise that I wouldn't wear them again. He showed me that guns were only made for enforcing the law, not breaking it."

Neither boy answered, and after a moment they moved on down the street toward the hotel, passing a dozen people as they progressed. One or two nodded casually to West. Several merely stared. The rest ignored him. No one spoke until they rounded the corner and came face to face with Bruce Gimble and Al DeMember, the sheriff.

West stopped, for the men were standing side-by-side, blocking the sidewalk. He started to smile, then let his lips straighten as he saw no welcome in either of their faces.

Gimble's first glance had been at West's waist as if he had hoped to catch the young doctor wearing a gun and therefore breaking the town ordinance. Then he saw the two boys and scowled at them. "You kids get out of here." Both Andy and Sam Dillon were taken by surprise. They stared at him, not moving, and red crept up under his deep tan. "Hear me, you move!"

West said mildly: "What's the matter? They aren't doing anything wrong."

Gimble glared at him. "I'll be the judge of that. We want to talk to you and we don't want them hanging around. Now, get."

They got, retreating reluctantly, looking back across their shoulders. He waited until they rounded the corner. DeMember had not spoken. He was a big man, placid and unhurried.

Gimble said: "A lot of our better citizens don't take kindly to you coming back here. They don't think a train robber will make a good doctor."

West said calmly: "The railroad doesn't object. The Chicago office knew my history before they hired me. I'm not going into general practice, Gimble. I'm working for the railroad."

The marshal scowled at him, baffled. He was not a bright man and his mind worked slowly. "And you're a troublemaker," he said. "You hadn't been in town five hours before you were in trouble."

"What kind of trouble?"

Gimble was growing angry. "Don't try and play innocent. You had a fight with Bo Benton, didn't you? I tell you, West, we don't want you here. We want you out of town."

Hy said idly: "Have you ordered Bo to stay out? He started it."

Gimble's face gained color. He was very conscious of his fear of the Bentons. "That's different," he muttered. "The Bentons kind of belong here."

"So do I," West said. "Or have you forgotten?"

He had been trying to hold his temper, having expected something like this from the first. They were standing close together and Gimble made a mistake.

"I mean it," he said, and dropped his hand to his gun. He actually did not intend to draw it; he was only trying to emphasize his words. But Hy West's reaction was instinctive. The moment Gimble's right hand dropped, West's left shot out. He caught the marshal's wrist in a vise-like grip and crossed his right to Gimble's jaw.

The marshal fell. As he went down, West jerked the gun from Gimble's holster. Swinging on the balls of his feet, he jammed the heavy barrel into the stomach of the amazed sheriff.

DeMember gasped, the air partly driven out of him. He was a man who avoided unnecessary violence at all times. Not as able a man as Dave Lawrence had been, nor as smart, he still had little love for Gimble and had not realized what the marshal had in mind. He spread both his big hands out, well away from his body, palms down to show that he wanted no part of this. "You didn't have to poke my stomach in, Hy. Gimble was out of line."

West had recovered from his quick, momentary flash of anger and embarrassment crept into his voice. "Sorry, Al. He caught me unexpectedly."

"Which was what he intended." DeMember's voice was dry.

West reversed the marshal's gun and extended it to the sheriff, butt first. He did not look at Gimble who was getting slowly to his feet. He moved on past the sheriff, knowing that the man turned as he passed and watched him, muttering under his breath. He neither knew nor cared what DeMember said. He was shaking a little from reaction by the time he entered the hotel.

The lobby was quiet and he paused inside its shadows to hold up his right hand, looking at it curiously. It was trembling and he smiled wryly. *I've got to get hold of myself,* he thought. *I'm letting the town get me down. I knew that there would be trouble when I came back, but I pictured nothing like this.*

He went on into the kitchen then, expecting to find Laura Hall with Mrs. Lawrence. She was nowhere in sight. Belle Callahan was alone, seated at the kitchen table. She looked up and put one finger to her lips.

"Mary's asleep."

"How is she?"

"The nurse said she was all right." She accented the word *nurse* slightly and he gave her a sharp glance. Obviously Belle didn't like Laura. It was so very easy to tell when Belle did not like someone. There was almost no pretense about her.

He said in defense: "I'm very glad Laura was here last night. I would have hated to operate without her." He knew he was making an effort to justify Laura, and was surprised that he felt the necessity. "Where is she now?"

"She went to lie down. She was up half the night."

He nodded and asked for a cup of coffee. She brought it to the table and sat down beside him. "So you aren't going to stay, Hy?"

He looked at her in surprise. "Not stay? Where did you get the idea?"

"Miss Hall told me. We had quite a talk. I don't think your Miss Hall likes me much. She asked me a lot of questions about you. I think she sensed a romance between us."

He grinned, stirring the sugar into the coffee. "Did you tell her that you were too smart to have anything to do with me?"

Her smile in return was faint. "I agreed with her that you were a damned fool to come back to Soda Springs. She told me about the offer from Doctor Forbes. Why did you come back here, Hy?"

It was the question he had been asking himself all morning, but he temporized. "Maybe I got homesick. I've been away a long time."

She said, almost roughly: "Stop evading. I know why you came back. Even your Laura knows. Don't tell me you aren't as smart as we are."

His grin widened. "All right, Miss Portia, tell me . . . why did I come back?"

"Because," she said, "you're a chuckle-headed son-of-a-long-tailed-mule."

He laughed outright. "Such language."

"I learned my language in the Army," she told him, "and that's an old expression of my father's. He reserved it for each new set of green recruits. Don't you remember how shocked the teachers were at the way I swore?"

He did remember. "You've developed into quite a lady."

"Stop it," she said. "We never kidded each other, Hy, even when we fought."

"No," he said, "we never kidded each other." He looked at her and felt a sudden warmness that he had not experienced since his return. He was easy with Belle Callahan;

that was the word, easy. With her he never had to pretend. With her he could relax the defensive mask that he had built up to protect himself against the world. He tried to analyze the reason for this. Perhaps it went a long way back. Perhaps it was because out of the whole school he and Belle had been the two outsiders, the ones on whom the other children looked a little askance. They'd both had chips on their shoulders, knowing that they were not accepted: he, because he was associated with the Bentons, she because her father had been an Army sergeant, and now ran a saloon.

"That's the only reason I'm talking to you now," she said. "Because we've never kidded ourselves and it's a little late to begin. It's none of my damned business, Hy, but somehow I feel a little responsible for you." He looked at her in surprise and she colored faintly. "You don't need to begin to get worried. I decided a long time ago that marriage was not for me. I saw what it did to my mother, and to the other women on the post. This is a man's world, Hy. The women sit at home and knit."

He had a momentary vision of Laura. No matter what else she did, Laura would never sit at home.

Belle was not smiling now. Words had never come too easily for this girl and she was having trouble making her reasoning plain to him. "There's nothing for you in Soda Springs. You can stay here for twenty years and without a miracle they will never accept you . . . and you are a person who needs to be accepted. I remember how hurt you were, down inside, when the school kids used to call you an outlaw and a train robber. You wanted to fight back because you were hurt. But the more you fought, the farther apart you set yourself, the higher you built the wall that separated you from the town."

He knew she was right and he found a moment to marvel at her ability to understand. But then he realized that the understanding came out of her own deep bitterness. "What you're saying applies to you as well as to me."

"It does."

"Then why don't you take your own advice and get out?"

"Because I'm a coward." She said this frankly. "I'm not happy here. At times I'm lonely, and I always have the feeling that, if I went away, things might be better. But I'm afraid to put it to the test. I have no training. I've never been a hundred miles away from here. What little I do have is centered in this town. But you're different. You've already made the break. You have your training and your future before you. You have a pretty girl to marry and a chance to work with Doctor Forbes. Again I tell you . . . stop being a long-tailed mule. You came back here to prove something, to prove to yourself that you can break down the prejudice against you in this town. You can't. People resent those who are different from them in any way."

"I'm not entirely sure."

"Because you won't face facts as they are, because you hate to admit that you've been wrong for six long years. Nothing has changed here since you left. If you don't believe it, get a horse and ride out to the Benton ranch."

"An idea, that."

"A poor one, but it might bring you to your senses. A look at the house where you were raised and the people you were raised with might show you how very far you've traveled in six years. Go on, go. Don't worry about Mary. Miss Hall's here, and, although I freely admit I don't like her, I think she's competent with the sick."

He went then, and, as he crossed the lobby, he knew a sudden eagerness that he had not expected. On the porch outside he was stopped by Andy and Sam Dillon. Andy was bubbling with excitement.

"It's all over town," he said. "The way you knocked Bruce Gimble down. I'll bet that will make people stop and think. I'll bet from now on they'll be careful to let you alone."

That, West thought as he descended the two steps and moved up the sidewalk toward the livery, was the trouble. Everything that had happened to him since his return seemed to be building the wall higher. He had wanted to come back to Soda Springs to gain respect from the people who had once sneered at him. He realized that fully now, and these early setbacks troubled him all the more because of his knowledge.

It was such a nebulous thing, and yet so very important to his self-esteem. He might run away, back to Dr. Forbes and the hospital, telling himself that the fools who made up the population of the town did not matter. But he was as honest with himself as he had tried to be with Belle. They did matter. Even a fool like Bruce Gimble mattered. At the moment a word of grudging praise from Gimble would be more important than a citation from the President. He smiled wryly.

The horse that Wentworth rented him was a bay. It had been in the corral for days and it wanted to run. Once free of town he made no effort to curb it. Fast riding gave him a sense of freedom that he had not known for a long time. The empty country stretched away toward the distant hills, limitless, unhampered by buildings or fence. The high, dry air was so clear that the mountains stood out against the sky like cut-outs, yet three-dimensional and massive in their towering hugeness. He knew each foot of this wild land. The whole place was a maze of trails, and the land here was so dry that tracks that had been made months before seemed to have the clarity of yesterday.

He rode, and the horse, having had its blowout run, settled into the steady gait that would carry it on for miles and miles. The country roughened, and spurs of rocky shoulders ran out now into the uneven plain. The trail climbed, and the vegetation altered, and now there were tiny streams in the cañon bottoms, racing torrents that would lose themselves to the south in the ever-thirsty sand.

He knew a sudden urge to keep riding, into the mountains, beyond the mountains, until he had completely lost himself, and a desire never to see Soda Springs again, to leave the Railroad Hospital behind, to forget Condon, and the Bentons, and even Laura Hall. But he knew it was not for him. Some people were fiddle-footed. Some people could shed responsibilities as they would remove an old coat, but this was not for him. He knew that he would go back, that he would stay in Soda Springs, stay there until he had whipped the town or it had whipped him.

Side trails were splitting off to right and left now, reaching out like the ribs of a fan into the small mountain meadows where the solitary ranches hid their weathered buildings. He had known these people. They were like the Bentons, suspicious of strangers, violent, resentful of those who chose to live in town. Theirs was a marginal existence. They hunted a little, ran a few cattle, and were not above branding a stray calf or running off a few horses. An unarmed stranger was not safe in these hills, and he had armed himself, wearing Bo Benton's gun in a borrowed holster, carrying the rifle he had borrowed from Wentworth under his knee.

It was not that he expected trouble, yet he knew that, if he ran into Bo Benton or Fred, there might well be another fight. He had no intention of ducking them. This ride was a kind of test. He could not remain in this country indefinitely and quarrel with the Bentons every time they met. He wanted to talk to Ma. A word from Ma Benton would curb her war-like sons quicker than anything else. But just as he reached the mouth of the cañon that led to the Benton ranch he had a sudden impulse and turned the horse into a steep, rocky trail that wound up through the timber to the cañon rim overlooking the Benton house. At the top the trail ended abruptly in a little promontory, and he stepped down, setting the horse free to graze on the scattered tufts of mountain grass.

He walked to the rim and stood looking down on the roofs of the place that had been his home, the only home he could remember. It was a typical mountain ranch, the house of logs, its corral of poles, its sheds and outbuildings grass-roofed. It sat at the head of a bottle-shaped cañon, facing the neck, some two hundred acres, fenced by the natural rise of the cañon sides. It was seldom that anyone save the Bentons rode into the valley. But even as West reached the rim he saw a horseman coming up the trail through the lower cañon. The rider must have been fairly close behind him on the main trail. The thought crossed his mind that the rider could have been following him, but then he dismissed the idea as ridiculous. There was no reason for anyone to follow him out from Soda Springs.

He hunkered down, idly picking a stem of the dried grass and twisting it between his lips. He had always liked this spot as a boy, and he had climbed here often to escape the turmoil in the valley below. His eyes centered on the rider as the horse climbed the steep pitch of the lower cañon and the man grew in size as he approached. There was something familiar about him, but at the distance West failed to realize who it was until he reached the corral fence and stepped down to walk toward the house. Then recognition came. There was no mistaking Dr. Condon's walk.

Someone came from the house porch to meet the doctor, and they paused for an instant in the center of the yard, then turned and moved back to the house. West waited motionlessly. His first thought was that someone in the house below him was sick. He wondered who it was and decided that it must be the mother. And suddenly he had his idea. It pleased him. He would simply walk in, a doctor, offering his aid. Bo must have told Ma Benton about his return, but she would still be surprised to see this boy who she had raised, entering as a doctor.

The stream ran down on his right, dropping over the rim in a series of short rapids to fall the last a hundred feet to the cañon floor in a direct drop that landed in a round, deep pool above the house. Beside the stream zigzagged the path. It was a footpath only, too narrow and steep for any horse, but he had climbed it many times as a youngster. If he rode back to the cañon mouth, it would take almost an hour to reach the house. By the path, he could make it in less than ten minutes.

He started downward, still carried forward by impulse, feeling his way cautiously. The going was steeper than he had remembered and he sighed with relief when he reached the level ground beside the pool. The woodshed was between him and the house and he came around it with a curious feeling of nostalgia. His memory naturally inclined to retain the nice things that had happened rather than the bad, and he had not been too unhappy at this ranch.

The yard itself was filled with remembered things: the tree from which he used to mount his horse before he was large enough to reach the stirrup; the old tin target that he and Vance and Bo had trained their first guns on, still tacked to the woodshed door;

the old milk house beside the stream where Ma had cooled her butter crocks; the open forge where Prince had showed him how to cinch on a shoe. He climbed the pole fence and came up into the main yard, and then he stopped suddenly. Vance Benton had come from behind the house and Vance was carrying a rifle in the cradle of his arm.

Hy waited for a cheerful greeting. He had always felt closer to Vance than all the rest. He had even looked up to the older boy. But the greeting he expected failed to come. There was no smile to twist Vance's thin-lipped mouth, no welcome in his dark, flat eyes.

"What are you following Condon for?"

Hy West could not have been more surprised if he had been accused of stealing drugs from the Railroad Hospital. He started to grin, thinking it a joke. Then his grin faded as Vance shifted the rifle.

"Give me your gun," Vance said.

West had the impulse to pull Bo's gun and take his chances with Vance. But he had not come here to fight. His intention had been to make his peace with Ma Benton. He said slowly: "Bo's in there, and spoiling for my blood."

"Then why'd you come?" Vance stared at him coldly.

West told him then. He said: "I wanted to see Ma. I haven't seen her for over six years, and I wanted to patch things up with Bo. What the hell, Vance, I'm going to stay in this country. I don't want to carry on a feud with you Bentons. After all, you're the only family I ever had."

There was still suspicion in Vance's eyes. "Then why'd you try and sneak in the back way? Why didn't you ride up the cañon?"

West tried to explain. "Remember how we used to play up there on the rim? I suddenly thought of it as I rode in, and took the hill trail. Then from the rim I saw Condon. I thought someone was sick, so I came down to help."

He watched Vance's face as he spoke, trying to decide if he had convinced him. He couldn't be sure. Vance said: "You'd better give me that gun."

West drew it slowly and extended it, butt first. Vance glanced at it and his thin lips curved a little. "Bo's?"

West nodded.

"I'll tell him you rode out to return it. That may quiet him a little. At any rate I'll see he doesn't start anything as long as you aren't armed."

VII

Ma Benton was exactly five feet tall and never in her life had she weighed more than ninety pounds. Her husband had been six feet two and every one of her five sons stood over six feet. But she was the brains of the family, and always had been. Hers was the driving power that stirred them into activity, and, although all the boys were now fully grown, she still tried to dominate them as she had dominated them as children.

Condon had always found her both interesting and amusing, and it had been for amusement as much as anything else that he had first become involved in the Bentons' illegal enterprises. He was a man turned bitter by life, who resented what organized society had done to him, and he had begun to take a sardonic revenge in plotting the minor crimes which the Benton boys and their wild-riding neighbors carried out. That he had gotten involved far deeper than he intended was due to carelessness and accident, and to his ever increasing drinking, and the fact that his practice hardly managed to pay his enormous bar bills. As he grew older, he had become more and more careless, but when Duke and Prince finally waxed ambitious and planned the hold-up of the express car with its box that was reported to contain over $30,000, he had drawn back. He, far more clearly than they, understood that there was a vast difference between holding up an isolated stage and robbing a few passengers, and holding up the through limited and thus bringing down upon themselves a flood of railroad detectives and Pinkerton men. But although he had refrained from having any part in the hold-up planning, he had done his best, once Duke, Prince, and Hy West had been captured, to secure them the lightest sentences possible. Although never appearing openly, he had arranged for the lawyer from Fort Smith, and paid for the defense out of his own pocket, knowing that if he refused, the Bentons would turn on him like hungry animals. But now, even though he had done everything a man could, they were yapping at his heels, threatening him with exposure for Dave Lawrence's murder.

There was no arguing with the Bentons. Their ignorance was so enormous that plain logic made not the slightest appeal. He had drunk himself into a stupor, trying to think of some method that might stand even a slight chance of freeing the two brothers from the Territorial Prison, and had thought of nothing. But he dared not admit to the

Bentons that there was anything to which he could not somehow find an answer. His only hold on the unruly family came of their belief that once he really put his mind to it he could figure out anything. He had taken half a dozen drinks and was sweating profusely as he dismounted at the corral fence and moved up across the sloping yard. He still had no answer, but the liquor had given him courage. He would tell them he had formulated a rough plan, but that it would take several weeks to develop. In that time anything could happen, and Condon's alcohol-soaked brain told him that anything was better than a showdown now.

Fred came out into the yard to meet him, and together they mounted to the sagging porch and entered the square front room. Bo was seated beyond the stove. He did not even bother to get up.

Ma Benton said: "So you decided to come out." She sounded sarcastic. She had a voice like the high-pitched call of a water bird. Condon knew at once that he was in for a bad time. He pressed his big, beefy hands against his throbbing temples.

"Look, Ma, I. . . ."

"You're no good, Doc." She said it without emphasis as if she were stating a well-accepted fact that brooked no argument.

"You never were any good, and you've been lording it high and mighty around here for a long time, telling us what to do. Well, now it's our turn to tell you."

Condon looked around. Fred had followed him into the room and shut the door. Fred was grinning.

The mother went on: "I guess the boys laid it on the line last night. I guess they scared you or you wouldn't have come busting out here this morning."

"I've always come when you've asked me to." He tried dignity.

She sneered at him. "So now I'm asking you to figure a way to break Prince and Duke out of that prison. Have you figured it out yet?"

He said slowly, conscious that her round, black eyes were watching him intently: "I've been thinking about it. I thought about it all last night."

"You're a liar." She was staring at his puffy face. "You drank yourself stupid last night, Doc, like you usually do. But you're going to think about it now."

"I tell you I've got to have time. . . ."

"I've been doing some thinking myself," she said tartly. "Maybe I ain't as smart as you, Doc, but I get ideas. For one thing I know that prison doctor calls you in when

185

they got sickness up there. That gets you on the inside. Maybe you could take some guns in to the boys. Maybe they could do the rest themselves."

He was horrified. The last thing in the world he wanted was to be involved directly in a prison break. "I couldn't do that," he said. "They search me every time." This of course was not true, but he had to say something and it was the first thing that came into his mind.

"Then how do we get them some guns?"

He shrugged. "I told you I'm working on it. I'll think of something." They might be able to fight their way out with guns, but he doubted it. "Once they're outside they'll need help."

She was not concerned. "That's easy. The boys have enough friends in these hills."

"And we'll have to arrange to get them across the border."

She was startled. "Mexico? Why can't they come back here? There are plenty of places to hide in these hills."

He tried to be patient with her ignorance. "When Prince and Duke break out, every able-bodied man in the territory will be in the posse, and every soldier from the fort. Don't forget, that is a federal prison and these hills will be combed until a rabbit couldn't escape. And it will take money, a lot of money, to stay safe below the line. You'll have to pay off the authorities down there."

"We'll get the money." It was Fred.

Condon glanced at him, wondering what foolishness was cooking up in Fred's brain. Then he shrugged, looking back at the old woman. "Remember," he warned, "this will take time to arrange. It can't happen tomorrow or the next day."

Her face hardened. "It better not take too long. The boys warned you they'd talk to Al DeMember, and they weren't fooling. You fail us on this, Doc, and I'll live to see you dance at the end of a rope."

She broke off as steps sounded on the porch. Everyone turned. Hy West came into the room with Vance at his heels, still carrying his rifle.

"Look what I found climbing down the cliff," Vance said. "He claims he rode out just to say hello to you, Ma."

Condon was staring at West with bulging eyes. Bo rose with a muttered curse and kicked his chair out of the way. Fred Benton held his place beside the door, not moving.

West looked around. His first thought was: *There's something out of the ordinary going on here. They don't look natural and Ma isn't sick. No one is sick. What is Condon doing here and why are they so nervous? It isn't like them to be nervous. Ordinarily they don't know what nerves are.* He looked at Condon with renewed attention. He had never understood the man. He had never solved the mystery of why Condon, of all people, should have taken him in after the train robbery. Condon had never actually mistreated him, any more than Condon had mistreated the coyote dogs. In fact, Condon, when sober, had talked to him now and then about medicine. That had first captured his interest. He realized, without knowing how he knew, that under his drunken exterior Condon had a real love for his profession.

But Condon had so seldom been sober, and Condon drunk was an entirely different person. Hy had hated the old doctor when he was drunk. He had kept out of his way as much as possible. For Condon's tongue was razor sharp, and he spared no one. He had railed at the boy then, calling him ignorant, stupid, uneducated. He had told him over and over that he could not be trusted. At times it had seemed almost as if Condon had hated him, had seen in him something that Condon despised. He looked at the doctor now, wondering how Condon felt about him actually, and saw only fear in the prominent eyes. Condon was afraid. You could almost smell the fear within the room. Condon was afraid, and not of him. It must be of the Bentons, and that hardly made sense. Condon had sometimes railed against the Bentons, but West had never thought too much about it. He had been too occupied with his own misery. He had supposed that it was merely the doctor's way of trying to wean him from the influences of his foster home.

Ma was looking at him in that studying way of hers. He remembered the same look when he had been very small. He had learned early that there was no good in trying to lie to her. She could ferret out a lie faster than anyone he had ever known. She seemed to have a sixth sense that warned her when he had not been telling the truth. She had whipped him in those days, using a piece of an old harness strap, but she had not whipped him more than she did her own sons. She had been very impartial about that.

"So you came back," she said. "I never expected to see you again."

"I came back," he said, and wondered at his own lack of feeling. This woman had raised him, had fed him and clothed him, and at times had shown him a certain amount of kindness. And in those days he had not wanted to be an outsider. He had wanted to be a Benton.

Bo never let him forget that he was an outsider. Vance never mentioned the fact, and the older boys had usually ignored him unless he got in their way. The Bentons were bound together by a tight, rigid clan instinct that had little or nothing to do with real affection. And as a boy he had wanted affection. He knew this now. In medical school he had used himself as a kind of case history, trying to analyze his own emotions, and he had realized in a half sentimental way that the Bentons were the only family he would ever have. But seeing them now brought only a quick curiosity as to why they had gathered in this room, as to what Condon was doing at the ranch, as to what made them so suspicious of his own presence.

"I came back," he repeated, and put a smile upon his lips although he felt no mirth, "because I wanted you to know that one of your boys went and got educated as a doctor."

"One of my boys?" She repeated it to herself as if the words came as a surprise. "At least you've grown. You used to be a puny little runt."

"You take the credit," he said, and meant the words. "There never was a better cook than you."

That touched her. Ma Benton had always prided herself upon her cooking. She wiped her hands on her apron and relaxed a little. "You didn't give me too much trouble." She had softened as much as she would ever soften. "You didn't give me as much trouble as some of my own, but I didn't expect you to bother to ride out." A trace of bitterness crept into her voice. "I thought you were all through with the Bentons."

He said quickly: "I couldn't come before I went away. The judge said that, if I ever came back to the ranch, I'd have to go to prison. I was on parole."

She didn't understand the word. She had never understood why Prince and Duke had been locked up and this boy freed, and remembering it hardened her mouth. She did not blame him for their being in prison, but she resented him because he was free. "So you had to come back, spying around?"

He sensed the renewed suspicion in her tone and said: "Would you call it spying if Vance had been away and suddenly came home?"

"Vance belongs here."

That, he thought, was the basic difference,

the thing that Belle had tried to make him see, the reason she had sent him to the ranch. In the Bentons' eyes he did not belong, just as in the eyes of the Soda Springs people he was an outsider to be treated with constant suspicion. "All right," he said. "I guess I made a mistake in coming. I won't bother you. But I'm going to stay in Soda Springs, and I don't want to have to fight Bo and Fred every time we meet."

Bo said angrily: "It's damn' lucky Callahan was there with his shotgun last night."

West looked at him. He had the impulse to remind Bo that he had already shoved a gun into Bo's stomach before Callahan had moved with the shotgun. He didn't.

Vance said: "Trouble with Bo is that he thinks you're trying to take Belle away from him. Truth is, she won't even look in Bo's direction."

Bo's anger switched to Vance. "That's a damn' lie."

Fred could not resist saying: "At least she put her brand on Bo yesterday."

Bo had forgotten West in his anger against his two brothers. He turned and went through the kitchen door, slamming it behind him.

Ma shrugged. "You and Bo will have to

work it out. You and he never got along too good."

That was true, and he realized from the flatness of her tone that he would get no help from her. He thought of something else. "I never asked you who I was, Ma, where you got me, or who my parents are."

She looked at him for a long moment, and, when she spoke, her tone was curiously gentle. "You wouldn't be any happier if I told you, Kid. Now go on out with Vance. I want to talk to Doc."

He was dismissed, and he knew the dismissal was final. "Good bye, Ma."

She did not even answer, and he went back to the porch with Vance at his side. Fred followed them, closing the door. Fred seemed to hold no rancor for the preceding night. "How was it in Chicago, Kid?"

"All right," West said.

There was envy in Fred's voice. "Someday I'm going to take me a trip. Someday I'm going to see that town. I hear it's really something."

He did not follow them across the yard, but Vance stayed at West's side and West noticed that Vance had left his rifle in the house. They reached the foot of the cliff and he paused. "No need for you to climb, Vance."

Vance shrugged. "Haven't gone up there in years. Might be fun."

West couldn't decide whether Vance was following him to make certain he actually rode away, or merely for companionship. They reached the rim, both a little short of breath, and turned to look back down at the buildings below. He did not offer his hand, and Vance did not expect it. He had been much closer to Vance than the other brothers, but now there was an air of reserve between them. He caught his horse and stepped into the saddle. "See you in town."

Vance looked up at him. "Watch out for Bo. He's crazy where Belle is concerned."

West nodded. "For your information, I'm not marrying Belle. I'm marrying a girl from Chicago."

Vance shrugged. "None of my business." He was silent, considering. "What in hell did you come back here for? There's nothing in this lousy country for anyone."

"Why do you stay, then?"

Vance spread his hands. "What's a man to do?"

West did not know the answer. Suddenly he was a little sorry for Vance. He felt older than Vance, aged by his wider experience. And then he thought of something else. "I didn't ask down there, but what is Ma cooking up with Doc Condon?"

Vance's face changed, grew sullen, making him seem more like an Indian than ever. "I taught you never to ask questions when you were a kid. Maybe you forgot it back East, but in these hills people mind their own business."

Without another word he dropped over the rim, disappearing as if the earth had swallowed him.

VIII

All the way back to town West puzzled about Condon's visit to the Bentons. He kept telling himself that Vance was right, that it was none of his business. Certainly he had enough trouble of his own without searching for more. But he could not get it out of his mind. Nor could he forget that Ma Benton apparently knew where he came from. It had never occurred to him that the Bentons knew his identity. He had assumed that he was a foundling, picked up perhaps from some ambushed wagon train. Such things had been all too common in the territory twenty-five years before. But now the knowledge that, if she chose, Ma Benton could tell him who he was added a chafing irritation to his already uneasy thoughts.

Somehow, some way he would make the old woman tell him.

He rode into town, using the alley to reach the livery, turning the bay into the outer corral, leaving the saddle and bridle on the fence, and walking through the runway past the open door of Wentworth's office. The man waved, but West did not pause except to return the rifle. He stepped out onto Railroad Avenue, but before he had traveled halfway to the hotel, he heard someone call his name. Turning, he saw Andy Lawrence running toward him across the station yard. He came up, panting, saying as he arrived: "Omstead wants to talk to you. He sent me looking for you an hour ago."

"Who's Omstead?"

"The super, and you'd better talk to him quick. That Dutchy doctor at the hospital was in there, and he's got his knife out for you."

West was surprised. "Gruber? Why should he have his knife out for me?"

"He's scared," Andy said with quick wisdom. "He's afraid you'll get his job. He's a fake."

"What makes you say that?"

"I heard Doc Condon say it. Doc Condon says he wouldn't let Gruber doctor a horse, even if the horse wasn't sick and even if he didn't like the horse."

West grinned. That sounded like Condon after he had been drinking. "Is there anything about this town you don't know, Andy?"

The boy shook his head. "Nope. A fellow's got to know how things are if he's to get ahead."

"How's your mother?"

Andy's eyes glistened. "She's just fine. Laura says she never saw an operation go better. Does it take a lot of practice to learn to operate?"

"It takes a lot of schooling," West said.

Andy was thoughtful. He had never cared particularly for school. He led the way across to the station building and showed West the stairs that led to the offices above. It was very obvious that the boy would like to be present at the interview, but knew the superintendent would not permit it. He stood at the bottom of the steps, watching West climb as if he were watching a friend going to his execution.

Clay Omstead was a small man, and a tough one. Now sixty, he had fought his way up through the ranks to head the railroad's desert division, the longest division of any in the huge, interlocking system. Nor did he like the job before him. He hated to try a man without a hearing, and that perforce was what he was about to do. But it was not only Gruber's complaint that swayed him. He had received twenty complaints that morning from various citizens of Soda Springs.

He looked at West curiously as he came in. He saw a tall man with a strong thin face and quiet direct eyes, and wondered if someone had not made a mistake.

"You're West?" He never wasted time beating around things.

"I'm West," the doctor said, and watched the man behind the desk.

Omstead was known to his employees as a driver, but a fair one, and he said now: "This is a job that I don't care for, but one that I trust you will understand is impersonal. I've had a number of complaints about your appointment to our local hospital. I understand you were involved in a train robbery some years ago."

"I was." West's voice was quiet, unhurried. "The Chicago office knew all about it when they hired me."

Omstead had not known that. He said slowly: "Your former association with the Bentons makes you a kind of marked man. I'm surprised that the Chicago office assigned you here. It would have been much wiser if you had been sent to some station where you were not known."

"I requested Soda Springs."

Omstead's estimate of this quiet man rose rapidly. For himself he did not like Gruber, and the opinion of the foreign doctor had very little weight with him. His blunt fingers strayed across the desk, picked up a penholder, and toyed with it. "I'm in a peculiar position." He was watching the penholder now, not West. "Actually the hospital staffs are not directly under the operating department. They are hired and paid directly from Chicago. I have no authority to ask for your transfer, even if I desired to do so. You are under Gruber directly, and Gruber has made it plain that he does not care for your services."

He stopped as if expecting West to comment. The doctor remained silent. Omstead sighed. This was one of the situations that he disliked thoroughly, a clash of personalities among employees. "All I can say is that, if I were you, faced with this kind of a situation, I'd ask for a transfer."

"I doubt it."

Omstead's head jerked up with surprise. "Doubt what?"

West was smiling faintly. "Doubt that you would ask for a transfer. You're a fighter, I think, and stubborn. I suspect you wouldn't want to be run out of a town any more than I do."

Omstead matched his grin. "I think," he said, "that maybe you'll be a match for Gruber at that." He stood up, offering his hand. "Good luck."

West took the hand. Omstead was the first person who had actually wished him success since he had returned to Soda Springs.

Andy was waiting for him at the foot of the stairs. Andy, he realized, had adopted him, and he could expect the boy to be underfoot at almost any time.

Andy was watching his face. "You get fired?"

"Not quite."

The boy sighed his relief. "I didn't know. Never can tell about old Omstead." He fell into step, and together they walked to the hotel.

Laura Hall was at Mary Lawrence's bedside in the laundry. She looked up to see West standing at the door, and then spoke to the woman on the bed.

"Here's the doctor now."

He crossed to the bed and smiled down at Mary, at the same time lifting her wrist to check the pulse. "How do you feel?"

"She has some gas pains," Laura told him,

"but she's coming along nicely."

He talked to Mary Lawrence a few minutes, then moved away with Laura at his side. She said curiously: "Belle said that you went to see your outlaw family. Were they glad to see you?"

He shrugged.

"And how long are you going to stay in this horrible town?"

To his surprise he found himself defending Soda Springs. "It's no worse than any other town. All of them have faults."

She was pouting a little. "And what about me? You were a fool to ever come back here. Even your little country girl knows that."

"I told you Belle isn't my girl."

"She's in love with you," Laura said. "I have a good notion to go back East and leave you two stuck with each other."

He was suddenly angry. "Does that mean you don't want to marry me?"

Laura Hall never quarreled with any man except on her own terms. "We'll not talk about it now," she said. "If we do, we'll both say something we don't mean." She walked away before he could answer. She usually managed to have the last word.

IX

The Bentons were planning to wreck a train. They planned it as calmly and cold-bloodedly as if they were considering the building of a new fence. The discussion had started as soon as Doc Condon had ridden away, for once an idea found its way into Ma Benton's mind, she never rested until it was acted upon.

"Doc says that we'll have to have money to take Prince and Duke into Mexico."

They stared at her. They were all standing on the porch of the ranch house. Vance didn't say anything. They all knew that Vance was not in favor of the prison break. Vance did not think it could be done.

Fred asked: "How much money?"

The old lady did not know. "A lot," she said. "We'll want to buy a ranch or something down there."

They considered. They had never earned more than a few dollars honestly in their whole lives. "Condon will have to think up a job for us," Bo said.

His mother shook her head. "I don't trust Condon now. Since we're putting pressure on him, he might just set up a trap for us. What's wrong with planning a job ourselves?"

They looked at each other. Vance said: "You fools. Haven't we got trouble enough? You want to get Duke and Prince out of prison, not join them."

Bo said angrily: "I don't like the way you've been acting."

"Don't like it then." Vance stepped off the porch and walked to the corral. They watched in silence as he caught up his horse and rode out through the cañon.

Fred said: "I just don't understand Vance. Sometimes he don't act like a Benton at all."

"Hell with him," Bo said. "We can get the Dovell boys and Hale and the Armstrongs. That's all we need."

"But what are we going to do?"

Bo said thoughtfully: "The Eastern Express always carries a heavy mail shipment, Eastern banks sending funds to the West Coast. We could stop it at Desert Center."

Fred said: "How are you going to stop it? The Express rolls through there like a bat from hell."

Bo grinned. "The mixed freight always pulls off on the switch to let it pass. Suppose we fixed it so the freight wasn't quite clear of the main line?"

Both Fred and Ma Benton peered quizzically at him.

"That would stop the Express," Bo said. "Chances are the engine crew and the men on the express car would get killed, and the rest would be too shook up to bother us."

"When?" Fred asked.

"What's the matter with tomorrow morning?"

They eyed him for a long moment in silence. Fred started toward the corral. "Let's ride over and talk to the Dovells," he said.

Their mother watched them go, then walked back into the house. She was smiling to herself. Things were beginning to move. One day, not too far away, Duke and Prince would be free.

Fred and Bo rode directly through the hills to the Dovell ranch where they talked to old Ab and his two sons. Then they crossed the ridge and dropped down into White Feather Valley where the Armstrongs had their place. It was arranged that the Dovell boys and the Armstrongs would meet them at Desert Center with pack horses and mounts for Bo and Fred. Afterward the Bentons rode on to Soda Springs.

They reached town late in the afternoon and without asking permission hid their horses in Condon's barn. Then they loitered about, trying not to attract attention. It was their plan to ride the mixed freight when it left Soda Springs after midnight, staying concealed until it pulled into Desert Center shortly before daylight. They would then overcome the freight crew and leave enough of the freight on the main track to cause the wreck. The plan was as simple as it was brutal. From a room in one of the cheap hotels across from the station they watched the people on Railroad Avenue. Just before 6:00 Bo gave a sudden grunt.

"What's the matter?" Fred asked.

Bo pointed, and Fred saw Hy West come along the street, cross it, and head for the Railroad Hospital. "We're taking him with us tonight," Bo said.

Fred gaped at his brother. "Have you gone crazy?"

Bo shook his head. "It's a chance to get him out of this town without us killing him. Maybe he'll be wiped out in the wreck. We'll stick him in one of the front cars. If not, I'll take care of him then."

Fred didn't like it but he had to agree. He had no real feeling about West, but he knew how Bo felt about Belle, and, when Bo got that Indian look, there was no arguing with him.

They timed their invasion of the hospital well. They waited until nearly 11:00, then slipped across through the station yard and came up to the platform. Chance played into their hands, for just as they were creeping toward the small building, West stepped out for a smoke.

He stood there, watching as the puffing switch engine busily made up the freight, and did not sense that he was not alone until Fred shoved the gun against his back. Bo searched him for a weapon and found none. West studied Bo with care as he stepped back. He knew these boys. Neither had much more judgment than a ten-year-old.

"What's this?"

"You're taking a train ride." Bo had been drinking, but he was not drunk. "We're giving you a nice free ride."

Fred said to his brother: "Where's his tools? We'd better send his tools with him. No one would believe a doctor would leave without his tools."

Bo looked at West. "Where are they?"

West decided that they did not mean to kill him, at least not there, and said: "In the office." He was waiting for a chance to grab the spare gun from Fred's belt. Bo brought out his bag and led him across the welter of tracks. He stopped beside an empty boxcar close to the head of the train.

Fred took the bag from Bo. He tossed it into the open door of the car. As he did so, West grabbed his extended arm. He swung Fred around, between himself and Bo, at the same time trying to jerk Fred's gun free. But Fred was like an eel in his grasp. He needed both hands to hold him, and Fred didn't content himself with struggling. He let his legs go slack so that all his weight hung on West's arms, bending him a little forward. That was all Bo needed. He reached across his brother's shoulder and brought the long barrel of his gun down across West's head in a slashing blow. West collapsed, falling forward with Fred under him. Bo stooped, dragged his inert body from Fred, then helped his brother to his feet.

"OK?"

Fred nodded. Together they heaved the unconscious West into the car and rolled the door shut. They crept forward and found places for themselves directly behind the tender. Everything was going on schedule and Bo was happy. Whatever else happened, he felt that he did not need to worry about West again.

X

West returned to full consciousness slowly. He was at first puzzled by the jolting of the train, then he remembered the Bentons and how he had gotten there. He had no idea how long he had been unconscious, but gray light was filtering in through the crack beside the almost closed door. Dawn came early at this time of year, but it still must be at least 4:00 a.m.

He lay, not caring. The motion of the train jolted him on the hardness of the splintered floor. There was a little hay in the bottom of the car, but not enough to make a real cushion for his aching body. He lay there a long time and finally realized through his half stupor that the train had stopped. He considered this and found it puzzling. He dragged himself upright then, and on rubber legs moved toward the door.

His instrument bag lay where Fred had thrown it. He opened the bag and searched until he found the pills he wanted. Afterward, he moved to the door and peered out at the sweep of desert land beyond. They were not in a railroad yard; that much was plain. It was, he guessed, some lonely siding, and this was confirmed in his mind a moment later by the distant *hum* of an approaching train.

He was thirsty, and the lump across the top of his head ached dully, and he felt a little tender in the pit of his stomach. The *rumble* of the oncoming train grew louder, and the loose ground on which the track was built trembled from the vibration of the wheels pounding toward them. He sat, waiting for the train to pass — and then came an impact that rolled him from his sitting position and sent his body almost to the far end of the car. There was a grinding *crash,* like nothing he had ever before experienced. The car jiggled like a bucking horse and slowly rose, tilting as the freight train tried to telescope under the thrusting motion of the driving express. Then it buckled as the coupling broke, and the car seemed for a teetering instant to stand upon its end before it fell sidewise to the desert beyond the right of way.

West was battered and bruised. He lay for a moment utterly quiet, and after the smashing, grinding noise the world was suddenly as silent as a tomb. His mind had lost its capacity to judge time. Time was endless. It seemed that the splintering collision had lasted for hours, and afterward the period of silence was endless. But finally the screaming began. It brought him to full consciousness as nothing else could have. The car about him was a crumpled thing, twisted out of any recognizable shape. He lay there, a timber across him, pinning him down, holding him in place yet not hurting him. He had time to wonder about this even as he struggled to free himself. The screams continued. And then he smelled it: a touch of smoke that drifted back through the broken car sides. He smelled it, and he heard the *crackle* of the flames, and now above the screams he heard the shouts of the rescue workers.

The flames ate their way into his vision, running along the dry wood, aided and nourished by a steady breath of desert wind, growing as they inched along, a wall of fire that seemed to be closing down upon him, licking at him like the forked tongues of a million angry snakes, tightening until he knew that there was no escape. He called. He never knew what he said. He did not hear the shots from without as the Bentons with their friends dragged the sacked mail from the express car and threw it onto the pack horses. But those shots kept help from coming because they held the crew of the passenger train at bay. The freight crew, those who still lived, were locked in the caboose.

XI

Vance Benton did not know exactly what his brothers' plans were, and he did not want to know — at first. But as he rode away from the ranch, something prompted him to circle back by the hill trail to the rim, where he could watch their actions. Then he had followed them across the hills, first to the Dovell ranch and then to the Armstrong ranch, and afterward into Soda Springs. He saw how they hid their horses at Condon's and sought seclusion in the cheap hotel, and he watched the hotel from the entrance to Wentworth's livery.

When they left it, late at night, he trailed them across the station yard and from the shadows he saw them load West into the empty boxcar and then seek places for themselves on the train. He guessed now what they planned to do, and swore under his breath. In his eyes they were fools who could bring nothing but trouble to the family. The clan feeling remained strong in him, and he almost went to join them. Instead, he went back to Callahan's. He wanted to be certain that he would be seen, that his presence in town would be remembered. He sat in one of the poker games, and stayed with it until after daylight, winning over $100, thus establishing his alibi.

Afterward he ate breakfast in the railroad lunchroom and went to Wentworth's livery where he had left his horse. But instead of saddling the animal and riding out, he loafed in the sun, not quite knowing what to do.

He saw her coming along the sidewalk and knew at once that this must be the girl who had followed Hy West from Chicago. Her clothes were different, and her pink and white face showed no marks of the sun, and her hair was worn differently. To Vance Benton she seemed the prettiest girl in the world.

She passed him in the entrance, lowering her eyes, but not until she had looked into his for one deliberate moment. Then she spoke to Wentworth who stood in the office door.

"I'm looking for Doctor West. He isn't at the hospital and I thought he might have ridden out somewhere. Did he rent a horse from you?"

Wentworth wagged his old head. "He took a horse yesterday, but he brought it back and I haven't seen him since." He called to Vance: "You seen Hy this morning?"

Vance said — "Nope." — and, as the girl turned to look at him, he came forward.

"I'm Vance Benton, miss. You must be the girl Hy was telling me about. The one he's going to marry."

Laura Hall gazed fascinatedly at Benton. So this was one of the outlaws she had been hearing about. Funny. In her mind she had built up a picture of bearded men in shabby clothes. Vance was young, not more than a year or two older than West. He was as tall as West, and in some ways more handsome. His thin face had darkened under the desert sun, and his eyes were black and proud. He stared at her with a boldness she found disconcerting, but she rallied to say: "And you must be the outlaw he was raised with. The one he told me about."

At the word *outlaw,* Wentworth glanced sharply at Vance. It was one thing to refer to the Bentons as outlaws when they were not present, but quite another to use the word to their faces. In their own way the Bentons considered themselves average citizens who broke the law because they refused to be bound by the conventions other people had created. But Vance showed no displeasure at her words. Instead, it seemed to please and amuse him that she had heard of him.

"So the Kid mentioned me to you?"

"He did."

"Well, what do you know?" He gazed at

her with open admiration. "Shame I didn't meet you first."

"You've met me now," she said, "and I'm glad. After all, you and your brothers are the only family Hy has."

It was a new thought to Vance. While he had never teased the younger boy as Bo had, he still had never thought of West as a member of the Benton clan. He thought fleetingly of West on the freight train, speeding east. He wondered if he should tell her, and decided against it. He wondered what would happen to her here, with West gone, and found the prospect interesting. Vance Benton had known his share of women, most of them from the dance halls of the Southwest, and he had never considered any of them worth more than a second thought. But he had never met anyone like Laura Hall. She was pretty, very pretty, but he had seen other pretty girls. It was her poise that struck him, her self-assured manner. It seemed as if she expected everything and everyone to bend easily to her purpose. She was like a high-strung horse, proud and willful, and the thought crossed his mind that it might be fun to break her.

They stood there for a long moment, appraising each other, trying to guess the strengths and weaknesses that the other might have hidden. And it came to Laura that the man before her was dangerous. She had not found most men dangerous; in fact, her relationships had been highlighted by her own aggressiveness. But some instinct warned her that Vance Benton was different, that anyone who in any way associated with Benton would follow a pattern he set up. And while she stood there, trying to think of the proper words, the best way to handle this stranger, a whistle shrilled suddenly from the roundhouse, long and piercing, reaching the farthermost corner of the town.

"A wreck!" It was Wentworth, and with agility surprising in one of his age he dashed past her, out into the runway and on into the street.

She turned, surprised, and, as the whistle continued its shrill message, she followed the livery man. Vance was at her heels. They came together into the sunlight in time to see the dusty length of Railroad Avenue fill with excited people, all running toward the yards. Laura ran too, not because she thought that the wreck concerned her, but because she was caught up by the crowd excitement.

Vance ran at her side, and, when she stumbled, he put a quick hand under her arm to steady her. He knew, or figured he knew, what the wreck was about. And as they ran on, he wondered how Hy West's death would affect her. It might be hard to comfort her, but it sure as hell would be fun to try.

XII

Pinned under the splintered beam, Hy West watched the leaping flames inch their way closer, and figured that he had only a matter of minutes to live. Surprisingly the danger had cleared his head, and he found that the pain was almost entirely gone. He did not panic. From the time he was able to walk he had faced danger of one kind or another with no one to rely on but himself. He was lying half on his side, half on his stomach, with one arm folded under him, the other outstretched. His legs were extended, one pinned tightly by the broken piece of the car's siding, so that he could get no purchase for his knees in an effort to raise himself. But he tried. The sense of survival was very strong within him. He lifted on the arm that was crooked under him, trying to bring the other back until he could get a purchase with his elbow. He was so engrossed with the effort that he did not hear the freight conductor who was running along the shattered train toward where the two engines had merged in a twisted heap of battered metal.

But the man saw him, and stopped, and then tore into the pile of wreckage that held West a prisoner. The freight conductor worked frantically. He managed to lift the bar across West's shoulder. He managed to free the pinned leg. And somehow West dragged himself to his feet. As he straightened, his toe caught the black bag that had been hurled to the end of the shattered car. He stooped to pick it up and raced after the running man.

They both stopped as they got their first clear view of the wreck and he heard the man beside him sob. "The murderers. The damn' murderers."

West turned to look at him. "What are you talking about?"

"The murderers. The two men who locked us in the crummy and left the freight engine sticking out on the main."

A cold feeling like a ball of ice settled at the pit of West's stomach. He steadied himself as he said in a strange voice: "Who were they . . . where are they now?"

The freight conductor seemed dazed, as if he were suffering from shock. "I don't know.

They were masked. They broke out the registered mail and the express and rode away. Someone must have met them here with horses."

He ran on then, with West after him. The Eastern Express had been traveling at better than fifty miles an hour and the mail coach and express car and the first Pullmans were a twisted jumble of burning wood. Already the passenger crew was laboring to put out the fire, and one of them had climbed a pole with a jumper instrument to tap the telegraph and send the news of the wreck to the division point.

Both engine crews were dead. Eight passengers were dead and most of the rest injured. West had no clear memory of the next three hours. He worked with the others, halting the fire, prying the injured from the broken cars. Looking at the twisted train, it seemed impossible that anyone would have survived, but most had, and the children had fared the best. Not one child was seriously injured.

West worked as he had never worked in his life, spreading blankets on the ground and caring for the victims as they were brought to him. He was hardly conscious of the arrival of the wrecking train, of Omstead taking charge, of Gruber, red-eyed from his night with the bottle. But Gruber had brought medicine and morphine and he worked at West's side without comment.

Omstead was everywhere. He listened to the reports on the masked men who had raided the mail car, and himself climbed the pole to wire the news to the sheriffs up and down the line. Already men were tearing up the switch track, using the ties and rails to build a shoofly around the wreck. The crane dumped the broken boxcars from the right of way, and before darkness came the line was open again for through traffic. But West knew nothing of this. He worked savagely, endlessly. Gruber was not too much help and West ignored him. When the special came, he supervised the removal of the injured to the hospital at Soda Springs.

One woman died during the ride, four more were borderline, the rest had varying injuries from broken bones to black eyes. Omstead had noticed West when he first arrived, but not until late afternoon did he find time to ask the freight conductor how West happened to be there.

The man shrugged. "He was in one of the boxcars, beating his way I guess. I hauled him out and was damned glad to find he was a doctor. Who is he?"

Omstead did not bother to answer. He

had other things to trouble him. For one thing he had just learned that Andy and Sam Dillon had managed to stow themselves away in one of the toilets of the special, and had escaped the brakeman until they arrived at the scene of the wreck. The boys immediately attached themselves to West. He sent them on a hundred errands while preparing to load the more seriously injured aboard the special. Afterward, he made room for the walking cases, and not until all of these were safely in place did he permit the uninjured to board the train.

When they arrived at Soda Springs, he again brushed Gruber aside, and went about setting up the ward as best he could. He sent Andy and Sam out to find Laura, Belle, and any other town women who would volunteer.

When Laura came, he put her in charge, avoiding her questions as to where he had been and how he happened to become involved in the wreck. Soda Springs was a railroad town, and it was affected by the wreck in the same way that a mining village is affected by a disaster underground. The people turned out in mass, and Condon appeared almost at once, offering his services. West accepted gratefully. He had lost all patience with Gruber, and he simply did not have enough hands to do everything that was required. For three days he lived in a kind of nightmare and a number of things happened of which he was only vaguely aware. First was a telegraph order in response to Gruber's protest. West was relieved at Soda Springs and ordered to report to the home office.

Gruber brought the order on the second morning after the wreck. There was whiskey on his breath and triumph in his round, brown eyes.

"You can leave today," he told his former assistant. "I'll take over from now on."

West looked around him. There were still twenty-seven patients in the small, overcrowded hospital. The others had been patched up and sent on to the coast. Three of those remaining would not live. West was certain of that, although he and Condon had done everything they could. Strain, coupled with his anger at Gruber, made his voice sharp. "You'll get out of here," he said quietly, "and you'll stay out as long as any of these people remain here."

Gruber started to bluster. In the world from which he had come an underling did not question authority, but West wasted no further words. He walked around the desk, catching the older man by his coat collar and swinging him about. He walked Gruber down the hall and threw him through the door to the platform beyond.

Gruber went to his knees. He started to get up, then saw West still in the doorway, waiting for him to rise. He turned and scuttled away on hands and knees. He had almost reached the corner of the building when Condon rounded it and stopped in surprise. Gruber scrambled to his feet and beat a hasty retreat. Condon stared after him in amazement. "What's happened to Dutchy now?"

"I threw him out."

For the first time he could remember he saw approval in the old doctor's bloodshot eyes. "Wish I'd gotten here three minutes sooner. Anyway, you'd better go talk to Omstead. I'll take over here."

West nodded and, after showing Condon the charts, left the hospital for the first time since bringing the patients from the wreck, and walked toward the station. Omstead was in his office. He finished dictating an order to a clerk, then swung around to face West as the clerk left. "Been meaning to see you, but I've been so damn' busy with the wreck and the hold-up."

West had a sudden flash of guilt. He had meant to tell Omstead about the Bentons, but he, too, had been busy. Now he tried to make amends.

Omstead heard him out, carefully expressionless. "You're sure it was Bo and Fred Benton?"

"Certain. I've known them all my life."

"But you don't know that they had anything to do with the hold-up. They might have dumped you on that train and not gotten on themselves?"

West had to admit it was possible. "I'd guess, though, that they rode the train and that Vance met them with some horses."

Omstead frowned. "Then you'd guess wrong. Vance Benton played poker at Callahan's all that night. He was here in town when news of the wreck reached us. Maybe the others were in it, but Vance was not. We've been checking on them all, naturally."

"And what did you find?"

The super shrugged. "Nothing. Bo and Fred claim they were at a dance at one of the hill ranches, someone named Armstrong. Of course, the people there may be lying. All those people hang together out there, but we can't prove it." He sounded discouraged. "And I'm afraid your story won't help much. A lot of people in this town are wondering how you happened to be on that train. Several have reminded me that you were mixed up in one hold-up, and that merely because you turned to and helped take care of the injured doesn't mean you weren't tied in with the robbers."

West flushed.

"I don't believe it," Omstead told him, "and don't worry about it. By the way, there's a telegraphic order relieving you of duty."

West's flush deepened. "Gruber came to tell me. I threw him out of the office."

Omstead laughed, then sobered. "I don't blame you, and, as far as I'm concerned, you can stay here as long as you like. But you can't keep Gruber out of his hospital. I'll have a talk with him and try to straighten it out. Now go back and get some rest. You look as if you haven't slept in days."

West went back to the hospital and found that Condon and Laura seemed to have everything under full control. Then he went into his own office and stretched out on the couch. He fell asleep almost at once.

In the ward West had just left, Condon was studying Laura closely. He had to admit that she seemed to be a good nurse, but he did not like women in general and he found that he did not like this girl in particular.

Laura was quick to sense his attitude. She had watched Condon during the days as he helped with the wreck victims, hoping that she could catch him in a slip that she could turn to her own advantage. She resented him for his apparent hold on West, and she was also a little afraid of him. But her manner when she addressed him was always carefully correct.

She came over to speak to him now, reminding him that they were out of morphine and that none had arrived on the afternoon train.

He nodded, still busy dressing a burn. He pulled the keys to his own medicine closet from his pocket, tossing them to her and telling her how to find his house. Ordinarily she might have resented being sent on this errand, but this afternoon she was pleased to get away from the hospital. She felt free as she moved up the street, ignoring the stares of the people, until she saw Vance Benton riding toward her.

She told herself that she had no interest in the tall man, that she would be a fool to get mixed up with the Bentons. But despite this denial her interest did quicken, and she could not resist the impulse to raise her hand in greeting as he rode up.

Vance was never a person to stand on ceremony. All his life his actions had been direct. He had taken what he wanted when he was strong enough to get it, and he had decided during the last few days that he wanted this girl. He stepped from the horse, looped the reins over the rail, and ducked under it to join her on the sidewalk. His clothes as usual were worn but clean, and also he was clean-shaven. Somehow this impressed Laura. She had seen many other riders during her short stay in Soda Springs, and few of them were either shaven or clean. He came to her side with the easy, cat-like grace that marked all his movements, and took her arm as if by right, saying in his drawling voice: "How's my nurse?"

She was very conscious of his nearness, of the touch of his fingers on her arm. This for her was a new experience, this quick awareness, and to her it rang a small bell of warning. She who all through her short life had been the huntress had suddenly become the hunted. It was pleasing to know that a man wanted you, that you had made him want you, and yet be able to stand as one detached, to remain objective about him, even when you were pretending to surrender to him. But with Vance she sensed that it would not be a case of token surrender. He would take what he wanted at the first opportunity. For once in her life she had met a person stronger and more ruthless than she was. To mask her unease she made her voice light, saying pertly: "And how is my pet outlaw?"

His white teeth showed for one instant in his dark, wind-burned face, and then he walked along beside her, indifferent to the interest that his presence caused the shoppers they passed. Beyond the small tight business section he told her easily: "Your reputation here is ruined for all time. You were seen on the streets with a Benton. What are you doing up this way?"

"Morphine," she said, and explained that Condon had sent her to his office.

Vance swore under his breath. "The old fool, sending you up here to face those mongrel dogs."

"I'm not afraid of dogs."

There was open admiration in his eyes. "I don't believe you're afraid of much of anything. Another girl would be afraid of me."

She knew better than to ask, but she could not resist: "And why should I be afraid of you?"

He grinned down at her. "You know the answer to that one. A man sees a woman, what does he want?"

She knew that she should stop this conversation, but she found herself saying: "That depends upon the man . . . and the girl."

Suddenly he was gravely serious. "I'm talking about us, Laura. We're different from ordinary people. We take what we want."

"Do we?" She knew that her voice was not quite steady. Damn him. What right did he have to make her feel this way?

"We do," Vance said, and then stopped. They had reached Condon's gate and the dogs came charging out, leaping high against the firm planks.

In spite of herself Laura flinched, and Vance laughed at her. "Not so bold now."

She said: "Those horrible animals. They sound as if they would tear me apart."

"You're all right with me," he told her. "They know me. I've been here a lot."

She found a moment to wonder why Vance should have spent much time with the old doctor. Then he opened the gate and began kicking the cringing dogs out of their path, cursing them as he did so. The animals fell back, disappearing around the corner of the house, cowed by his presence. Vance led her up the path and pushed open the door.

As she stepped in, she peered curiously around the untidy, dirty room. Her hatred of Condon sharpened her interest as she noted the cluttered table, the old desk, and the medicine cabinet. She unlocked the cabinet's battered door and found the morphine. She relocked the cabinet, and turned. And as she turned, she saw the tintype above the desk.

The beauty of the face astonished her. She wondered who the woman was, wondered how anyone so lovely could have had anything to do with the monstrosity that Condon had become. She sensed a story here, and she nodded at the picture. "Do you know who that is?"

Vance said without interest: "Someone the old doc really hates, I guess. I've seen him stand and curse her for half an hour when he's drunk, but when I asked him once, he told me to mind my own damn' business."

Laura continued to study the picture, and she noted the photographer's name and Philadelphia address on the frame. Abruptly she obeyed an impulse. She let Vance lead her out to the sun-baked yard, then muttered an excuse and ducked back into the room. When she rejoined Vance, the picture was safely concealed beneath her dress, and for some reason she felt gayer than she had in days.

"Vance," she said, "do me a favor and take this morphine over to Condon. I want to go on to the hotel and get some breakfast."

He accepted the medicine and the key. "When am I going to see you?"

"I don't know."

"Go riding with me tonight."

She pretended embarrassment. "You know I can't do that. I'm engaged to Hy West."

He caught her arm roughly and swung her around. For an instant she was afraid that he was going to kiss her there on the street, and knew suddenly with a feeling of weakness that she wanted the feel of his mouth, hard against her own. "Stop playing with me." There was a savagery in his voice she had never heard before. "Meet me behind the livery at eight."

"And if I don't?"

He held her by both arms, so close that she could feel his warm breath against her cheek. "If you don't, I'll come and drag you out, no matter where you are."

He was gone then, releasing her as suddenly as he had grabbed her, striding away, cutting directly across the wide street to the hospital building without looking back.

For an instant she stood helpless, her knees so weak that she feared to move. Then slowly she walked on toward the hotel, knowing as she went that whatever happened she did not dare meet Vance Benton that night.

But at 8:00 p.m. she found him in the deep shadow, near the corral, standing beside two saddled horses. Neither spoke, neither made a sound as he lifted her into the saddle, and then mounted his own animal. He led them out, circling the town by a little used path. To the right were the far-flung lights of the railroad yard. Ahead to the east were the fainter lights of the fort three miles away. Above them a million stars turned the dark arch of the sky to a milky hue.

Laura never knew how far they rode. She only knew that finally Vance pulled his horse from the trail and they followed a small, side cañon, the matted grass deadening the sound of their horses. Then they dismounted and the *gurgle* of the stream sounded somewhere to the right, and the trees above them made a ragged outline against the sky, and suddenly Vance's arms were about her, his teeth hard, pressing against her lips. She had never known anything quite like this. The innate savagery of the man stunned her. She felt that she should fight him, but her desires stopped her.

They were on the grass now, and she experienced something that she had never before known, that she had believed did not actually exist. Her body came alive for him as it never had for anyone else. It was as if it moved of its own volition, without control or direction from her mind. She was crying softly, her fingernails digging into his bare shoulders as if to hold him to her always. Afterward they did not talk. They lay quietly for a long time, and then slowly, reluctantly they rose and went back to their horses.

Belle saw them ride up to the rear door of the hotel. Belle was not trying to spy. Belle had come into the kitchen to get a glass of water for Mary Lawrence. She heard their horses in the alley and was surprised. She looked out in time to see Vance help Laura from the saddle. She watched them kiss for a long moment before she turned away. But she could not get out of the kitchen before Laura came in. Laura stopped, just inside the door.

"So you've been watching for me," Laura said. "Well, I hope it does you as much good as you think it will."

She stalked past Belle, went through the dining room, and up the stairs.

XIII

Hy West knew nothing of Laura's ride with Vance Benton. Laura did not tell him, and

Belle did not mention it, and he was much too busy trying to save the injured. He hardly left the hospital. He slept on a cot in his office and took his meals in the kitchen.

Gruber had come back, but by Omstead's orders he left West strictly alone. Omstead had wired Chicago that he could not spare West. He got no reply, and then the pox struck, and he along with the others forgot all about it.

It was Gruber who discovered the pox. He came into West's office to find Laura Hall and West checking supplies that had arrived on the morning train. West looked up as Gruber came in, expecting some kind of argument. It seemed that he and Gruber did nothing but argue whenever they met. But Gruber was too tense with excitement to remember his differences with the younger doctor.

"It's the smallpox!" he half shouted. "The smallpox. I am not mistaken. I tell you I know the smallpox when I see it."

West took three quick steps forward and grabbed Gruber's arm. "Keep your voice down. What are you talking about? Who has the smallpox?"

Gruber tried to shake free. "The man in the bed at the end of the ward. The one who lost a hand in the wreck."

"When did you find this out? Who already knows?"

Gruber wet his lips. "Condon and one of the volunteer nurses. She ran away as soon as I told them what it was."

West swore under his breath. "The news will be all over town in fifteen minutes."

He was wrong. It was all over town within ten minutes, and Soda Springs reacted with quick fear. The frontier dreaded no scourge more than the pox.

West made his plans swiftly, but he knew that whatever they did, they were still in for trouble. At least fifty of the townspeople had been in and out of the hospital within the last few days.

"We'll have to vaccinate everyone who's been exposed," he said.

Gruber was gloomy. "In Europe you can force vaccination, but here . . . there is no law."

West said grimly: "We'll vaccinate them, law or no law."

"Have you sufficient lymph?" Laura Hall had recovered her composure and, as always, was being practical.

"I'll wire for more. In the meantime, we'll set up a quarantine of the hospital, and arrange for a pest house for anyone who contracts the pox."

"Where?"

He thought quickly. "In the baggage shed. Have one of the porters clear it out and clean the floor." But when he went to inspect the work an hour later he found that nothing had been done. The porters had vanished, fearful of infection. The volunteer workers who had helped so unselfishly with the wreck victims had disappeared. Even Condon had walked out, explaining that his private practice had to be cared for. West found himself with the whole hospital to run and no one to help him but Gruber and Laura Hall.

There were two more cases by the following morning, and he could only conclude that someone from the wrecked train must have carried the infection, perhaps someone who died during the accident without anyone knowing that he had been sick.

The next week became a nightmare, not only for West but for the whole southern end of the territory. Fear like a racing forest fire spread across the whole of the thinly populated land. Two cases had broken out among the volunteer nurses who had helped at the hospital. The supplies arrived from Chicago and West sent out a call for the Soda Springs citizens to come in and be vaccinated.

Only a few came. He appealed first to the sheriff, and then to the town marshal for help. Instead of assisting, they ignored his plea and set up a quarantine law of their own, manned by volunteers to keep anyone from the hospital from crossing Railroad Avenue.

West learned of this line from Belle Callahan, who had volunteered on the second day and was assisting with both the nursing and the cooking. She came into his office from the hospital kitchen, her face flushed, her eyes angry.

"That Bruce Gimble!"

West was very tired. He had been on duty for twenty-four hours without sleep, and one of his patients had died at daybreak.

"What's Gimble done now?"

"You know that man who died this morning. Well, we had two of the Mexican section hands . . . boys who had already had the pox . . . put the body in a coffin and take it out for burial."

He nodded.

"Gimble and his men drove them back. They say no one from railroad property is allowed to go uptown."

West's mouth tightened.

"And they're telling everyone that you are purposely spreading the plague."

He blinked at her, startled. "Spreading it?"

"That's right. Gimble made a speech. I heard him. He said you'd always been a cold-blooded killer at heart, and everyone in town knows you should have gone to prison, and you know how they feel and you hate the town because of it, and you'd be perfectly happy to see everyone in Soda Springs die. . . ."

"Surely no one is fool enough to believe that."

"People," Belle Callahan said, "are fools enough to believe anything when they're afraid. And they're afraid now. They look at everyone they meet on the streets, wondering who's carrying germs and who isn't. A good third of the population has already pulled out for the hills."

"The best thing they could do," West said slowly. "If they won't be vaccinated, the farther away they can keep from each other the better."

"And there are four new cases in town. They won't bring them here. They've set up their own pest house out at McClune's ranch. They've got some men who have already had the pox caring for them, and Condon is advising them on the proper treatment."

"So much the better. It leaves less for us to handle."

They were interrupted by the opening door. West saw Andy Lawrence standing in the entrance. The boy had been one of the few in town to submit to vaccination, but still West did not want him at the hospital.

"Son, you know better than to come in here."

Andy was almost crying with excitement. "I had to come. I had to warn you. They're fixing it up to hang you."

"Hang me?" West swung about. "What are you talking about?"

"Bruce Gimble. He's got ten men who've had the pox. They've volunteered to come in here, and they're going to move all the sick people on a train and send them away, and then they are going to hang you, and afterwards they're going to burn the railroad buildings. They think that burning the buildings will kill the germs."

West started for the door. "I've got to warn Omstead."

"They've already got Omstead." Andy was barring his progress. "And the ticket agent and the master mechanic and Boone Grantline. They've taken them to the far end of the yards, and they're forcing them to make up a train, and, when the train is ready, they're coming here."

Belle Callahan's face was very white. "You'd better slip out the back door, Hy. I'll get my father. Surely there must be someone left in town who hasn't completely lost his mind."

"No use," Andy said. "They've got their quarantine line all around. They let me through because they didn't see these, but they won't let anyone out." He pulled open his coat and showed his father's gun belts underneath. "I brought you these, Hy."

West reached out and helped the boy unfasten the heavy belts. For the barest instant he hesitated, feeling Belle's eyes upon him. Then deliberately he fastened the belts in place, lifting first one gun, and then the other, making certain that they were loaded.

Afterward he said: "Both of you stay in here. Don't come out no matter what happens."

He went quickly through the office door into the hall. He passed Gruber just inside the entrance and from the man's white face judged that he already knew about the mob in the lower yards. He had a momentary flash of contempt for the man's obvious fear, and then he stepped out onto the sunlit wooden platform.

From where he stood, he could see them working at the train, three cars behind the switch engine. He saw it move slowly, backing toward the station with the mob walking beside it. He glanced to his left, out at Railroad Avenue, and saw the thin line of men spread along the opposite sidewalk at the far side of the wide street. Andy had not been exaggerating. The railroad property was completely surrounded, with the hospital at the center of an irregular circle.

He stepped back a little, so that the hospital corner was between him and the street, and stood facing down the yards. He watched the makeshift train back slowly toward him, watched the mob close ranks behind Gimble and come on, heading for the spot at which he stood. He was not afraid for himself. He did not believe they would hang him although mob psychology was a peculiar thing, and undoubtedly some of them had been drinking. The hanging talk had only been Gimble's way of stirring them up. But he had no intention of letting them load the sick on that train. Such an action would result in several deaths.

They had seen him. Gimble pointed, and they increased their speed. They had seen him, but they had not yet seen the heavy gun belts crossed at his waist. They came on, and he knew by the way they moved that his guess had been correct. Gimble had fired their courage with alcohol. Alcohol and fear were a bad combination. Men had done many foolish things in the grip of alcohol and fear.

He watched them, feeling set apart, as he had so often felt when he was a boy, set apart and rejected. But for some reason he no longer hated them. Instead, he felt a very deep contempt for the mob that was following Gimble so blindly.

They were closer now, and he saw their flushed faces distinctly. There was six men behind Gimble, the rest halting as the train stopped beside the station. And still he waited until they stepped up from the tracks to the platform, hardly ten feet from where he stood. He spoke then to Gimble and at the same time opened the white coat so they could not miss the fact that he was wearing Dave Lawrence's guns.

"That's far enough, Marshal."

Gimble stopped, one foot raised, his eyes surprised as they fastened on the guns sagging at West's hips. Ever since the doctor's return to Soda Springs, Gimble had observed West closely, and this was the first time that he had seen the doctor armed. He had not expected it, and the knowledge

241

came as a shock. He had never seen West shoot as a boy, but there had been wild stories of his ability during the hearing following the hold-up, and Gimble was by nature a cautious man.

The men behind him surged on, pushing him forward until he was forced to use his elbows to hold them back. "Wait a minute!"

A bearded man who West did not recognize seemed not to be impressed. His liquor-slurred words carried clearly along the platform. "What's the matter? Let's get him."

West said mockingly: "Is that your idea, Gimble . . . to get me?"

The marshal was sweating. It had seemed so very easy when they planned this move in Callahan's bar. All they needed to do was to seize the station and the roundhouse, force the railroad employees to make up a special train, load up the sick people from the hospital, and send them down the line. He had spoken of hanging West. He had done that merely to inflame his audience. He didn't really care what happened to the doctor. But he had not expected any opposition once they had control of the station, and it angered him now that they should be so close to their objective and yet be blocked by one man.

He controlled himself with an effort, managing to say in a fairly normal tone: "We want no more trouble than is necessary. Keep out of this while we load the train. You can ride with your sick if you like. We don't care what happens then, but this town does not want the plague."

"No one wants the plague." West's voice was low, but it had a carrying quality that reached them all. "But you are not moving anyone this morning. These people stay where they are, and they stay until they have recovered completely."

Gimble almost lost control then. His voice cracked from sheer nervousness: "Don't be a fool. Look around. We have fifty armed men at least."

"You can have a hundred." West still spoke in that calm voice. "You can't move these people."

Gimble's face contorted. "I'm giving you one last chance. Stand aside while we load them."

"No, Gimble. No other town wants the pox. If we move them, we chance further infection. I'll kill you if you try to move them. I'll kill as many as I can of those with you, but I'll kill you first."

For a moment no one stirred. He watched them all, but mostly Gimble, seeing the sudden raw desire in Gimble's eyes. Gimble was trying to steel himself to the point where he would reach for the gun at his hip. Gimble had killed three men in the line of duty. West watched his eyes. He saw the purpose grow. He saw the man's fingers spread and then fan down suddenly toward the butt of his single weapon.

West's hands dropped. He pulled both guns, just as Gimble got his free of the holster. West fired, his bullet tearing the gun from Gimble's grasp, spinning it away. A smear of blood grew on the marshal's finger. Gimble stared down at it stupidly, not realizing for an instant what had happened. Then reaction set in and he started to shake.

West had fired only one gun, the right one, and fired but once. The other gun covered the men behind the marshal. None of them had moved. They stood like so many leaderless sheep, uncertain and afraid. West knew a crowd, and he knew that there were moments when you could sway them and moments when you would fail.

"Had enough?" His words were thrown at the marshal, but they included the men behind him.

And Gimble broke. With a muttered curse he turned and headed for Railroad Avenue, clutching his injured wrist. The men who had followed him only minutes before hesitated, staring at the lone figure before them, at the big guns still steady in his hands. They still wanted the plague sufferers driven out of town. They hated the quiet man before them and would have hanged him had they dared, but their cohesion was gone. They were no longer a mob, following blindly, given a feeling of security by their numbers. They were individuals, threatened by the guns in the hands of a man who had shown that he was both able and willing to use them. Suddenly they, too, broke, hurrying off as if each dreaded to be the last one on that platform. West watched them go, but he did not budge. Where he stood, he was screened from the men patrolling the far side of Railroad Avenue, but if he were to step forward, he would be exposed to their fire and might easily lose the victory he had just won.

He held his place, calling to those members of the mob who still guarded the special train: "All right, boys. Get off railroad property and stay off."

They hesitated. They might well have shot at him, but they had seen Gimble go and the men with him follow, and they felt deserted. First one edged away, and then the whole crowd dispersed, hurrying now as if they would not feel safe until they had crossed the town's main street.

At once, the railroad crowd they had been holding as prisoners on the train came thronging down the steps, Omstead in the lead, angry now, spoiling for revenge.

Despite his lack of size, Omstead was a born fighter. He had not relished being herded aboard the train at gunpoint, but he was level-headed enough to realize that this was not the time for a pitched battle between the railroad workers and the town. He came along the platform, extending his hand to West. "This is the second time you've proved yourself," he said as they shook hands. "First at the wreck, now here. I'll tell you now that you can stay in Soda Springs as long as I am running this division. I don't care what Chicago says." He turned to Boone Grantline who was at his heels. "Wire Kansas City. Tell them to send a dozen railroad police with rifles, men who've been vaccinated or have had the pox. If Gimble wants to play rough, we'll show him how. In the meantime, dig up some guns. Arm the wipers and the switchmen. Throw a guard around the yards and the station and tell them to shoot the first son-of-a-bitch that crosses our lines without permission." He wiped his face with a handkerchief. "That was real fancy shooting, Doc. Did you mean to get his hand or just knock his gun down?"

West gave him a small grin. "I meant to hit him in the belly. I guess I'm kind of out of practice."

Omstead could not decide whether to believe him or not.

XIV

Dr. Albert Condon had no love for his fellow men and in a way he found himself amused by the reaction of Soda Springs to the threat of the plague. Nor was the gripping fear confined to the town. The whole southern half of the territory lay in its grasp and every settlement looked on each newcomer with sharp suspicion. But it was not until Condon received the wire from the doctor at the Territorial Prison that he sensed the scope of the terror that embraced the countryside. The wire told Condon that one of the inmates had developed suspicious symptoms and in panic asked if Condon could co-operate in vaccinating all the prisoners. It was then that the solution to his problem flashed into Condon's mind.

Condon answered the call as he had

answered the others in the past, for the prison doctor was entirely incapable and often summoned Condon's aid. He rode the thirty intervening miles in the local's smoker, as the only passenger in the dirty car. People were not exposing themselves to the possibility of infection unless absolutely necessary. Condon sat gazing through the clouded window at the broken hills that stretched away southward toward the border, and tried to complete his plan. Once or twice he almost discarded it as unworkable, but after he reached the prison and saw the terror with which the officials viewed the possibility that the plague might break out within the walls, he decided to go ahead with it.

The prisoner had the pox; there could be no doubt about it. Condon had him isolated, promised to send for lymph in sufficient quantity to vaccinate the others, and returned to Soda Springs. Less than an hour after he arrived at the yellow station he was on his horse, heading for the Benton ranch.

He had not expected a warm reception, but was totally unprepared for the welcome that he got. Before he could step down from his horse beside the corral fence, both Bo and his mother appeared from the house, and Bo was carrying a rifle.

"That's far enough, Doc."

Condon dismounted, ignoring the rifle, and walked toward them. "What in hell's the matter with you now?"

"The plague," Ma said. "We don't want it here."

Condon swore, but kept walking. "I hope you all get it and die of it," he told them. "Put that damned gun down. The plague in this part of the country is about over. Why in the devil didn't you come in and be vaccinated?"

They looked at him uncertainly. Bo said slowly: "What brings you out here anyway?"

"I promised to think of a way to free Duke and Prince."

Nothing else could have driven the fear of the sickness so quickly from the old woman's mind.

"You've got a plan?" she said. He nodded, and she said: "Come up to the porch but don't step inside. The germs might be on your clothes."

Condon didn't argue. For the first time in weeks he was thoroughly enjoying himself. His thinking had always had a sardonic quality. He enjoyed the mechanics of plotting, the feeling that he was sitting behind the scenes and motivating the actions of others as if they were puppets controlled by strings. He wasted no time. He explained exactly what had to be done, and why the prison break had a better than average chance of success. "The warden is a fool," he said. "The prison doctor is worse, and they're scared to death of an epidemic within the walls. They know if anything like that happens, there will be an investigation of conditions within the prison, and they can't afford that. Now our main problem is that both Duke and Prince have been anything but model prisoners. They've spent more time in solitary than they have out, which makes it doubly difficult to get guns in to them. But if they could fake being sick, they would be removed to quarantine, especially if that dunce of a doctor thinks they might be coming down with the pox. Whenever anything like that happens, he always sends for me."

Ma Benton's face lighted. "Then you'll take the guns in to the boys."

Condon swore at her. "I won't. After the break I'd be the first to be suspected if I'd so much as seen them." He let his voice change quickly. "Don't worry, I have it all figured out. They've asked me to help vaccinate the prisoners. I'm sending Pedro Martínez down with the lymph. He's had the pox."

Bo laughed suddenly. "Pedro's the biggest horse thief that ever came out of the breaks."

"And he owes me a favor for saving his boy last year. He'll do what I tell him. Now, here's what you have to do." He was looking at the woman. "You are to go to the prison tomorrow. You are to tell the warden that you haven't much longer to live, that you want to see Duke and Prince once more before you die." He pulled a small package of white powders from his pocket. "If they search you and find these, you can say it's your own medicine. Give these powders to the boys, tell them to take two apiece. It won't kill them but it will make them vomit. They're to wait four days after you've been there before they take the powders, and then they're to complain of headaches and pains in their backs. They're to rub the skin of their foreheads with dust or pebbles or something close to the hairline so that it's reddened. The doctor will be so sure that it's the pox that he won't be too thorough in his examination."

"Then what?" They were both watching him closely.

"I've sent for lymph from Chicago. The doctor will have isolated Duke and Prince, probably in the old stables. He'll want me to see them, but I'll swear that I haven't the time. However, I'll leave Pedro as a nurse. In his bag of medicine he'll have the guns. They'll wait until the following night. You, Bo, get as many riders from the hills as you can trust, and some spare horses. Be in the arroyo behind the prison just after sundown. With the guns, Duke and Prince will break into the yard. If they're lucky, they'll get out the main gate without too much trouble. Then the lot of you will head for the border, taking Pedro with you. If there's any question about the escape, the blame will be on him. He can stay below the line. He has fifty relatives down there."

The pleasure that had been building up in Ma Benton's face died. "That's the only part I don't like. If they could just come home sometime."

"They can never come home," Condon said flatly. "I suppose you've got enough money stashed away from that train wreck." He looked at Bo who met his glance blandly. Condon said: "That was a damned fool thing to do. The country still thinks you did it. The only thing that has saved you so far is the fact that Vance was in town all that night. They can't understand the Bentons riding without Vance riding with them."

Bo could not understand that, either, but he did not answer. Condon rode away, feeling relieved. If the Bentons succeeded in breaking their brothers out of prison, none of them would dare cross the line from Mexico for years. That was fine with Condon. He was through with the Bentons, no matter what happened. And if the break proved successful, the chances were that most of them would be killed. If any survived, they would certainly be fugitives. Either way, it was all right with the old doctor, and for the first time in his life he felt that he was growing old. He rode up to his place, dismounted heavily, unsaddled, turned the horse into the little corral, and with a sigh of relief headed for the house, ignoring the dogs as they crowded forward for his greeting.

He entered the cluttered front room, tossed his hat to the table, and sat down in the chair before the desk. He was very tired. It seemed to him that he had scarcely slept since the train wreck, and he had not permitted himself more than a few casual drinks. He bent forward, opened the lower drawer, and pulled out a partly filled bottle. As was his wont, he raised the bottle in a sardonic toast to the picture that hung above the desk. His hand paused, shaking. The picture was not there. A lighter square on the soiled wall showed where it had hung.

For a moment he sat motionless, staring at the wall, trying to recall when he had last noticed the picture in place. Had he been drinking through the last few weeks he might believe he had destroyed it in one of his drunken rages. He had been tempted many times during the past years. But he'd stayed sober. . . .

He rose, pulling the desk away from the wall to be sure the picture had not fallen to the floor. Then he searched through the piles of junk that had accumulated in the various corners. The picture was not in the room. Either he had thrown it away, or someone had taken it. His first thought was of West, but he discarded that almost at once. The boy had shown no curiosity regarding the picture, even during the two years he had lived in this house. Someone must have stolen the picture. But who? How had they gotten past the dogs? It might have been one of the Bentons. He frowned at the thought, then discarded it, also. Puzzled, he drank deeply from the bottle. For some reason that was not entirely clear to him the loss of the picture came as a shock. He drank again, and yet again, and afterward he slept in the chair.

XV

Riding home well after midnight, Vance Benton considered his own future. He had never given it a great deal of thought before, but he was not a person who set out deliberately to deceive himself. The impact of Laura Hall upon him had been far greater than he had expected. At first it had been little more than a game with him. It had amused his bitter sense of humor to attempt to take the girl for no other reason than that she was different from the women he had known and therefore offered a challenge to his vanity. But as the affair had progressed, he found it harder and harder to do without her. Love was something that he hardly understood. His feeling for his family was a clan relationship, a certain responsibility that was not complicated by any other emotion. But now, amazingly, he was stirred by ambition, by a desire to get away from these hills, a desire to make something of himself. This stemmed directly from Laura. After that initial ride together she had refused to see him again, but he had met her the following night, and the next, and the next.

For the first time in her self-centered existence Laura found it impossible to follow the level dictates of her cautious mind. In

Vance's arms everything else faded to nothingness. She was in love. She knew it, and resented it, and fought against it. But something within her cried out for Vance and she surrendered herself to him again and again although she swore that each time would be the last. Sobbing in his arms, she lashed out with bitter words as she felt the structure of her carefully planned world slip away from her.

"This is crazy!" she had almost shouted. "What do you expect me to do . . . live in a mountain cabin, away from people, like a coyote skulking in a hole, while you go out and steal a few horses?"

"To hell with that," he'd said roughly, stopping her words by kissing her fiercely. "I'll pull out. We'll go away, away some place where they have never heard of me. Hy West did it. Why can't I?"

Why couldn't he, indeed? His resolve was taken now. He would go away. He had no actual idea of where he would go, or what he would do. At the instant he felt as much in prison as if he had been sharing the cell with Duke and Prince. He gave no thought to the fact that Laura was supposed to marry West, that there had been no break between them, that West had been too engrossed with his work to learn about his relationship with Laura.

He rode through the cañon mouth into the ranch yard, stepped down, and pulled his saddle from the weary animal. Loosing the horse into the corral, he walked toward the house.

Bo had heard him coming. Bo was waiting on the porch. Bo's voice shook a little from his inner excitement. "We're going to get Duke and Prince out of prison."

Vance stopped. He and Bo had hardly spoken since he had refused to help in wrecking the train, and he had been so involved with Laura that he had forgotten all about the possible prison break.

He stared at his younger brother. "How are you going to do it?"

Bo told him, his voice rising with tension as he talked. "I've already lined up a dozen men to ride with us. It's all set. We've got the money from the train wreck hidden, and, if Condon and the Mexican do their parts, it can't fail."

Vance leaned against the post. His tone gave no indication of the despair within him. "So we head for Mexico." Before his mind rose a picture of the Mexican villages he had seen, the mud and straw huts, the dust, the heat, a backward land filled by a sleepy people. A fine prospect for anyone.

Certainly no place to take Laura Hall. He said: "The whole idea is crazy."

Bo never thought beyond the next move. Bo's voice hardened. "What's happened to you? I believe you're scared."

Vance looked at him squarely. "Yes, I'm scared, but you wouldn't understand what I'm afraid of. I'm afraid of the years ahead, of what that kind of life will do to me, of being cheated of everything I want, of going on and on the way we are now."

"I don't get what you mean." As always when he failed to understand, Bo turned sullen.

"I didn't expect you would. You're in love with Belle, aren't you?"

Bo's sullenness increased. "What's that got to do with it?"

"You going away and leaving her?"

Bo considered. He began to see what Vance meant. This was the jumping-off place. If they went through with the prison break, he would never again ride freely into Soda Springs, never again see this ranch. "I might take her with me," he said without conviction. "Think she'd come?" Deep in his heart Bo knew that she would not. Even with his exalted ego he could not fully persuade himself that he stood any real chance with Belle Callahan. Until this minute the idea of possessing her had been a nebulous thing, a part of a dream with which he had lulled himself to sleep on more than one lonely night. "I could make her," he said, his resolve crystallizing. "By God, that's an idea. If I had her down there, she'd be damn' glad to marry me."

Vance did not answer. He knew from past experience the futility of arguing with his brother. He started away from the porch.

Bo said quickly: "Where are you going?"

He answered without troubling to turn. "Back to town. I want no part of this."

Bo sucked in his breath. It was inconceivable that any Benton would refuse to side with his clan. "Hey, wait, you can't run out on us." He came down off the porch with a small rush, and Vance unwillingly faced him. "I know what's the matter with you," Bo said. "It's that damned nurse. She's making a fool of you the same way that she's making a fool of Hy West. She's man hungry, and everyone in town knows it."

Vance hit him then. He struck once, his knuckles cracking into Bo's jaw, lifting the younger Benton clear of the ground and dumping him into a sitting position on the hard earth.

Vance did not even look at him again. He walked quickly to the corral, picking a rope from the fence and stepping inside to catch up a fresh horse. He saddled and mounted. Bo still sat where he had fallen, fingering his aching jaw. Vance rode away.

It was almost daylight before he reëntered Soda Springs and rode down the alley to the dark livery. He turned the horse into the corral, went inside, and stretched out on the bedding in an empty stall. He lay on his back, staring up as the first morning light found the chinks between the warped siding. He did not sleep. He tried to think, but no matter how hard he puzzled, he could not unwrap the twisted pattern of the future.

When it was full light, he could remain quiet no longer. He rose, walked out to the rear trough, stripped off his shirt, and plunged his head and shoulders into the chill water. Afterward, feeling refreshed, he went to use the comb that Wentworth kept on a shelf in the office. Then, hearing a rig, he stepped into the still shadowed entrance of the runway.

A buckboard was coming toward him along the street. He recognized it at once. Bo was driving and his mother made a small figure at Bo's side. He knew even before they passed him and entered the station yard that this was the start of his mother's trip to the prison, that Condon's scheme for releasing his brothers was already in motion.

Vance held his place until the train came in from the east and he saw his mother board it. Having no desire to meet his younger brother, he left the livery by the rear door and found a scanty breakfast in a Mexican restaurant. Later he sought the barbershop and was shaved.

Finally he went to the Apache Hotel and strode into the lobby. Andy Lawrence stood behind the desk, and the boy looked up in surprise as Vance came in. Benton was not an ordinary visitor at the hotel.

"You want something?"

"To see Laura Hall."

Andy, along with half the town, had been watching the meetings between the Eastern girl and Benton with sharp interest. More than once Andy had considered relaying what he knew to Dr. West, but a reluctance that was almost entirely foreign to his nature kept him from talking. Now, however, he hesitated. West had come in only a few minutes ago, the first time he had left the hospital since the morning when Gimble's mob had tried to load the patients onto the train. There had been no more trouble. Omstead, with the help of the imported railway police, had patrolled the grounds night and day until the epidemic ran its course. The last patient had been sent out yesterday afternoon, the makeshift ward was empty, and West had turned the hospital back to Gruber.

Andy said: "I don't think she wants to see you." He said it resolutely, but not too certainly. He was a little afraid of Vance Benton.

Vance was in no humor to be put off by the boy. "Supposing you let her decide that, bud."

Andy resented being called "bud", but there was a look in Vance's eye that he did not like. He slid from his perch on the high stool and started toward the dining room. Then he stopped. Hy West was coming down the stairs.

West looked at the boy, and then at Vance, and the question in his eyes was plain. Obviously he had heard what had been said. He came down slowly. He reached the bottom of the stairs and said in a low voice: "Go on out front, Andy."

More than anything else in the world, Andy would have liked to remain, but he knew Hy meant exactly what he said. He passed Vance Benton and went out, letting the front door swing shut behind him. Left alone, the two men eyed each other in studied silence.

West finally broke it by saying: "I'd like to know why you want to see Laura."

Vance Benton was uneasy before West's steady gaze, and this feeling of uncertainty gave him a touch of quick anger. "Does that mean you pick out the people Laura can talk to?"

West said evenly: "There's something here that I don't quite understand."

"What is there to understand?" They were fencing and they both knew it. It was very unlike Vance Benton to attack a subject indirectly.

"I didn't even know you knew her."

Vance's smile was paper-thin. "There are a number of things you don't know, Doctor. While you've been nursing the plague, life goes on. There's no reason not to tell you. I know her real well . . . maybe a lot better than you do."

West's own reaction puzzled him. Perhaps the emotional vacuum that so often follows surprise explained his seeming lack of feeling at the moment. He started to say something, and then changed his mind. "I'll get her," he said, and went into the dining room. Laura was at the kitchen table, eating a delayed breakfast. At sight of him she looked startled. She had not known he was through at the hospital.

"Why, Hy. . . ."

"There's someone in the lobby to see you."

Surprise narrowed her eyes. "To see me?"

"Vance Benton."

For a moment she did not move, but color swept up into her rounded cheeks. West saw the color and understood at once that this relationship had gone very far indeed. For her part, the girl was trying desperately to think of the proper thing to say. She had known, of course, that sooner or later she would be faced with a showdown of some kind, but she had not expected it to come so soon, certainly not this morning. Vance had never dared come openly to the hotel before. She gave up finally, letting her eyes fall away from West as she rose and went quickly out through the dining room. West's head twisted to watch her, and, when he turned back, he found Belle Callahan watching him.

She had been at the sink when he came in, and he had been too abstracted for the moment to realize that she was there.

"How long has this been going on?" he asked simply.

She answered without hesitation. "It isn't

my affair, Hy."

"I'm sorry. I shouldn't have asked you. I'll ask her." He came over to the table and sank tiredly into a chair. She took one look at his face, and then lifted a cup from the shelf. She filled it from the coffee pot and set it before him.

"It's been going on quite a while. I think everyone in town knows but you."

He closed his eyes. He was not a person who indulged in self-pity and he was not indulging in it now. He wasn't even thinking of himself. "But why Vance Benton?" He sounded puzzled. He was puzzled.

"He's a man," Belle said. "That's about all there is, I guess. A man and a woman. I don't pretend to like her, but I have seen her face after she's been with Vance. She looks like a different person."

"She might have told me."

Belle came over and sat down at the table. "I suspect she's been fighting it," she said. "I think she didn't want you to know because she hoped it would pass."

"She didn't want to burn her bridges. Is that it?"

Belle found no answer.

He let his breath out slowly. "You'd have to know Laura to understand how impossible this is. She's the original girl who

265

wanted things. She had a hard time when she was young. She never told me how hard, but I probably guessed more than she realized. She had her life all figured out. That's why she refused to come back here with me in the first place. She wanted me to take a resident's job at the hospital. That meant security and a fair degree of comfort. How can she hope to have either with Vance Benton?"

Belle said slowly: "I don't think she does. I don't think she wants to marry him. I've watched her during these last few days. It's almost as if she were trying to escape from a trap . . . and yet she can't seem to stay away from him. It's hard on you, to find out this way since you loved her."

He looked at the girl sitting across the table from him, so utterly different from Laura, as different as night from daylight, big where Laura was small, calm where Laura was nervous, seeming content with her niche in the world, wanting independence enough to take this job at the hotel. "Don't waste too much sympathy on me." He gave her a wry smile. "I suppose I loved her in a way. I suppose I still do. I was very young, and I knew nothing about women, and I was extremely lonesome and uncertain of myself. She taught me a lot. She helped me find a strength I didn't know I had, and I let her down by coming back here merely to prove to myself that I could make this town accept me on my own terms."

"You have," she said. "Even the ones who joined Gimble's mob are saying now that without you half the town might have died."

He said: "I've had no indication of it."

"And don't turn bitter because you've lost your girl."

"I'm not bitter," he said, "and I don't accept the fact that I've lost her, as you put it. In a way I've won the battle that I came out here to fight. I hadn't realized it until this moment. I no longer care what this town thinks of me. It's ceased to be important. I can look back at the people saved from the wreck, and the ones who had the pox, and know that I did a satisfactory job."

She showed her first unease. "Does that mean you're leaving here?"

"I don't know. I suppose Doctor Forbes would make a place for me if I went back. I had not intended to do it, but now that Laura has got herself involved perhaps it would be better. I think I owe her that much at least."

She was watching him, a faint frown growing between her brows. "Don't do it, Hy. Don't pattern your life to try and save her.

You'll fail. You can't help her now."

He peered at her curiously. "You seem to know a lot about it."

"I do," she told him. "I'm a woman. Sometimes we don't reason like men. Sometimes we think only with our emotions."

"This from you, the girl who always said she wouldn't marry?"

She gave him a strange wry smile. "You may be a good doctor, Hy, but you still know very little about women." She rose and went back to the sink. He watched her in silence.

In the lobby, Vance Benton was finding out that he, too, did not yet know all about women. Laura came quickly through the dining room, saying as she came: "You had no business asking for me here this morning. What will Hy think?"

Vance had been alone with his troubled thoughts for most of the night, and his patience was near the breaking point. "What difference does it make what he thinks?" He tried to take the girl in his arms but she avoided him.

"Vance, stop it. Not here. Are you out of your mind?"

"Probably," he told her savagely. "Can you be ready to leave this town today?"

"Leave town?" She was thoroughly surprised. "What are you talking about? What's happened?"

"Never mind," he said. "We're leaving. I've made up my mind."

A trace of her old manner returned. "Now just a minute. You're going a little fast. I've never taken orders from anyone and I'm not about to start now."

"Look," he said, "I'll marry you, if that's what you're worrying about."

"Oh, so now you'll kindly marry me."

"God damn it!" He caught her shoulders, shaking her harder than he intended. "This is important. You don't think I'd let you go back to Hy West after what's happened between us?"

Under his touch some of her resolution crumbled. "Vance, stop, please. I can't think clearly when you're pawing me. What's happened? Don't you think that I have the right to know?"

He almost blurted out the whole story, but he was not completely certain of her full loyalty, and the code that had held him to his brothers was too strong. "I'm in no trouble," he said harshly. "But I've split with my family. I'm getting out. There's no reason for me to stay in Soda Springs. I'll go anywhere you want to go so long as it's a long way from this town. Isn't that what you wanted?"

She didn't know what she wanted. She seemed to be a huge well of uncertainty. She could not make up her mind. "Let me think."

"Think, then."

"Not now. I can't seem to think now. Give me a day or two. Give me a week. This is all so new, and so horribly important."

Black despair seemed to engulf Vance. A week. He did not know exactly what day the prison break was planned for, but he doubted if they would wait a week. And he had to be out of Soda Springs before the break, he had to if he wanted to stand clear of it and the events that would follow.

"To hell with it then." He let her go. Ignoring her protesting cry, he slammed his way from the hotel. She stood straining after him, almost running after him. But at last she started toward the stairs. She had gone halfway up when West's voice reached her.

"Laura."

She stopped, but did not look down at him.

"Hadn't we better have a talk?"

Her voice was listless, as if all emotion had been drained out of her. "What is there to talk about?"

He said with a tinge of irony: "I'd think there were several things. Won't you come down? I hardly care to stand here shouting."

She came back down the stairs like a sleepwalker who has no control over her legs. "All right. What is there to talk about?"

"Vance Benton. What was he doing here?"

"He came to ask me to marry him." She was rapidly recovering her old poise. The need to defend herself renewed her confidence.

"And you answered?"

She did not deny his right to know. "I asked for a few days to think it over."

"Which means you're considering it?"

"Which means I'm considering it."

They stared at each other for a moment like two strangers. He said: "This is no good, Laura."

A trace of listlessness returned to her voice. "Nothing's very much good, Hy. I'm sorry, but sometimes people can't help the way they feel."

"They can't," he said. "But have you thought about the future?"

"It's all I've thought about." It was a cry, words of desperation. "How can I marry him, Hy?"

"You can't." He said it bluntly. "Marriage

is more than an emotional disturbance, more than the act of giving yourself to a man. It's a partnership. How can a person like you be partners with Vance Benton?"

Suddenly she was crying, softly, but as if her whole control had given way. "I can't get along without him, Hy. I can't. I never felt this way about anyone else, not even you. I'm not sure it's love. I guess I don't know what love is. I only know that when his hands are on me I can't refuse him anything."

He looked down at her bowed head. He had never seen her like this before, humble and afraid. "What's he want you to do?"

"To go away with him today. Something is pushing him, Hy. I don't know what, and he won't tell me. Could you find out? Would he talk to you? I think he's scared of something. He said he'd split with his family and there was no point in staying in Soda Springs. He said he didn't care where we went so long as he went a long way from here."

"And you told him?"

"That I had to have time to think. But thinking does no good. Nothing does any good."

"All right," he said. "I'll talk to him. In a way I got you into this. I guess it's my business to try to get you out."

XVI

The main building of the Territorial Prison dated back to early Spanish days. The place had been rebuilt and enlarged, but enough of the original structure remained to give it a marked resemblance to a medieval castle. Abel Hunt owed his appointment as warden to the political ring that flourished in the capital, and he had paid his debt by filling most of the positions at his command with friends and relatives of his political associates. The prison doctor was no exception. Dr. Mathews had learned what little medicine he knew by rolling pills in the office of a small Missouri town doctor, and had purchased his diploma from one of the diploma mills that flourished through the country in the 1880s. But general practice had proved both hard and unremunerative and he gladly accepted this prison post that a brother-in-law had secured for him.

A nervous man, uncertain and apologetic before his equals, he could be vicious and cruel, and he was hated thoroughly by both the prisoners and guards. The prison itself held the prize collection of criminals that could be gathered from all over the Southwest, murderers and thieves whose names were bywords of robbery, of rape, and of ruthless killing. But even in this select company the two Bentons had managed to build a small notoriety for themselves. As usual, they were confined in solitary when their mother arrived.

The doctor was in the warden's office when word came that Mrs. Benton wished to visit her sons. She was carrying a letter from Dr. Condon explaining that because of age and failing health it would probably be her last chance to talk to either of the prisoners. The warden was a careless but not an unkind man, and both he and Mathews owed Condon favors from the past. He read the letter, shrugged, and gave his permission.

Ma Benton walked along the stone corridor to the visitor's room, looking small and tired and old. The prison building awed her as nothing else had ever done. It was so huge, so massive, so obviously strong, that she began to understand Condon's evident reluctance to undertake the break. Considering these stone walls, it did seem that no man could possibly hope to escape.

She sat waiting, and her iron composure almost cracked at her first glimpse of her sons. Both had aged, and their thin dark faces bore a certain pallor that is mostly associated with death. Nor was the pallor the only mark. Their eyes burned with a light that showed a hint of madness and made her almost fear them.

She waited until the guard had retreated to the door, and then she told them what was planned, repeating Condon's instructions minutely. Later she watched them being led away and offered up a silent prayer that the next time she saw them the boys would be free.

Afterward she left the grim old building and walked slowly to the railroad track, feeling weak-kneed and more tired than she had ever been in her life. It was with real relief that she saw Bo waiting for her beside the station in Soda Springs. She let him help her into the buckboard for the long ride to the ranch.

She saw the bruises on his face and asked how he'd gotten them. When he told her about his fight with Vance, she listened with her thin-lipped mouth tight as a steel trap. When he finished, she said: "Find Vance. Let me talk to him."

He left her beside the station, but although he searched the town, he found no trace of his brother. It was Andy who told him that Vance had ridden out. Andy and Sam had watched from the station as the older Benton left the livery stable, but Andy did not know where Vance had gone. No one seemed to know. So finally Bo was forced to return to his mother with this information. He took her out of town at a high run, whipping the horses needlessly as a way of working off some of his suppressed anger.

Two days later Duke and Prince were reported sick. No one at the prison associated the fact with the visit from their mother.

The news reached Mathews while he was at breakfast. In the ordinary course of events he would have ignored it until he finished his meal. But such was his fear of the plague that, when the guard reported the symptoms, he hurried into the dark, lower tier that was commonly called the Hole. Both Bentons lay on their bunks, and Prince was groaning softly, complaining of his aching head, the pains in his back, and sickness at the stomach.

Mathews made certain that both had fever. He noted the redness along the hairline, and at once ordered them to the row of outbuildings that flanked the courtyard and had previously been used as stables. Then he wired Condon and sought the warden in his office.

"More pox."

The warden was short and fat and not inclined to worry unnecessarily. But he worried now. They waited for Condon to come; they got an answering wire instead. The lymph from the East had not yet arrived, but he was coming on the next train, bringing with him a Mexican who had had the pox and who he had used to nurse some of the cases in town. Mathews relaxed. He had an ignorant man's respect for Condon's knowledge and there was no reason why they should mistrust him or his Mexican companion.

Pedro was short and squat, and his face bore mute evidence of the pox's ravages. He moved with his bag of medicines into the empty stable next to the sick prisoners and from that moment took over their full care, bringing the food from the prison kitchen, and keeping the guards out of the improvised cells entirely.

Condon went back to Soda Springs on the evening train. He rode out to the Benton ranch long after dark to warn Bo that everything was working perfectly. He told Bo to gather his riders and be ready outside the prison at sundown on the fourth day. Then he returned to Soda Springs.

Andy carried the news that the doctor had

been summoned to the prison when he came in for lunch, and he reported in the evening that Condon had returned. "I guess they've got the pox," Andy told West who was eating beside him in the long dining room. "At least he took a Mexican up with him as a nurse."

"How many cases?"

Andy was chagrined that he did not know. "I'll find out," he volunteered.

"Never mind," West said. "I'll talk to Condon tonight. Maybe it would be better if I went up there to help."

He glanced across the table at Laura Hall. His first impulse was to suggest that she might accompany him to the prison, that there might well be sufficient work for a proper nurse. Work would do her good. She had been like this for three days, ever since Vance had walked out of the hotel. She had not mentioned Vance's name. She was pleasant and reserved with everyone, but the spark had gone.

He glanced toward Belle. Belle had been wonderful these last few days, bestowing kindnesses on the other girl without appearing to. Belle had seen that Laura was kept as busy as possible during the daylight hours.

He rose and left the room, walking along

the street. Several people spoke to him as he passed, people who a few short days ago would have pointedly ignored his presence. He had won his place here, all right, won it with the help of the train wreck and the epidemic. And now that he had won it, he did not care. He felt at loose ends for the first time in years. There had been so little time for real thought since coming back to Soda Springs.

He wondered if the change in Laura was responsible for his inability to make up his mind about the future. It seemed very curious that they, whose lives had been so close, should suddenly find themselves little more than strangers. But he knew deep within himself that Laura had nothing to do with his purposelessness. It went deeper than that. He was like an athlete who had practiced all his life for one event, and won it, and now saw no other purpose for his developed proficiency. His medicine had been a means to an end, a means of establishing himself in this town, of claiming what he thought of as his rightful place. And now that he claimed it, the whole thing seemed empty and without real purpose.

I'm just tired, he thought. *I'll take a few days until I get my feet under me, and then I'll go back to Chicago and see if Forbes will still give me the residence job. I may find enough to occupy myself in hard work.*

He reached the fence before Condon's house. He peered over the fence, found the house dark, and thought: *I should have known he'd be at Callahan's.*

He turned away just as the saddler came from his shop and paused to lock the door. Then he called across: "Looking for Condon?"

West nodded.

"He took his buggy out about two hours ago. I haven't seen him come back."

West thanked him and walked aimlessly along the street. He came to Callahan's, hesitated, then went in. The big room was nearly three-quarters full, men lined along the lip of the big bar, four poker games going at the rear tables. He ordered a drink, the second since he had returned to town. He carried it to the rear, setting his shoulders against the old wall and watching the play of the cards at the corner table.

Behind the bar, Callahan had watched him come in. He continued to watch without appearing to, studying West, analyzing him, and somehow being dissatisfied with his thoughts. Two or three of the players had turned their heads and nodded. It was a motley crowd: merchants from along

Railroad Avenue, riders from the outlying hill ranches, and half a dozen soldiers from the fort who formed a hard knot at the front end of the bar, not mixing with the townsmen, taking their drinks in quiet silence, thinking of other pleasures that they might find later above the dance hall beyond the tracks.

Three times there were empty seats at one of the games and three times West almost sat in. He had no real desire for cards, but he was inwardly restless.

This was the town. Every shading of its social structure was represented within the room. If he were to remain here, these were the men with whom he would be associated, and he thought with a detached bitterness that there was not a friend among them. They were no longer hostile. They had accepted him on a kind of sufferance. Some of them even felt a little guilty at remembering that they had joined Gimble's mob in its attack on the station and the Railroad Hospital, but none of them made any real motion to include him in their circle.

Belle had been right, he thought. He had unconsciously held the world a little away from him. A man had to give something of himself before he had any real friends. Throughout his years in school, and his internship at the hospital, others had formed into small cliques, sharing their joys and their problems, while he stood almost alone. He had accepted this as his natural lot until Laura forcibly broke down his reserve. And then he had clung to her, holding fast to her in an effort to escape loneliness. He knew now that he had never loved Laura. Always he had suspected her associations with other men, but time after time rejected the suspicion out of fear that it would break the relationship he had come to depend upon. And suddenly he realized that the severance of the relationship brought relief. Actually his unconscious mind always had rebelled at the thought of binding his life to that of Laura. But without her, what would he do? Would his work be enough? Could the hospital and its never-ending duties replace his desire for the tight companionship of a family that he had always wanted and never had?

His glass was empty. He walked to the bar for a refill and found himself facing Callahan. He looked at the man curiously as the ex-sergeant set the bottle of whiskey upon the bar. Callahan had made a success here, a far greater success than he had ever been able to contemplate while wearing a uniform. But he had traded much to achieve that success. He had lost his wife and now his daughter. He was alone with no one save a crowd of saloon loafers for companions. He wondered, if Callahan had a chance to go back and live his life over again, what would his choice be? He was almost tempted to ask the man, and then, meeting the steady eyes, he held back the words. Callahan was a person he never could get close to. Callahan neither invited confidences nor returned them. Callahan had selected his road and plowed along it with all the determination of a headstrong bull.

West swallowed his drink, heard a rig in the street beyond the batwing doors, and walked the length of the room to peer out. It was Condon. He saw the doctor travel the block and turn into his own drive and pull up at the barn. West stepped out. It was nearly midnight and there were few loiterers. Bruce Gimble cruised down the far sidewalk, making his late rounds, and saw West and pointedly avoided him. West stood there for a moment, undecided, then moved up the street toward Condon's.

Condon came from the barn in response to the clamor set up by the dogs, and found West in the shadows. He felt a stab of quick fear, wondering if in some way the young doctor had learned of the planned prison break. Then his self-confidence came rushing back as he decided that this was impossible.

"Come in." His tone was ironic. "It's been a long time since we had the pleasure of your company here."

West did not speak as he followed the older man across the baked hardness of the yard and into the cluttered messiness of the consulting room. He took a chair, tilting it back against the wall, and watched as Condon cleared the table by the simple expedient of sweeping the litter to one end. Then without a word the older doctor produced two dirty glasses and set out a bottle from the desk's lower drawer. West watched while Condon poured a small drink into one glass and then half filled the other, raising it in a kind of silent salute before he downed the contents at a gulp.

"I've been expecting this visit."

"I've been rather busy." West's grin was mirthless. "I heard that they're having some trouble at the prison. I thought I might be of help."

Condon raised his eyebrows.

West felt his face redden slightly. It had always been thus between them, a gulf that for some reason neither could seem to bridge. Condon had the knack of making him feel that he was in the wrong, even when the older man did not apparently intend it that way. "I'm through at the Railroad Hospital," he said. "There's hardly enough work for one man under ordinary circumstances, and I doubt if I'd stay even if Gruber were not here. It isn't what I want."

"What do you want?" Condon had poured new drinks without even asking West's desire.

"You asked me that once a long time ago," West said. "You were sarcastic then, and your question along with other things sent me away from here. I've never thanked you, either for that or for taking me in at the time of the trial."

There was an expression on Condon's face that West had never seen there before and that he did not understand. "I might have done more for you." The older man seemed to be talking to himself. "Perhaps I should have . . . and yet, I doubt that you would have come out as well. I'm rather proud of you."

West was startled at that. Despite everything that had happened he had never expected praise from Condon.

"Life's a funny thing." The older man was still speaking almost to himself. "We all make mistakes, stupid mistakes. But sometimes things turn out better than we have any right to expect." The whiskey seemingly had loosened his tongue, but instead of sharpening its bitter edge as drink usually did, it mellowed him to a point that West had never before observed. Then the tone changed, hardening a little. "Keep away from that prison, boy. They almost got you once, and it's better not to enter those walls. Besides, there's no real problem there, nothing for you to do."

He broke off to empty the bottle into his glass without offering any to West, and drank it at a gulp as if his throat were burning. Then, his speech noticeably thickened, he added: "Get out of Soda Springs. There's nothing here for you or for anyone else. I've found that out. It's a trap." The words died. He stared at his visitor apparently without seeing him. Then he laid his head upon his hands and slept.

West blew out the light and left the house. The street was entirely empty as he made his way back to the hotel. Lights still burned in Callahan's but there was no noise from the bar, only the steady *clanking* from the distant railroad shops and the *chuff* of a switch engine as it made up the eastbound freight.

He came into the lobby and was surprised to find Belle Callahan sewing under the light of the center lamp. He said: "Don't you work enough in the daytime?"

"It's Andy's shirt," she said, holding it up for his inspection. "Since Mary's been sick, the kid is almost out of clothes." She looked at him intently. "Some coffee?"

He nodded and she led the way into the kitchen. Putting the pot on to boil, she asked: "Out celebrating?"

He grinned at her. "If you can call it that. I went down to ask Condon if I can help at the prison. He was out on a call so I visited your father's place." She winced a little at that, and he leaned across the table impulsively, putting one hand over hers. "Can a doctor give you a bit of advice?" Her expression was neutral, neither rejecting nor asking for his words, but he said quickly: "Your father's getting old, Belle. Don't cut yourself off from him too long. You might be sorry when it's too late. A family is a nice thing to have."

She did not argue. Instead, she nodded slowly. "I'll think about it, Hy. What about yourself?"

He said lightly: "Nothing about me. My only chance is marriage and that doesn't look promising at the moment. Not promising at all."

XVII

Andy Lawrence knew something was going to happen. He didn't know exactly how he knew it but he was as certain as if someone had told him. It was kind of like sensing that it was going to rain. He'd had this feeling before, he confided in Sam Dillon. They were sitting on an empty baggage truck behind the express office and Sam's blue eyes squinted as he listened to Andy.

"It's this way," Andy told him. "It ain't just an idea I got. There's real trouble brewing. You just wait and see."

Sam did not argue. He was a year younger than Andy and he usually followed the older boy's lead. "You think the Bentons are up to something?"

Andy scratched his leg. "I just don't know. I figured maybe Vance and Doc West would start shooting each other over Laura, I did for a fact. But, shucks, Doc acts like he don't even care."

"Maybe he's afraid of Vance."

"Shucks, he ain't afraid of nobody. Look at the way he stood up all alone to Gimble and that mob. I'll bet you Vance Benton wouldn't have done that. You know something . . . I think maybe it's him being a doctor. I was talking to him and he was telling me about the oath a doctor has to take, something about saving life and such. Maybe doctors feel that it just ain't right for them to kill people."

Sam was thoughtful. "Come to think of it I never saw even Doc Condon wear a gun."

"He's got a shotgun," Andy said. They brooded on this in silence.

"What's Doc West going to do now?"

Andy hated to admit he didn't know. "He's just sitting around, doing nothing. I asked him was he going back to Chicago and he just grunted. I sure hope he does."

Sam was surprised. "I thought you liked him."

"Sure I like him, but if he was in Chicago, maybe I could stay with him while I studied medicine." He glanced carelessly up the street, and then stiffened. "Hey, there's Vance Benton riding in now. First time I've seen him in three or four days. I bet Laura will sure be tickled to see him. I heard Belle tell Ma she was plumb eating out her heart since he went away." He slid from his perch, followed by Sam, and together they started for the livery, a kind of unofficial welcoming committee.

Vance Benton did not see them coming.

Vance's mind was busy with more important things. When he had ridden out of town, he fully intended to keep on going until he was out of the country, and right now he was cursing himself for not following his first impulse. But ten miles above the Benton ranch he had halted, then swung back, knowing that his mother would still be on her way to the prison, and that Bo probably would wait in town. Fred was away when he rode up, the ranch deserted. He packed food and coffee into a sack that he tied behind his saddle and then took the hill trail, winding onward until he found a vantage point on the flank of Mount David.

From this place he could watch the comings and goings of the hill ranchers. Often in the past he had amused himself by spying on his neighbors. But this time there was more than amusement in his mind. For three days he watched, checking on both Fred and Bo as they rode in and out of the side cañons. He guessed that they were alerting the men who they had chosen to ride with them on the prison break, and the knowledge made him all the more uncertain and restless. For the first time in his life he seemed unable to make up his mind, and finally on the morning of the sixth day after his mother had gone to the prison he could stand it no longer.

He caught up the horse that he had kept hobbled in a little box cañon, and set out for Soda Springs, making a wide detour to avoid the possibility of meeting either of his brothers. He rode in, tired and dirty and unshaven, in the shank of the afternoon. He left his horse in the corral and started along the alley, ignoring the two boys who watched him from the rear barn door. He paid no attention to anyone, made no attempt to conceal his progress as he stalked along. He was a man with a purpose, and nothing would turn him aside from that purpose.

He reached the entrance to the hotel kitchen and came in without knocking, his arrival startling Belle Callahan so badly that she almost dropped a bowl of stewed apples. She managed to set it on the table, and then she scanned his unshaven face.

"What is it, Vance?"

"Laura. I've got to talk with her."

Belle did not argue. Without a word she left the kitchen, climbing the stairs to knock on Laura's door. "Who is it?"

"Belle. Vance is in the kitchen."

The door opened almost at once. Beyond the girl, Belle had a view of the bed, an open letter, and an unwrapped package. Laura's face was white, her eyes troubled and uncertain. "What shall I do?"

Belle was practical as always. "You'd better talk to him. He looks as if he's had a bad time."

"I can't. It's no use."

"Look." A hint of annoyance had crept into Belle's practical tone. "Go ahead and talk to him. If a man wanted me as much as Vance seems to want you, I'd at least talk to him."

There were tears in Laura's eyes. "I'm afraid to. If I see him again, I'll probably agree to anything he wants."

"Why not? I understand he's broken with his family. Let him take you away from here."

Laura gave her a thoughtful look, then went past her. Belle hesitated. It was time to start supper but she must stay away from the kitchen. She went into Laura's room and sat on the bed.

The package lay open and she saw a picture inside. She was about to shove it out of her way when she noticed that she had seen the picture before. She sat there several minutes before she remembered. Yes, of course. It was the tintype that for years had hung above Dr. Condon's desk. She picked up the letter that lay beside the package and read:

My Dear Miss Hall:

The enclosed picture which you forwarded to Messrs. Gill and Brush of Arch Street is a likeness of my daughter Mary. This picture was given to her husband, Dr. Silas Jordan, at the time of their marriage. I am extremely anxious to know where you secured this picture as I have spent the last twenty years in a vain effort to trace Dr. Jordan.

When he and my daughter separated, he took their two-year-old son with him and we have never heard from either since. Any information concerning the whereabouts of the doctor or of the boy will be very very welcome to an old man. My daughter died long ago and there is no one left but me.

Very respectfully,
Phillip DeLong

Belle Callahan read the letter twice. Condon must be the missing doctor, but the boy . . . ? Why should Laura have had the picture? Why did she send it East? Did Laura think that the missing child was Hy West? She pored over the letter, her quick mind exploring the possibilities, the implications. If West were Condon's son, that would explain why the older doctor had taken the boy in at the time he was threatened with prison. But why had the boy been placed with the Bentons to raise? And why had Condon failed to tell the boy who he was, saddling him instead with the ridiculous name?

She had no answers. She walked impatiently into the hall. She wanted to talk to Laura. She wondered how soon it would be before the girl finished her conversation with Vance.

Half an hour passed before Laura came through the dining room into the lobby. Belle hurried downstairs to meet her, carrying the picture and the letter.

Laura was radiant, too excited to notice the letter in Belle's hands. "It's all settled." She was nearly crying. "Vance and I are going east on the midnight train. There's a man in Texas who will give Vance a job. We'll be away from here and I can find out if I can stand ranch life."

Belle said — "That's wonderful." — and meant it. She held up the letter. "I found this on your bed."

Laura was still too filled with her own affairs to pay much attention. "Yes, it came on the afternoon mail."

Belle hesitated. "Isn't the picture the one that used to be in Condon's office?"

Laura nodded. "One day I went there to get some morphine. . . ."

"You stole it?"

Laura flushed. "I don't know why. I haven't liked Condon ever since Hy told me how he was treated when he was a boy. And I had a hunch. I felt that Condon was hiding something. I didn't know what. So I took the picture and mailed it to the photographers."

Belle said slowly: "And you think Hy is Condon's son?"

"It could be. Why don't you have Hy ask Condon?"

"Why should I be the one to tell Hy?"

"Because you're in love with him."

Belle gasped.

Laura took both her hands. "Belle, Belle, stop trying to fool yourself. I knew it when I first came. I resented you because I thought I wanted Hy myself. But since I met Vance, it's different. You're the only friend Hy ever had in this town. He used to talk about you, back in Chicago. I was jealous of you, even before I came."

Belle didn't answer.

"Show him the picture," Laura said. "Let him read the letter. He's all mixed up. You can straighten him out if anyone can."

She turned away, running upstairs to

pack. Belle stared after her, then slowly went on through the dining room to the kitchen.

XVIII

Ordinarily there was but a single guard in the prison courtyard, but as soon as the Bentons had been transferred to the old stables the warden put an extra man on duty. All day, Prince and Duke had been too restless to lie on their bunks. Only the Mexican, made stoic by his Indian blood, waited patiently for the coming of darkness. There was no way in which they could be certain that Fred and Bo would be posted in the arroyo with their men for the rendezvous at sundown. It was a chance they had to take.

The sun dropped slowly, the shadows lengthened across the yard, and the two guards stirred restlessly at their post. One was tall, the other short. Nondescript men, unimportant. The tall one was named Brem, the short one Curly Bill. They stood together in the shadows and Joe Brem said: "I don't like it." He spoke too loudly as a weak man often does in an effort to reassure himself. "I never did care much for this job and with the pox it's worse. The head guard doesn't like me. He always gives me the dirty jobs."

Curly Bill spat on the worn stones. He was a rider out of the wasteland to the west and only accident had put him here as a guard rather than an inmate. He was guilty of a hundred petty crimes. "No danger us catching the pox as long as we stay in the air. My brother died of it. I was with him. We was prospecting the Gila country. I just kept away from him, and I didn't catch it."

"Then how'd the Bentons catch it? They were in solitary."

Curly Bill did not know the answer. He did not want to think about it.

Inside the old stables, Duke Benton sat fingering one of the guns that Pedro had smuggled in with his bag of medicine. Duke was a big man, the biggest of the five brothers, but no longer as strong as he had once been. Prison had softened his muscles and turned them flabby. "Time yet?" His tone was irritated and impatient.

The Mexican moved to the tiny window and peered out. "Bo say half an hour after the darkness."

"It's that now. Let's get going."

Duke stood up. The Mexican nodded. He slipped the gun under his belt, opened the door, and vanished into the courtyard. Duke and Prince waited, the guns in their hands, ready.

Curly Bill saw Pedro emerge. This was standard procedure. The Mexican would cross a corner of the yard to the kitchen wing and return with the prisoners' supper. But Pedro was getting closer to him than Joe Brem liked. The man would be carrying germs on his clothes.

"Get back, keep away from us!" Brem called.

Pedro turned away, but, as he turned, the gun came from its hiding place below the belt. He fired twice, accurately, his bullets dropping them both. He ran in then, seizing Brem's rifle as Duke and Prince bolted from their doorway to join him.

There was a guard on the wall at the corner. He foolishly stepped into view, and Prince dropped him with a shot from Curly Bill's rifle. Then they raced for the heavy gate, tearing at the chain that fastened it, finally shooting away the massive lock.

Bo came yelling into the yard, leading an extra horse. Duke lifted himself into the saddle.

Prince never got to his horse. They did not know from which direction the bullet came. It must have been fired from one of the windows of the main building. The whole place was in an uproar.

The outlaws now had control of the courtyard and the wall guard station, but of course they could not break into the main building. It never occurred to anyone within the massive structure that the men in the courtyard would try to get in. The prisoners were escaping. The only thought in anyone's mind was to stop them.

The warden himself opened the main door and led the rush of the guards into the courtyard. The warden was one of the first to die. The guards who survived the first volley tried to retreat, to bar the door, but Bo Benton seemed to go crazy at their attack. He had been marshaling his men for withdrawal when the guards came out. He swung, riding directly into them, clubbing about him with his heavy-barreled gun, blasting into the faces of the guards, taking a wild, savage joy in the battle and excitement. Eight guards were killed in the courtyard before Bo rode his horse into the main hallway. The doctor was almost the last to die. He died in the warden's office where Duke Benton had forced his way in, searching for the master keys. The doctor died without a fight, knocked from his chair by Duke's bullets.

The outlaws were in control of the main

prison. The surviving guards had retreated into the stone tower that stood above the solitary cells and barred the door. The whole building was in tumult, excited prisoners clamoring for release, shrieking their curses as Duke passed them by.

Duke made his selection with care. He picked only men who he had learned to respect within the walls. But after he had freed those he had chosen to accompany him, he flung the keys into the nearest cell, not caring whether or not they were used to release the rest.

He had freed eleven men, but there were not horses enough for them. It was necessary to raid the prison stables before they could be mounted. As they dashed from the stables, there was a red glow from the kitchen wing, and a minute later the windows burst, the flames shooting out to lick upward toward the sky. The whole action of the break had taken less than ten minutes.

Cat-Eye Smith had been the leader within the prison walls. Cat-Eye was one of the toughest killers the border country had ever produced, and he tried to assume leadership of the mounted men as if by natural right.

"Let's move." He reined in beside Duke Benton. "This place will be swarming with marshals by tomorrow."

He was interrupted by Fred Benton who pushed forward, leading a horse across which he had thrown Prince. "We've got to get a doctor," Fred said. "Prince is hit bad."

Duke grunted. He hadn't known that his brother was wounded. Cat-Eye glanced briefly at the unconscious man. He said: "Leave him. We got no time to waste."

Bo bad come up on the other side of Smith, still carrying his rifle. Bo still had the wild glaze of excitement in his eye. He did not know who Smith was and did not care.

"Shut up," he snarled. "I'm giving the orders here."

Smith looked at him, his light eyes muddy with anger in the growing glare from the burning prison. Bo held the rifle ready. The men from the hills swung behind Bo in a tight knot.

Smith was no fool. His chances of escape would be better if he held company with the Bentons and he knew it. "What do you want to do?" he demanded.

It was Bo who answered, Bo in the emergency showing unexpected leadership. "Two of you ride over to the railroad and make sure the telegraph wires are cut. Fred, you head for Soda Springs and get Doc Condon. Bring him to the ranch if you have to drag him at the end of a rope."

Smith had no idea where the Benton ranch was. He was not familiar with this portion of the country. He said: "Is that heading toward the border?"

"Never mind the border," Bo told him. "We'll get Prince to the ranch and hide him back in the hills. Condon and Ma can look after him. Then we'll head for Mexico. Let's ride."

They rode, twenty-three men in all, heavily armed, the prisoners carrying weapons captured from the guards. Behind them they heard the shrieks of trapped men as the fire gained in volume until it seemed to fill the sky. Bo had Prince before him, on his horse, trying to hold his wounded brother upright, not knowing whether or not he would live until they reached the ranch.

At almost the same time Hy West came into the hotel kitchen, finding Belle there by herself. She turned and nodded, then went on frying the steaks for dinner. "There's something on the table you might be interested in seeing. Did you ever really wonder who you are, Hy?"

He looked at her curiously, pondering what prompted the question. "Of course.

Anyone would in my situation."

"Does it make a lot of difference?"

He sighed. "I guess so. At least it would have once. Now I'm not so sure." He walked over to the table, where the picture and letter lay enclosed by the loosened wrappings, and pulled them out. He recognized the tintype as the one that had hung in Condon's office and stared at it in puzzled surprise. He glanced toward Belle for explanation, but her back was turned. He picked up the folded letter, noting as he opened it that it was addressed to Laura Hall.

Belle continued to concentrate on the stove, so he read the letter, a frown deepening between his brows. When he finished, he said in an unnatural voice: "Where did you get this?"

"From Laura."

"And how did she happen to have it?"

Belle pushed the skillet back off the fire and came over to him. "Sit down," she said.

He had the picture in his hands. He sat down, poring over it, not lifting his eyes as she told him of Laura's stealing the picture, of her mailing it to Philadelphia.

At last he said: "So you think this is a picture of my mother?"

"We both do."

"And I'm Condon's son?"

"It seems so. It makes a certain amount of sense that way. It would explain why he took you in instead of allowing them to send you to prison. All you have to do is to ask him."

He said slowly: "If he'd wanted me to know, he'd have told me before this. What's to keep him from merely saying that the baby mentioned in this letter died? Maybe it did."

"Maybe."

"And I'm not too sure I want to claim Condon for a father. Perhaps I'd be happier not knowing who I am."

She said steadily: "You know what you told me about my father and myself."

"That's right."

"I know how you could find out without approaching Condon. Ride out and talk with Ma Benton. Tell her you know Condon is your father and see what she says."

He folded the letter thoughtfully. "Where's Laura?"

"Upstairs, packing. She and Vance Benton are leaving on the midnight train."

He showed no surprise. She watched him, recalling what Laura had said to her. She had always known that she was in love with him. Through all the years of his absence he had seldom been out of her thoughts. It came as a real shock when he returned, and a worse shock followed when Laura appeared. She had resolutely tried to put him out of her mind, and she had failed. She yearned over him as he sat holding that picture. She wanted to reach out and comfort him. She wanted to take him into her arms and hold him close. She knew how he felt. It must be confusing, even upsetting, to discover that after all these years he might have living relatives, that this stranger who wrote from the East might be his grandfather, that Condon might be his father.

He rose, stuffing the picture and letter into his pocket. "All right, Belle. I'll talk to Ma."

"And then?"

He shrugged. "It will depend on what she tells me. And after she talks, it will take some thinking." He started toward the dining room door, but stopped just before he reached it. "Say good bye to Laura for me, and wish her luck. It's better that I don't see her, I think." He was gone then, leaving the hotel and walking up the street.

He had traveled less than half a block when Andy ran across from the station to fall into step. "Where are you going?"

He hesitated. There was no real reason why he should not tell the boy. "Out to the Benton ranch."

"Why?"

They had reached the corner of the livery stable. "I want to talk to Ma."

"What about?"

"Look," West said, "when you get to be a doctor, then will be the time to ask questions. A doctor is supposed to ask questions and find out all he can about his patients. But other people aren't. It's kind of impolite. Now, run on home. Belle was already cooking the steak when I left."

Andy hesitated, but could think of no way to refuse. He scuffed slowly back along the street as West went on to the corral after a horse.

Vance Benton watched West saddle, wondering why West was going out to the ranch. Twice Vance almost walked out to stop him, but he stayed hidden in one of the stalls. He could not be sure that the break was set for tonight, and, if it was, his brothers would certainly head for the border and not go anywhere near the ranch.

After West rode away, Vance rose and brushed the straw from his clothes. He stepped into the dark livery office and checked the clock with the aid of a lighted match. It was 7:00 p.m., five hours until train time.

Vance was not a praying man, but he hoped with all his soul that nothing would happen in the next five hours, that he and the girl would be on the train, headed away from trouble. He washed at the trough and ate in the railroad lunchroom. Then, as he had done on the night of the train wreck, he went into Callahan's and sat at the poker table. He was too nervous to enjoy the cards, but he wanted to be certain that, if the break did come tonight, a number of people could swear he had been thirty miles away in a poker game. He played so intently that he did not see Condon come in and seat his bulk in his usual place, but the doctor stared at him so fixedly that he finally turned.

For Condon it was something of a shock to see Vance quietly playing cards while Bo and Fred were helping Duke and Prince to crash their way out of the prison. He had chosen to be seen in the saloon for the same reason that Vance had joined the card game. He waited with increasing nervousness for the flash to come, telling the town of the escape. The fact that Vance had held clear of the plot was troubling, since he had much more confidence in Vance's judgment than in that of the other boys. The game dragged on, a series of small pots, with no forging ahead of a real winner. At 11:00 Vance tossed in his few remaining chips and moved past Condon to the bar. He was standing there, having another drink, when the batwing doors swung open and Fred eased into the room.

Vance saw him in the backbar mirror and stiffened. His brother spotted him, gestured guardedly, and slipped back into the night. Apparently no one had noticed Fred's arrival — at least no one paid any attention.

Vance moved casually to the door, pushed it open, and stepped outside, his heart thumping so loudly that it seemed everyone in the saloon should have heard it.

Fred leaned against the corner of the building, white-faced and exhausted. He told Vance what had happened in quick, terse, choppy words. He had almost killed his horse getting here. He could hardly stand.

"Send Condon out to the ranch," he said. "Send him quick." Vance cursed under his breath. Less than an hour more and he would have been safely on the train. But Fred stopped that hope, also. "We cut the wires," he said, "and pulled up three rails. That was Cat-Eye Smith's idea. There won't be a train through for some hours."

A pall of depression settled over Vance. He still wanted no part of this. He thought of getting horses and taking Laura into the hills. But the city-bred girl would not be able to ride far, and, as soon as the news of the prison escape was broadcast, the hills would be safe for no one.

"Go to Condon's," he told his brother. "I'll get the doctor there as soon as I can. And a couple of horses, too."

He drifted back toward the saloon entrance, savagely resentful. Why had Prince had to stop a bullet? Why hadn't they headed for the border as originally planned? The whole thing seemed a conspiracy to involve him. If he went into the saloon now and dragged Condon out, everyone in the room would later associate the act with the break. And then he heard someone whistling and saw Andy leaving the railroad station and cutting across the street toward home.

He called softly and stepped out into the center of the street to meet Andy. He slipped a dollar into the boy's hand. "Look," he said, "Laura and I are leaving tonight."

Andy had already wormed the information out of Belle.

"I want to see Doc Condon before I go, but I don't want everyone in the saloon to know I'm leaving. Get Doc. Tell him someone's hurt and waiting for treatment at his place. Don't tell him it's me or he may not come."

The boy nodded and ducked toward the saloon door. Vance disappeared into the livery, caught up two horses, and had saddles on them by the time Condon came along the street. He followed, not noticing that Andy also was following farther down the block.

Condon did not hear Vance. The doctor entered the yard, went up the path, and pushed open the door. He saw Fred Benton and stopped. "What are you doing here?" he rasped.

Vance was almost at his heels, thankful that the dogs knew him and had not set up a clamor. He put a hand against Condon's back and pushed him into the room.

Condon swung on him savagely. "What's going on?"

Vance said tonelessly: "They broke into the prison as you planned. Prince stopped a bullet. He's at the ranch."

"At the ranch? What in the hell are the fools doing at the ranch?"

"They took Prince there. They had to take him somewhere, and they sent Fred in after you."

"Not after me." Condon's jaw set. "I'm all through. I've had enough. I warned them to get across the border as fast as they could ride. God damn it, the fools should know this country will be alive with men as soon as the news gets out."

Vance was in no mood to argue. "I've got horses saddled, Doc. You and Fred better ride while there's still time."

"No. I'm through."

Vance took a step toward him. "You aren't through, Doc. You're going."

For an instant Condon seemed to be measuring Vance Benton. Then a crafty light glowed in his eyes. "All right, I'll get my bag." He turned toward the desk as if to reach for the bag. Vance sensed what he was about, and before Condon brought the gun free of the drawer Vance shot twice. Both bullets struck Condon fully in the chest. The old doctor dropped his gun. He fell forward and lay still. Vance did not even give him a second glance. The dogs were howling outside. He opened the door to swear at them, and, as he did so, he saw Andy Lawrence peering over the fence beside the gate.

Vance could move fast when he chose. He sprinted across the yard and through the gate almost before the boy could drop from his perch. Andy had no chance to run. Vance grabbed his arm and dragged him inside almost before Andy realized what had happened. But before Vance reached the

311

house with his young captive, the town behind him seemed to go crazy.

Vance stopped and listened. Whistles were shrilling in the roundhouse. Men were shouting. He heard the *slap* of several shots. Soda Springs had come to life with a bang. He dragged the boy inside, answering Fred's question with a snarl: "I don't know what's happened. Get some rope and tie this kid up. Gag him if you have to. Then wait here. I've got to get word to the boys that Condon isn't coming, that they've got to get away from the ranch. If I don't show up here by daylight, watch your chance and slip south. If they catch you, you're as good as hung right now. But you're safe here. The dogs will keep people away. Just don't answer if anyone hails the house and keep the light off. They'll think Condon's away or drunk."

He slipped back through the rear gate to the alley and along it toward the livery stable. And now he realized fully what had happened. News of the prison break had reached the town. Nothing else could explain the feverish excitement. He did not know that the news had been wired to the West Coast, and then relayed back along the eastern line to Soda Springs.

The message had been so garbled in

transmission that no one understood all of it. But the prison was still burning and a good many of the guards were dead. Most of the prisoners had escaped and many of them had scattered afoot over the rough country to the south and west. The track had been torn up and no trains could get through. This much was understood.

The first message had been received at the railroad station just as Vance stepped from the livery stable to follow Condon up the street, and the news spread across town, the sound of the whistles, and the resulting excitement blanking out the noise of the two shots that killed Condon.

Vance did not dare to appear on the street, and he had no chance to ride away from the livery stable unobserved. Already the sheriff was forming his posse in front of the building and requisitioning horses for his men. Vance crouched in one of the empty stalls, trusting to the darkness and the turmoil to conceal his presence, and from the stall he heard the sheriff conferring with Bruce Gimble and the major from the fort.

Messages poured in constantly, and the call boys ran them over from the station as soon as they were received. The situation was clearing somewhat. The deputy warden who had led the guards when they took refuge in the prison tower had sallied out and already he and his men had rounded up half a dozen of the lesser prisoners. The fire was still burning, and they wanted help at once. The territorial governor called on every peace officer in the southern district to form all available men into posses and appealed to Washington for the use of troops. The War Department granted permission and Major Clayborn ordered out three companies, leaving only a few men at the fort.

Omstead made up a special with boxcars for the horses, and the troops were loaded as fast as they rode into town. The rough plan was for the cavalry to be shipped the thirty miles to the prison. Using the prison as a base, Clayborn was expected to string out his men westward in an effort to close the border. The sheriff and his volunteer posse were to ride northward into the breaks in a giant half circle, hoping to drive the escaped prisoners between them and the screen of cavalry that Clayborn would fan out.

"The Bentons engineered this." It was the sheriff talking. "The word is that the fighting started when the Bentons broke out of the old stables where they were quarantined, and that they opened the gates to riders from the outside. And the Bentons know every foot of those northern hills."

"You don't think they'd be fools enough to go back to their ranch?" Bruce Gimble asked.

"I stopped guessing what the Bentons would do years ago," DeMember said. "If I was in their boots, I'd head directly for the border and get across before Clayborn could spread his line. But we've got to cover as much ground as we can."

The major nodded. "The department is sending a detachment from Yuma. I'll make contact and work back this way. They will cover to the west of the prison. A posse is working down from the capital and another from Sweetwater, directly north of the prison. If you can comb the breaks, and then pivot to meet my men, we ought to have them boxed in if they're still north of the line." He turned as an aide brought word that the special train was loaded. "Good hunting," he said, and left for the station.

Ten minutes later the posse rode out, almost a hundred men, leaving Soda Springs deserted save for women and a few railway workers. As soon as he felt sure they had gone, Vance slipped back into the alley. The corral behind the livery was empty and the two horses he had so carefully saddled were gone. For an instant he stood staring at the bare enclosure. Then he thought of the horse in the doctor's barn. He ran back down the alley and threw a saddle onto the animal's back. He would have liked to say good bye to Laura before he left town, but there was no time.

He swung out across the flat desert a good fifteen minutes after the posse, but he was not worried about reaching the ranch first. He knew the slanting mountain trails as he knew the lines of his hand. Without trouble he could cut a good ten miles off the route that DeMember's men would follow. The question was: could he get back out again, bringing his brothers with him?

XIX

Hy West had taken the main trail to the Benton ranch, and he came into the valley unchallenged. He stepped from his mount at the corral fence and crossed the yard toward the lighted house. He did not realize that Ma was sitting on the shadowed porch until she rose and sent her query across the darkness.

"Who is it?" She had been waiting there since sunset, waiting for news from the prison, knowing that one of the hill boys who had ridden with her sons would circle back and bring her word on his way to his lonely ranch. Most of the men who had gone with Bo and Fred meant to come back. There would be nothing to link them directly with the prison break, and therefore no reason why they should accompany the Bentons to Mexico. But she had not expected West, and she did not identify him until he answered her hail. She stood at the edge of the porch, trying to keep her voice steady, trying not to conceal the nervous anxiety burning inside her. "What are you doing here? What do you want?"

He moved up into the path of light from the front window, saying quietly: "I want to talk to you, Ma. It's important."

To Ma Benton, nothing was important save news from the prison. She had been sitting alone, cursing her age that would not let her accompany her sons, an old woman, bound by a weakness she hated to admit. "There's nothing for us to talk about, Hy West." She had to get rid of him before the messenger arrived. She did not want him here when news of the break came. She did not trust him. In fact she would have trusted no one on this night.

"There is something," he said. "I've found

out who I am. I want to ask you some questions."

She was surprised.

"I asked you a few weeks back," he said. "There's no real reason why you shouldn't tell me everything you know."

She bit her lip, trying to think quickly. "If I tell you, will you go? Now?"

For the first time he sensed her nervousness. He had thought it strange that she should be alone on the dark porch, that there were no horses in the corral, and he wondered suddenly what the Bentons were up to this night. "What is it, Ma? Where are Bo and Fred?"

She said angrily: "That's none of your business. Did you come out here to spy?"

He felt sure now that something was wrong. He knew her too well not to recognize her uneasiness, but the last thing he wanted was to be mixed up in the Bentons' affairs. "Why should I spy on you? All I want to know is why Condon never admitted he was my father."

She was startled, then relieved. "Have you talked with him?"

"Not yet. I wanted to talk to you first."

She said slowly: "I don't know too much. He brought you here when you were just a baby. He paid us to raise you. He didn't explain anything then, but once or twice, when he got drunk, he talked. He'd gotten into some kind of bad trouble back East. A woman he operated on died, and his wife left him because of it, and he couldn't practice. I don't know the whole thing, but he admitted that he stole you from your mother and brought you out here. Your mother's father was hunting him and hunting you, and he was afraid that, if they found a doctor with a little baby and no wife, they might trace him down. Besides, he couldn't take care of you himself."

"I can see that. But why didn't he tell me later? Why didn't he tell me at the time of the trial, when he took me to live with him?"

She hesitated. "You're asking too many questions . . . some you'd be better off not to have answered. He hated your mother for not standing by him when he was in trouble, and he was drinking a lot. He told me once that Condon wasn't his real name, and that there was no use giving it to you. I think he loved you, Kid, in his own way. But he was also afraid that, if you knew, you'd ask questions about your mother, about his former life. Questions he didn't want to answer. He isn't much of a man."

West didn't comment. They remained there, silent in the darkness, and suddenly there came the whispered sound of many horses coming up the trail. The old woman stiffened with a gusty little cry. The number of horses scared her. There should be only one messenger, two at most. What had happened? Was this a posse already coming, looking for her sons?

West turned, staring down across the dark yard. "What is it, Ma?"

She did not answer. She stood speechless, one bony hand clutched to her thin old breast. And then they burst into the valley and were at the corral fence. He could not judge their exact number, but they made a black knot beyond the row of poles. Duke and Bo came toward the porch, supporting a sagging form between them, and Ma rose and ran forward with a sharp moan. They brushed by West, carrying Prince, still dressed in his prison garb.

Inside, they stretched Prince on the old couch. West, who had followed to the doorway, saw that the man's face already bore the grayish pallor of death.

Bo turned and saw West. "Hy? Good. You're a doctor. Have a look."

No questions as to how he came to be there, nothing in their excitement save the knowledge that he was a doctor. He stepped forward to bend over Prince. The bullet had gone in below the shoulder, and almost certainly it had nicked a lung. He was surprised that the man on the couch still lived. He heard them talking around him, heard them telling their mother about the prison break.

He bent over Prince again. He had not seen this man since the last day of the trial, and Prince had once been his boyhood hero. Strange, he thought, how your sense of values changes. He no longer identified himself in his own mind with these foster brothers. Then he was cutting away the bloody shirt, and asking for hot water, bandages. Bo was at his elbow, no longer hostile for the moment, asking how much chance Prince had.

He wanted to say: none. The bullet hole was a little higher than he had at first supposed. Perhaps it had missed the lung at that. But the shoulder was shattered and the bullet had lodged just under the shoulder blade. "I haven't my instruments." He was not speaking to Bo; he was thinking aloud. Prince should be dead. Only a man with the vitality the Bentons had could have survived so long.

"Condon's coming," Bo said. "He'll have some tools with him."

"He'll never come." It was Duke's bitter

voice. "The old doc thinks too much of his precious hide to venture into these hills tonight."

"He'll come," Bo said. "He'll come because he does think a lot of his precious hide. He knows that, if he doesn't come, I'll make certain that he hangs for Dave Lawrence's murder."

West had been sponging the blood from the broken shoulder. He stopped. "Say that again," he told Bo. "You mean Doc Condon murdered Dave Lawrence?"

"That's right. Condon shot him in the back. I saw him do it. Dave was on to the fact that Condon had been planning our hold-ups."

West turned back to the wounded man. Ma was standing across the couch. She handed him bandages, and then clasped her thin hands across her breasts. For an instant their eyes met, and in that instant West saw something in her face that he had never seen there before: compassion for him. He went on then, bandaging the shoulder now, and, when he looked up, Ma's shriveled lips formed a question: "Will he die?"

West shrugged. He did not know. He finished the dressing and stepped out onto the porch. Nothing further could be done until Condon got there. He wondered exactly how he would react when he met his father. He thought bitterly: *The one man I really respected here was Dave Lawrence, and my father has to be his murderer.* He looked out across the dark yard. He knew now why Ma had said there were questions about Condon that were better left unanswered.

Bo came out onto the porch, followed by Duke. Together they moved down to where the escaped men had built a fire, close to the corral. West trailed them, not because he was interested in the former prisoners, but because he felt that he had to get away from the house. Cat-Eye Smith had risen from his place beside the fire and came forward to meet the Bentons.

"How is he?"

"Bad," Bo said.

"We've got to move." Smith glanced behind him toward the cañon's bottleneck. "If they catch us in here, we're dead."

Bo's voice tightened. "We can't move until the doctor gets here."

The men around the fire heard him, and a grumble ran through the group. West listened to the argument with only half an ear, for he had caught the sound of a single horse, coming fast up the cañon. He stood still, analyzing his own reactions, wondering what he would say to Condon, what he could say to Condon, and then the fugitives heard the oncoming rider and were springing to their feet, catching up their guns. But the rider who came into the circle of firelight was not Condon. It was Vance Benton.

Vance pushed his horse directly at Bo and swung down. His younger brother gave a grunt of surprise. "Where'd you come from?"

"Soda Springs. I saw Fred. There's hell to pay."

"Where's Condon?"

"Dead."

A tremor ran through Hy West. He turned away, hearing Vance say behind him: "He wouldn't come. He tried to pull a gun on me."

West thought: *I suppose I should hate Vance. I suppose. . . .* But somehow he did not hate Vance. About his father he felt only a quick relief. Condon was dead. It closed the book as far as he was concerned.

Vance was talking rapidly: "The whole territory is up. The troops are out, and De-Member is leading the biggest posse I ever saw to keep you from crossing the border." They were silent, staring at him. Vance's anger turned on Bo. "I should leave you all to rot. It was bad enough making the break.

It was a fool's choice coming back here."

Bo said sullenly: "I suppose you'd have left Prince to die."

"We'll probably all die now. How is he?"

"Bad. West is here, but he hasn't got his tools. He says he'll have to operate. We were counting on Condon's medicine bag."

Smith walked back to the fire. Men gathered around him, ready to pull out. Vance glanced back at them. "How many men can you count on?"

"Four. The rest of the hill boys have taken off for home."

Vance was thinking. He said softly: "I've got an idea. Soda Springs is drained of men. There aren't more than half a dozen left in town. We could ride in there and Hy could operate in his hospital."

"Smith and the rest wouldn't go." Bo sounded disgusted. "They're hell-bent to get across the border."

"So much the better. Let them go. They'll take the main trail out of here and they'll run head first into DeMember and that posse. We can slip around to the east and take the short cut for town. DeMember and Smith's men are going to fight the damnedest battle you ever saw. That should keep them all occupied while we get away."

Bo sounded dissatisfied. "And when we

get to town, we'll be in a worse trap than we are here. The border south of there will be lousy with soldiers."

A devil had started to dance in Vance's dark eyes. "We've got a chance," he said. "That's all we can ask for . . . a chance. Remember when Gimble seized the railroad station during the plague? Remember how he pushed Omstead into making up a special to send the pox victims out of town? We can do the same thing. We can load our horses into a boxcar, and have the train take us fifty miles east. We can leave it in the desert, unload the horses, and ride for the border. It won't be guarded that far away."

Bo and Duke were catching his spirit. Bo said softly: "It might work. If we told Smith, he'd bring his men with us."

"To hell with them." Vance's voice was rough. "We need them to keep DeMember and the posse busy. When they run into the sheriff, they'll scatter like quail. DeMember will spend the next couple of days trying to hunt them out of these hills. I'm going to talk to Smith. Just keep your mouths shut."

He went to the fire. Hy West followed, wanting to hear what Vance was going to say. Cat-Eye Smith said hoarsely: "Well, what do we do now?"

"We're going to take my brother into Soda

Springs," Vance said.

"The hell we are!" Smith took a step toward him. "We've wasted too much time already. If we'd headed out for the border first, we'd be almost across the line by now." He vented his anger on Bo. "To hell with you Bentons. We're riding out."

Vance said: "Do you know the country?"

"We'll find our way. To hell with you."

Vance looked at him for a moment, then swung on his heel, catching Bo's arm and half dragging his younger brother away. Out of earshot of the mounting men, he said: "They'll take the main trail until they get clear of the hills. They'll have to or get lost. Once on the plain they'll cut westward . . . if they get out of the hills before they run into DeMember's posse. I'm betting they won't make it." Bo did not answer. Vance went on: "Dig out those four hill boys and see if they'll ride with us." He motioned to West. "What chance have we to get Prince to town?"

"None."

"We've got to try it."

"Yes," West agreed. "You've got to try it." He trailed Vance into the house. Vance had taken charge. Bo and Duke were following his lead. West tried to analyze his feeling toward Vance and failed. None of the events of this night had any sense of reality. He felt as though he were living through a nightmare. Condon was his father. Condon was a murderer. Vance had killed Condon. Of all the Bentons he had liked Vance the best. And there was Laura to think of. Laura and Vance. What would happen to them now?

He heard Vance speaking calmly to his mother, telling her not to worry, that he would get them safely across the border, that she could join them later in Mexico. He wondered how much of this Vance actually believed. Vance was no fool. He knew how badly the odds were stacked against him.

Then they were in the saddle, with Prince in a crude litter between two horses, following the curving way down through the cañon mouth, cutting off on the hill path that would swing them eastward of the main trail around the rough, rugged face of Bald Mountain. They rode as stealthily as Apaches — three active Bentons, four hill riders, himself, and the unconscious Prince. All of them had grown up in this harsh country, all of them had followed this trail a hundred times. They knew each break, each rock, each twisted bend. It was not until they mounted the shoulder and dropped over it that the whisper of distant rifle fire reached them from the west.

Vance, who was in the lead, halted them and they sat in their saddles, listening. It was too far away to tell exactly at what point the posse had run into Cat-Eye Smith and his escaping prisoners. As nearly as West could judge, it came from the western slope of Bald Mountain, which would put the battle a good twenty miles from Soda Springs. He had no doubt that Vance was right. As soon as they were attacked, Smith's followers would scatter back through the rough country behind the Benton ranch. It would take the posse hours, perhaps days to dig them out and run them down. Certainly there would be time for the Bentons to reach Soda Springs and perhaps escape eastward.

XX

The sun was half an hour high before they came into the railroad town, but around them people were already stirring. Vance had given his orders well. He moved directly on the station and the roundhouse, seizing the night operator before the man had a chance to flash the news up the line that the outlaws were upon him.

They got Omstead in his bed, and Grantline before the dispatcher had time to dress. They herded the night crew out of the roundhouse, the switchmen from the yards, and marched them over and locked them in Callahan's. It was done neatly, rapidly, and almost silently. Within five minutes they were in complete control of the town. The few able-bodied men who had not ridden out with the posse showed no inclination to fight the Bentons. They even seemed anxious to help the outlaws in their escape, prompted to this course by their desire to get them out of town as quickly as possible.

West knew very little of these activities. Prince Benton had been carried directly to the Railroad Hospital, and West sent Bo to the hotel for both Laura and Belle. Surprisingly Prince was still alive, but West doubted that even with his amazing vitality the man could survive the operation.

Bo came back with the two girls and stood gazing down at his unconscious brother while West made ready to operate.

"Think he'll make it?"

West shrugged.

"Can we take him with us?"

"He'll die for certain if you do."

"Even if we took you along to watch over him?"

West had not considered that. He had

been giving very little thought to himself. He looked at Bo levelly. "It wouldn't make any difference. The shock of the operation will probably kill him. I'd say that he has one chance in a thousand, but the bullet has to come out. However, if you're going to insist on taking him with you, there's no use to operate. He'll die anyhow."

Bo said savagely: "He'd rather be dead than go back to prison. Go ahead, start cutting." He turned and went through the door.

West scrutinized the two girls. Neither had spoken since entering the room. Laura's eyes were swollen. She had been crying. Her hands trembled as she placed the instruments to sterilize. He had never seen her this way before and he said sharply: "Steady, Hall."

She flinched. "What's going to happen, Hy?"

"I don't know."

"It's my fault." The blonde girl said it in a monotone. "Vance wanted me to leave with him earlier. If I'd gone, he wouldn't be involved in this."

West shook his head. He guessed that he had never really understood Laura. A prison had been burned, fifty to a hundred desperate man were in the hills trying to escape, the whole territory was up in arms, the town had been taken over by the Bentons — and her only thought seemed to be that, because of her, Vance remained here in danger. There was nothing he could say, and it was obvious that in her present condition he could put little dependence on her help.

He glanced at Belle. She was composed, as steady as always, but she, too, looked as if she had had little or no sleep, and his tone was sharper than he intended when he asked: "What's the matter with you?"

"It's Andy." She said it in a low voice. "He didn't come home last night. We spent most of the time looking for him."

He started. "But where . . . ?"

"We don't know. He was at the station just before eleven. The operator said he started home. Then, my father says, he came into the saloon after Condon, and told him there was an accident case at Condon's. He and Doc went out together."

A wave of cold fear washed over West. "Did you go to Condon's?"

She nodded. "But Condon wasn't there. No lights, and the dogs wouldn't let us into the yard. We went around back and looked in the barn. Condon's horse was gone." West seemed lost in speculation so she said: "The only thing we could think of was that Andy had gone along with Condon. You know how he is. He likes to get his nose into everything."

"I know." West found that his own hands were trembling as he turned back to the table. He did not tell her that Vance Benton had killed Condon. He was afraid now that Andy had witnessed the killing, and that they had done away with the boy. A sudden rage at the Bentons went up through him. His feeling for Andy was something of which he had not been quite conscious. Andy was a reflection of the debt he owed Dave Lawrence. The boy had no father, even as he'd had no father. He had so much in common with the boy. But it went deeper than that. Andy with his inquisitiveness, his alertness, and his boundless energy was likable for himself. He had been the first to greet West on West's return, and he had made it very plain that he thought the young doctor was wonderful. All those things — and now perhaps Andy was dead.

He focused his attention on Prince Benton's wound. He began to work. Prince died before the ether could take effect. West was neither surprised nor shocked. Among the many operations in which he had assisted at the hospital, there had been an average percentage of deaths. Death was something a doctor had to accept as his eternal opponent.

He rolled down his sleeves slowly, saying in an undertone: "You can tell Vance that he doesn't need to worry about Prince any more." He looked at Laura, then went into his own office.

Belle Callahan followed him. Belle was in the doorway when he pulled open the drawer of his desk and lifted out Dave Lawrence's guns. He turned after fastening the cartridge belt and saw her watching him with big, frightened eyes. It came to him as a shock that he had never seen her frightened before.

She said: "What are you going to do?"

"I have an errand, Belle. Go back to the hotel."

"You won't try to stop them?"

"We'll see," he said, and left by the side door. Actually he did not know exactly what he meant to do. First, he wanted to visit Condon's house. He found it almost impossible to think of Condon as his father. The term included so many things that had little or nothing to do with blood relationship. He knew now that he would always remember Condon, not as his father, but as a crusty, untidy figure who had little love for his fellows.

He stepped into the center of the street, looking up and down its length. It was startling to see it so nearly deserted at this hour of the day. The citizens who still remained in Soda Springs were conscientiously keeping well out of sight.

One of the hill riders stood guard at the door of Callahan's, holding the captives inside. Another was planted directly opposite the station, where his rifle could control the full length of the street. The other two and the Bentons were in the yards, overseeing the making up of the special train. West walked up the street toward Condon's, wondering if the men would challenge him. But he had ridden in from the hills with them, and they had known him as a boy, and they merely nodded as he appeared, apparently assuming that he was on an errand for the Bentons.

He passed the livery stable and moved on down to Condon's house, taking the precaution of drawing one of his guns before he pushed open the heavy gate. The dogs came at him in a rush, one of them springing toward his throat. He waited until the exact instant, and then knocked it down with a sweeping motion of the gun barrel. The dog lay for an instant stunned, then struggled to its feet, running toward the rear of the house, yipping as it went. Its companions had fallen back, watching him narrowly, their teeth bared, their ruffs high.

He seemed to ignore them as he went up the path. One of them dashed in to nip at his heel. He swung quickly and his lifted boot sent the wicked animal half across the yard. The rest drew away, their coyote blood making them cautious. West reached the door and paused for an instant, steeling himself for what he might find inside. Then he pushed the door open.

Condon lay where he had fallen, but Fred had thrown a blanket over the body. West stared at the lumpy shape, and then saw the boy bound on the couch at the side.

He crossed the room, seeing Andy's eyes widen above the top of the handkerchief stretched across the small face to hold the gag in place. West freed Andy, gathering the slight body tightly in his arms, holding him close. A reaction such as he had never known set in, and he was trembling as he finally set the boy on a chair and dropped to his knees before him, rubbing circulation back into the small cramped legs.

"You all right?"

Andy's tone was not quite as self-assured as usual. "Sure." He tried to smile. "It wasn't so bad as long as Fred was here, but he left when he heard the horses on the street, and I didn't much like being alone with him." He indicated the blanket-covered figure with a slight gesture of his head.

"I can imagine."

"Vance shot him."

"I know," West said. "Let's get out of here. Your mother and Belle are worried about you. They've been hunting you all night. Come on, if you can walk."

Andy could walk. He complained of needles in his legs and held firmly to West's arm, but after the first hobbling steps walking came easier. The dogs snarled at them from a distance but made no real effort to attack. They crossed the yard, using the rear gate rather than the front, and moved along the alley toward the Apache Hotel. Now that Andy was safe, West had no intention of trying to stop the Bentons. He shared the feeling of the rest of the town. The sooner they were out of Soda Springs the better for everyone. No matter what happened now, they would have a rough time below the border, and any punishment they deserved would in a sense be satisfied.

He and Andy came into the kitchen, the boy beginning to yell as soon as he was inside the door: "Ma, oh, Ma! I'm home!"

They heard a *thumping* from the right.

They approached the door of the small storeroom. It was fastened on the outside, so West pulled the bolt and pushed the door open. Mary Lawrence almost fell out into his arms. "Thank God you're here." She was nearly beside herself. "They've got Belle."

He steadied her to a chair, knowing that she had not yet completely recovered from her operation. "Who's got Belle? What is all this?"

"The Bentons. They came to the hotel to get Laura's things. The fool is going with them."

"Who came?"

"Vance and Bo. They got her things and came downstairs, and then Bo grabbed Belle and told her she was going, too." The woman stopped to catch her breath. "Belle tried to fight him off and I tried to help. Vance pushed me into the storeroom and bolted the door. . . ."

West was already running out through the dining room. As he crossed the lobby and burst onto the gallery, he saw the special train, already made up and standing beside the station platform. It consisted of a switch engine, a freight car into which the Bentons had loaded their horses, and an old coach.

He leaped into the street. The two riders

who had been left as guards were heading toward the station. Vance Benton's special was about ready to pull out. He ran harder. He saw Duke standing beside the engine, a gun in his hand, flanked by one of the hill riders. He saw Vance and Fred at the coach steps, motioning for the guards to hurry, and then he saw Vance turn and mount the car. There was no sign of Bo. The youngest Benton probably was in the coach, standing guard over Belle.

He shouted. He had to stop them before the train began to move. If he failed, there was no telling how long it would take him to catch up with them — and he knew with a flash of insight that, if the Bentons succeeded in getting out of town with Belle Callahan, he would never stop until he tracked them down.

He didn't run toward the coach. He ran toward the engine. The engine was the key. Without it they could not move the train. He ran, shouting, and then he threw a bullet at Duke who stood covering the engineer. He missed. He heard the *spang* as the lead slug crashed against the side of the boiler.

Duke had been caught entirely by surprise. Even before he recognized the running man, he snapped off a shot. It kicked up dust beneath West's feet. The rider beside Duke was firing, also, and Fred Benton and the two hill men from the street were shooting at him from an angle. It seemed impossible that all of them could miss him. And then he had unexpected reënforcements, for at the sound of the first shots the men imprisoned in Callahan's ventured to the door and, finding their guard gone, boiled out into the street.

The fireman and engineer took a hand. The fireman came down out of the cab as soon as Duke turned his back. He felled the hill rider with one blow of his scoop, and then charged at Duke. Duke whirled just in time to avoid the swinging shovel, and put two bullets into the fireman's chest. But he did not escape for longer than a second. The engineer leaped from the steps, his burly form crashing into Duke Benton, and crushing him downward to the worn planks of the platform.

Seeing this, West changed his direction and ran diagonally across the station yard toward the old coach. He might well have waited for the reënforcements from Callahan's, but it never entered his mind. His one thought was that Belle was on that train and he had to get her off. Behind him somewhere, he heard Andy's squeaking yell, but he had no time to wonder what the boy was up to.

He stopped halfway across the yard, because his running shots had been far from accurate. He fired once, deliberately, and saw Fred Benton throw up both arms, spin, and fall to the platform. He saw the hill riders duck under the car and start off across the yards. Then Bo Benton came leaping down the coach steps. He fired at Bo. His bullet pinged off the coupling of the coach. He saw Bo raise his gun and fire, and felt the smashing shock of the bullet as it tore through his upper left arm.

He stood for an instant, steadying himself, wondering if he could hold his feet. And then he aimed and squeezed with desperate concentration. Bo Benton bent double, crumpled, and lay unmoving on the sunbaked platform.

Hy West walked on, slowly, cautiously, his useless left arm hanging at his side like a broken wing. And then he realized that Vance Benton was on the train platform, a gun in his hand. Vance was descending the steps haltingly, like a man approaching a chore he disliked. There was none of the frenzy about Vance that had marked Bo's movement. His eyes went over West's head, measuring the men who had broken out of

Callahan's, but he had personally disarmed them before leaving them in the saloon, and he saw no guns in their hands.

It was West he had to worry about, and on West he centered his full attention. The game was already lost. He sensed this, although he had not seen the action beside the locomotive. He sensed it before he stepped down to the planks and heard West's call.

"Drop it, Vance! It's all over."

Vance Benton made no motion to obey. He took a half step away from the side of the train. His gun hung loosely in his hand and for an instant it seemed doubtful if he would try to lift it. "You've raised hell, haven't you, Kid?" There was no real anger in his tone, merely an acceptance of what had happened and what might yet happen.

West stopped and braced himself. Some twenty-five feet separated him from Vance. He held his gun a little higher than Vance but he did not aim it. "It's over," he repeated. "Let your gun drop, Vance, and step away from it."

"Sorry," Vance said, and sounded as if he meant it. "We're going through with this. There's no choice."

West didn't know whether Vance felt that there was still a chance to escape, or whether he thought his murder of Condon left him with no way out. And Vance gave him no time to decide. Vance's gun started to swing up. West squeezed the trigger, thumbed back the hammer, and squeezed again. Both bullets caught Vance in the chest. He staggered once, swayed, and then collapsed across Bo's still body.

West took no chances. He knew that Vance would have killed him if he could, would still kill him if he lived. He stood there watching, and he saw Laura Hall come down the car steps in a little rush and drop to her knees beside Vance.

Then the men who had been imprisoned in Callahan's reached him, and Omstead threw an arm about his shoulders, not seeing his wounded arm. It was Callahan who reached his daughter first. Callahan came up behind Omstead just in time to see Belle appear on the car platform.

He rushed forward with a growl, and she came down the steps into his arms, and she told him what had happened. He listened, his face growing redder by the second. He had been inside the saloon and had not known that she was on the train.

He released her and grabbed West's hand. "You're all right, Doc. I won't forget it. I won't, and you can count on that."

It was Belle who saw West's arm, and his white face. It was Belle who made them take him into the hospital, and found Gruber, and stood over Gruber while he set the bone and bound up the arm. There were other patients by this time. Duke had been brought in, more bruised than hurt. Fred was still alive with a bullet in his hip and a second in his side. One of the hill riders had a hole in his chest.

They had hardly been patched up when the first wounded from the posse's fight with Cat-Eye Smith's men began to come in. DeMember's men had hit them hard. Smith was dead, his followers scattered through the hills, and the sheriff was hunting them down, aided by riders from the capital. The wire that the Bentons had cut on both sides of the station had been repaired. Reports flooded in. More than half of the escaped prisoners had been recaptured and the circle of troops and posse men was gradually closing in on those still at large.

Belle brought West the news late that afternoon, and Andy came with her to add his version. It was Andy who told him that Laura Hall had had Vance's body loaded into a wagon and hired a man to drive her out to the ranch.

"She sent word to you," the boy told West. "She said to tell you that she didn't blame you. She said she guessed it had to work out this way, but she don't want to see you. She said she was going to take Ma Benton back East if the old woman would go with her." Both Belle and West showed their surprise. Andy went on importantly. "And they've already taken Duke to jail. He wasn't hurt bad. Fred is going to die. That's what Gruber thinks."

"The end of the Bentons." Belle said it softly.

"It sure is." Andy was too active to stay long in the sick room, especially while the whole town was still buzzing with excitement and news kept drifting back from the posse hour by the hour.

After he had gone, Belle said: "I was sorry to learn about Condon. Did you get a chance to talk to Ma Benton? Was he your father?"

West nodded. He didn't tell her that Condon had killed Dave Lawrence. It would serve no good purpose for her to know. "Don't feel too bad," he said. "The fact that we were related doesn't seem to mean very much."

"You can write to Philadelphia," she said.

"You can probably find out more about him in that way."

West didn't answer. At the moment he didn't want to think about Condon. His arm was aching and he was very tired.

"Speaking of fathers," Belle went on, "I made up with mine. He even offered to buy the Apache for me. Mary Lawrence is in no shape to run it."

He said: "Are you going to buy it?"

She hesitated. "I don't quite know."

He reached out with his good hand. "Belle, I've got something to say to you. I don't know what I'm going to do, whether I'll stay here or go back East. With Condon dead, the town needs a doctor, and I might undo a little harm that he did from time to time."

"That's not a good reason for staying."

He said: "I've got another. You're here."

"Please, Hy, not now. I. . . ."

"Listen," he said, "you once told me that you'd never marry a man unless he wanted you as deeply as Vance wanted Laura. Well, I found out one thing about myself today. That's the way I want you. As soon as I heard you were on that train, I knew. I knew that I'd follow you to the ends of the earth if necessary. I was going to let them go, without a protest from me, but when I heard about you. . . ."

She kept her eyes down.

"I should have known sooner," he said. "I think the real reason I came back here was to prove to you that I amounted to something."

"That's what Laura said." The words slipped out before she realized she was speaking.

His hand tightened. "What did she say?"

Belle's face was stained with color. "She said I was in love with you. She said if I wanted you, I should go after you."

He stared at her. "If you're thinking about Laura and me. . . ."

"I'm not," she said, and dropped to her knees beside the bed. "I'm not." She kissed him then, and his good arm tightened around her.

Afterward he said: "We'll stay here. We'll help Andy study medicine if he still wants to, and doesn't decide to be a railroad man instead."

She didn't answer. She was content to kneel beside the bed, content to let her cheek rest against his, content to let their future take care of itself.

ABOUT THE AUTHOR

Todhunter Ballard was born in Cleveland, Ohio. He was graduated with a bachelor's degree from Wilmington College in Ohio, having majored in mechanical engineering. His early years were spent working as an engineer before he began writing fiction for the magazine market. As W. T. Ballard he was one of the regular contributors to *The Black Mask* magazine along with Dashiell Hammett and Erle Stanley Gardner. Although Ballard published his first Western story in *Cowboy Stories* in 1936, the same year he married Phoebe Dwiggins, it wasn't until *Two-Edged Vengeance* (1951) that he produced his first Western novel. Ballard later claimed that Phoebe, following their marriage, had co-written most of his fiction with him and perhaps this explains, in part, his memorable female characters. Ballard's Golden Age as a Western author came in the 1950s and extended to the early 1970s.

Incident at Sun Mountain (1952), *West of Quarantine* (1953), and *High Iron* (1953) are among his finest early historical titles, published by Houghton Mifflin. After numerous traditional Westerns for various publishers, Ballard returned to the historical novel in *Gold in California!* (1965), which earned him a Spur Award from the Western Writers of America. It is a story set during the Gold Rush era of the forty-niners. However, an even more panoramic view of that same era is to be found in Ballard's magnum opus, *The Californian* (1971), with its contrasts between the *Californios* and the emigrant gold-seekers, and the building of a freight line to compete with Wells Fargo. It was in his historical fiction that Ballard made full use of his background in engineering combined with exhaustive historical research. However, these novels are also character-driven, gripping a reader from first page to last with their inherent drama and the spirit of adventure so true of those times.